RAIN
OF
SCORPIONS

RAIN
OF
SCORPIONS

AND OTHER WRITINGS by

ESTELA PORTILLO TRAMBLEY

**TONATIUH-QUINTO SOL
INTERNATIONAL**
Publishers
POST OFFICE BOX 9275
BERKELEY, CA 94709
USA

LIBRARY OF CONGRESS CATALOGUE CARD NUMBER 75-37178
ISBN   0-89229-001-3

TO MY HUSBAND

ROBERT D. TRAMBLEY

THE PARIS GOWN

"Cognac with your coffee, Theresa?"

"No, thank you, Gran . . . Clo." Somehow the word "grandmother" did not fit Clotilde Romero de Traske, sophisticated, chic, and existentially fluent. Theresa had anticipated this after dinner *tete a tete*. In her mind there were so many things unclear about this woman who had left her home in Mexico so long ago. The traces of age in Clotilde were indistinguishable in the grace and youthful confidence exuded from her gestures, her eyes, her flexible body, and the quick discerning mind. Clotilde Romero de Traske, art dealer at the Rue Auber, was a legend back home. The stories about her numerous marriages, her travels, her artistic ventures, and the famous names that frequented her salon were many. But no one had ever discussed how she got to Paris in the first place when the women of her time had had small freedoms. Her life abroad had become scandal in epic to the clan of women in aristocratic circles back home. There was a daring in her grandmother's eyes.

"How do you like Paris, child?"

"I love it! It's like . . . like. . . ."

"An opening up . . . as does a flower to the sun. That is the feel of Paris."

"Yes, that is the way I feel. I'm happy to be here."

"You should be. You are very lucky too. Everyone should see Paris before they are twenty-five. . . . I heard that somewhere. It is true. It is like no place else in the world."

"You never went back home, Clo?"

"My dear girl, no one can truly ever go back home. . . . for one changes and the home was a different you." The older woman spoke gently. "We journey; we find new tempests. These are good. This is the way beauty and trust are pieced."

Theresa sat silent. She had suddenly glimpsed into a beautiful clear depth in a human being. She felt sudden love and admiration for her grandmother. Clotilde's fragile, ember quality of spirit grew and filled the room. Theresa felt half-way beyond caprice into a giving. Theresa felt Clotilde had a deep and lasting comprehension of her place in the universe. How fresh and open was the world in this room. Theresa felt that the room itself was a composite of what Clotilde had become in the life process. Every piece of art and sculpture gave the impact of humanness. The colors were profuse and rich; they seemed to touch impulse and awaken still undefined passions. Yes, it was a room with a singular ferocity for life.

"I understand you are traveling with a university group?" Clotilde's expressive eyes searched her granddaughter's face.

"Yes . . . it is a way we are allowed to travel away from home; the old traditions still have strong ties. They teach us early that the world is too dangerous for innocent, young girls. I think it's silly!"

Clotilde smiled. "I agree with you one hundred percent." She put down her cup and walked to the mantlepiece over the fireplace as if she chose to observe her granddaughter from a new perspective. Theresa was somewhat startled by the impression Clotilde made with the room as background. A convex reflection of mood, the older woman was a human focal point against the subjectivity of artistic experience in meaningful arrangement around the room. Emotionally coded, Clotilde stood, a liberated form from civilized order. All this was a sensing to Theresa who knew little about art.

"The art in this room, Clo, it's so . . . so. . . ."

"What other artists call it . . . without doctrinaire implication. That says nothing, really, but it means that the artist makes his own rules for finding a strength out of the life experience."

There it goes again! thought Theresa . . . that flash of galvanic illumination . . . a look inside spirit again. Theresa asked: "You are an artist yourself?"

"A terrible one; it did not take me long to find that out when I first came to Paris."

"So you became a dealer in art."

"More of a lover of art . . . look!" Clotilde went up to a massive sculpture. She touched it reverently. "Have you ever heard the name Gaudier-Brzeska? This is his work. He has made out of stone and metal what I would like to make out of life, or have tried to make out of life."

Theresa leaned over in her chair; her eagerness to know was unmasked. "Explain it to me, Clo. . . ."

"Gautier was a man of great passion; many consider him a primitive. He plunged into the instinctual and emotional to surface with an energy, a feeling, an ability free of barbarism."

Theresa was somewhat puzzled. "Isn't barbarism equated with the primitive?"

"Perhaps I look at the world as if I were standing on my head, Theresa, and many artists do. For that reason we define barbarism different from Civilization."

"I remember, Clo, that history says that Civilization downed barbarism by making reason dominant over instinct."

"If you see it from a historical viewpoint. But look at it from a human viewpoint; barbarism is the subjugation of the instinctual for reason. I know that within the pretty works of the great Hellenes, reason is primary and instinct secondary. But man's reason is a boxed-in circumstance that has proved itself more violent against human beings than instinct. Instinct is part of survival law; it is also a part of what gathers a wholeness. Barbarism is a product of limited reason. And what reason is not, at least in part, limited? Instinct is an innate law without barrier. . . . It is important to leave the field of invention open in art . . . as in life."

Theresa almost jumped up from her chair, her arms outstretched as if to encompass the room. "That's what I feel about this room! It is an open field! I see how this room is your beliefs, your history . . . how beautiful!"

"And isn't history, really, a personal thing, not belonging to nations, but to individuals?"

She was pleased by Theresa's natural discovery. Theresa, with extended hand, touched the Gautier figure as if savouring the meaning of a new part added to herself.

"I understand now, Clo, why you never went back. In a world still archaic, women suffer the barbarism of men. An injustice." Theresa looked at her grandmother with questioning eyes. Clotilde touched her cheek with the tips of her fingers and smiled at her granddaughter.

"I used to think so . . . when I was very young."

"Don't you feel that way anymore?"

"No . . . I don't think so. Maybe, because I know that the instinct that respects all life, the instinct that understands equality, survives in all of us in spite of overwhelming, unfair tradition. Men know this instinct, too, although thousands of years of conditioning made them blind to the equality of all life. The violence of man against woman is a traditional blindness whose wall can be broken. Isn't that the objective of love . . . to break walls?"

"But the unfairness is still there, Clo, even today. The woman has a secondary role to that of the man, and the brutish mind accepts it. I can imagine how it must have been in your time!"

Clotilde maintained the crystal of her world. "Men have attempted fairness since the beginning of time; it's just that sometimes they are overwhelmed . . . overwhelmed." She walked up to the window and looked out as if trying to gather a memory . . . pain and all. Theresa sensed it and went up to her and leaned her head on Clotilde's shoulder. Both looked out into a garden with its own kind of freedom. It had no symmetry, no pattern; the lawn and trailing vines, the cypress trees and profuse flowers had only been given a kind of order, only to free the life from complete chaos. Everything reached for the sun in its own way. Theresa caught a lovely fragrance.

"Mmmmm . . . what is that?"

"It is Italian jasmine; it is a beautiful part of my life brought into my garden."

"Tell me, Cló, how did you escape the blind tradition?"

Clotilde laughed her silvery laugh. "I thought you would never ask!"

Theresa was intense about her question. "They never talk about that back home, only about the terrible things you do in Paris. Inside all our womenfolk, as they sit around the card table with their gossip, there is a wish, a wanting to be you . . . I felt it many times."

Clotilde hugged her granddaughter. "It is wonderful that you feel so much!" Theresa caught her grandmother's hands and led her to a settee.

"Come, tell me the story."

Clotilde did not resist. She sat back and cast off the years.

"How does one begin without condemnations, Theresa? When we are young, to condemn is simple and an easy way out for even our mistakes. I remember my indignant feeling of injustice! I felt like a victim from a very early age. But I would show them all! That was my battle-cry!"

Clotilde shook her head in memory and continued: "Yes, tradition was much heavier in my time. There was but a single fate for the gentlewoman . . . one variation of a cloister or another. To marry meant to become the lonely mistress of a household where husbands took unfair freedoms, unfair only because the freedoms belonged to them and were unthinkable for women! Children were the recompense, but children should not be a recompense; they are human beings belonging to themselves; and we should not need recompense. It can turn to bitterness, then we become the bitterness itself, a patterned, strict garden of dead things, poisoned things. If we did not marry, there was total dependency on the generosity of pitying relatives, with church and its rituals for comfort. The nunnery or running away with the stable boy offered many sacrifices and discomforts. No . . . no. . . . There must be another solution, I would tell myself!"

"How did you turn to art, Clo?"

"I don't know whether you remember uncle Gaspar. He was considered the bohemian in the family. He had tried painting, writing, the theatre, in his attempt to keep the gypsy spirit. I liked uncle Gaspar. When he was around, I felt the gypsy spirit. He made me laugh and feel important. That was a lot to a girl. One Christmas he gave my brother an artist's palette. He brought him some books on design and color. My brother, Felix, became engrossed in his attempt to paint. In time, he discarded the palette and went on to other interests. I found it one day with the books, and began to awkwardly sketch and paint. This became an outlet, a hope. Felix had little talent. I think I had little talent too. But I stuck to the practice; I worked at it everyday ... so naturally I acquired a certain proficiency and decided I had a talent and my brother did not. I had a compulsion to compare, to outdo him, because he was a boy with born privileges and I was a girl born into a kind of slavery. I poisoned my garden early in life, but to an extent, it was my nature to want freedom. I had a mind that craved and that weighed the inequalities as a gross injustice. I found ways of justifying my opinions, my martyrdom. My brother and I used to ride a lot. We had a pair of matched stallions, beautiful horses. Riding along the path of the high hills was an excitement that grew in the body and escaped in the wind. It was a taste of wild freedom. I was the better rider, or maybe it was my greater desire for the wildness that made me the better rider. It happens that way, sometimes, when you are fierce enough about things. . . .''

Her voice trailed off in memory. There was a brief silence that caught the languid mood of afternoon. Then Clotilde continued her story:

"My father would say. . . . A man must never allow a woman to outdo him. How typical of him! The way of the varón, and Felix was his varón. . . . I was just a daughter, an afterthought, so I thought. My mother would whisper to me. . . . Let your brother win when you race. It would please your father. . . . I did not wish to please my father with the accomplishments of my brother. To outdo him became my constant form of revenge. My father resented the fact and overlooked my ability to outdo, as if it did not exist. This was adding salt to my wounds. . . . I think I began to hate my father, poor father!" Clotilde caught Theresa's glance for a second. There was a slight sliver of anxiety in Clotilde's voice. "You must remember, Theresa, it was my poison."

"But it was unfair to you!"

"Yes, it was unfair. . . . It was. Felix wanted to get out of going into the banking institute; he wanted to travel. My uncle Gaspar had painted glorious pictures of Europe, specially Paris. There were stories about the left bank, Montmartre, where one could buy delicious madness for a few francs ... where people were alive. That was Gaspar's favorite expression. Felix told my father he wanted to go to Paris to study art. My father fumed and objected, but of course Felix got his way. My father excused it, saying the boy was sowing his wild oats! You know what I did? I decided to confront my father and ask him what he was going to do about my wild oats. Poor man! His reaction was violent. He accused me of insanity and wilfulness. Perhaps, he said, what I needed was a nunnery. He meant it too!"

"You had no freedom, Clo?" Theresa's voice was full of sympathy.

"That was the price the female paid for being *bien gentil!* I began to argue with my father, to rationalize, to reason, to prove to him what a fine brain I had; I deserved better than the fate women had in the town. I drove him half-crazy with the potency of legitimate complaint. It was then that his natural instinct of survival prompted him to do what he did."

"What did he do?"

"He decided to marry me off to a neighboring widower old enough to be my father. Mind you, it was more than just desperation on his part; it was also a good business venture. Don Ignacio was the wealthiest man around. It was the usual contract marriage between parents of means. Daughters did not have a say in the matter. It was an excellent way of joining two fortunes by blood."

"How cruel, Clo. It must have been terrible for you."

"I thought at the time that it was the end of any kind of hope as a human being. I was repulsed by Don Ignacio. I began to show it. My father punished me and threatened the convent again. So then I tried to starve myself, lock myself up in my room forever. I even ran away on my horse and stayed out in the hills until my father sent out a searching party who found me half starved and with a bad case of pneumonia. For the first time in my life, I felt the full attention of my parents. While getting over my illness, I prayed my father would forget about the proposed marriage. One afternoon my father came into the bedroom. He was gentle and kind and truly concerned about my health. I took advantage of my illness and asked him to promise not to make me marry Don Ignacio." Clotilde paused and walked slowly to the window again. There was a stir of wind in her hair. She whispered almost in a child's cry. "You simply do not unpetal a flower for your advantage. You give it the chance of life!"

Theresa knew the answer. "He refused, didn't he?"

"Yes, he refused." Her eyes roamed the great expanse of horizon as if trying to forget, not the pain, but a loved one's shortcoming. "I remember a similar garden while I was getting well. . . . no, now that I think of it, it was different. It was impressive and almost manicured to perfection. It was a showcase with swans in a pond and flowers arranged by specie. There was hedge after hedge where children played hide-and-go-seek. One afternoon, during my illness, I watched some children bathing in the pond. They were three or four years old, no more. There was a little boy who decided to join the bathing children, so he took off his clothes and waded in. His nurse caught sight of him and with great indignation caught him up in her arms and spanked his little bare back. It was a curious episode of innocence and the declaration of a truth. I remember going back into the house with the imprint in my mind. For the next few weeks, I felt a growing peace. I did not argue, or beg, or cajole, I simply enjoyed my time for contemplation. It was an attempt to accept. I tried, but I could not. One morning I awoke knowing the answer to my problem. I realized that my new-found calm was a part of the plan. So was my attempt to accept. I got well and offered no complaints about the proposed engagement. My father breathed a sigh of relief. I had come to my senses. I would obey him like a good daughter and marry the man that he had chosen for me."

Theresa's voice was somewhat incredulous. "You were giving up?"

"No . . . never. I simply had discovered a way out. But it took planning, calm and a feigned acceptance. I became docile and pretended a certain excitement over the plans for the engagement ball. The most difficult thing to accept was Don Ignacio's fawning over me. But I had to stand it; it was part of the plan. My father showed his generosity by telling me that expense was no object. I was to have the most exclusive, grandest ball anyone had ever had. He asked what my heart desired." Clotilde's voice broke momentarily. She quickly composed herself and continued. "I had devised a particular wish that would be part of the camouflage for my plan. I told my father I wanted a Paris gown. The most beautiful ever seen. I became very excited over the plans for designing the gown. I corresponded with French dress-shops and filled the dinner table conversation with detailed descriptions. My father was tremendously pleased I had finally fallen into the routine pattern of girls lost in their own frivolity. I had been saved. When the gown arrived, everybody was excited. It was a maze of tulle and lace and pearl insets. The ultimate of fashion. It was the most beautiful gown anyone had ever seen in that town. Every day was filled with the plans for the ball. There were gifts to put on display; there was the accounting and the usual courtesies before the engagement announcement. It was not a difficult thing to do. But, every night I would lock my room and put on the ball gown. For hours I would contemplate what I was going to do. I had to build the courage, for my plan included something completely against the grain of gentlewomen. It would scare me to even think of it. But I know I had to do it. I would stare at my image in the Paris gown and tell myself that it was the price of freedom. . . . there was no other way. That Paris gown was to become my final revenge against the injustice of men."

The afternoon sun had lost its full ardor. The pale coolness of early dusk melted gently in the sun. As the sun fell, the line of light chose among the garden freedoms pieces of shadow touching the world with a gentle sobriety. If there were a time in each day more suitable for sadness . . . or for finding gentle love . . . perhaps this time. . . . The modes of the now could not be forgotten for an old story. Nevertheless, the falling shadows upon light were a part of long ago as much as the story was a part of now.

Clotilde picked up the threads of her design of long ago: "I remember talking to my father about making an effective entrance. A champagne toast at the precise hour of nine after the guests had supped and drunk to their enjoyment, at a time when the music becomes a part of the breathing passion, at this particular time, my father would offer a toast to the bride and groom. Not until then would I descend the staircase leading to the main ballroom where the guests were gathered. My father was impressed. Yes, it would be very effective; it would show off the Paris gown to its fullest. Don Ignacio approved. It would show off his new possession. Yes, everybody was in agreement.

I stayed in my room the night of the ball listening to the rising talk and the sounds of the banquet. It was a foreign thing to me, for my thoughts were with the wind and a wide, wide freedom, soon, very soon. The gown was laid out on my bed in full glory. It was truly a beautiful thing. A few minutes before nine I began to put the final touches to the plan. I stood there before my mirror, full of an unknown terror at what I was about to do. I opened the door of my bedroom to meet the full force of happy voices awaiting my entrance. I heard the orchestra begin the music that was to signal my entrance. Then my father's voice, full of pride, was audible to me. He made a short, modest speech about the friendship between the two families about to be united. Finally I heard the words . . . May I present my daughter and the future bride of Don Ignacio Maez de Tulares. Let us toast the future of the ideal couple. . . . The glasses were now raised. I swallowed hard and slipped silently down the hall leading to the staircase. My throat was tied and my hands trembled, but I knew I could not falter. Soon I was at the top of the staircase. Immediately, I heard the cries and horrified exclamations among the guests. I thought at the moment of closing my eyes, but I was certain to fall. Also, I did not wish to appear afraid or ashamed, so I tried to look down into their faces. All wore the same frozen, shocked look of disbelief. I saw my mother fall into a faint, and the choleric face of Don Ignacio was punctuated by a fallen jaw of disbelief and anger. He threw his champagne glass and it smashed on the floor, then he turned and left without ceremony. No one noticed his departure, for all eyes were upon me. . . . All this I saw as I came down the stairs . . . *stark naked.* . . . "

There was a sudeen flurry of curtains and the light that gave life to the art in the room softened mysteriously to a promise. Clotilde touched the buttons of her blouse, still lost in that memory of what she had planned as a way of freedom. Theresa came up to her and kissed her cheek. "Oh, Clo . . . you were so brave, so brave!"

"I think now it was a kind of insanity finding its own method to fight what I considered a slavery. It was simple after that. My father could not abandon an insane daughter, but he knew that my presence meant constant reminder. He let me come to Paris with sufficient funds . . . and here I made my home. . . . my home."

"Do you miss the other home?"

"Yes, I left part of myself there and the people of my blood . . . of course there is a certain nostalgia . . . but no regrets. That's what I hope you will learn in your journeys . . . never to have regrets."

"You have found . . . the freedom . . . the equality?"

"Yes, my child, I have known the depth of feeling in all its glorious aspects." Both women looked out the window and caught the full colors of life.

THE TREES

The dead valley. Tombstones sprouted on a hill, scattered like old pennons along the valley, clustered in the shadows of a deserted house, and on the stamp of bank along a dead stream next to the hill. Dispirited, the wind moaned its own "Amen." Clusters of dry weeds hugged against the moan while rootless tumbleweeds found a path free-styled following the wind. **Unpredictable,** these jumbled skeletons of brush found refuge against tree stumps, doorways, and tombstones. There was no desperate plea for life in this deadness, but it was far from a nothingness. A nothingness . . . can the mind and heart conceive of such a thing? Even dead valleys cling to traces of something. This something is new because it is now in the instance of process. The process, in this case, was a part of eager lives until . . . human error? **Nature's** error? No one ever thinks in terms of nothingness or *is* in terms with nothingness. All is part of the change in process, errant and eternal. The reality now is different from the reality then . . . a life emerged, then, a desolation in the duration we call time. . . . Time . . . it is without creation. But things and people of the earth are creation and self-created by complexities beyond comprehension. That is why blame and condemnations of people should not exist, for they are but creations of a process, self created with ingredients from creations outside themselves. This valley thrived once; so did its people, following patterns known and unknown.

Close scrutiny will show that all the tombstones bear the same name . . . Ayala. They are sad finalities to the ways of men. All these tombstones came to be with a suddenness. No! wait . . . only some of them; the others cling like aftermaths, the consequence of greater things. But those that came with a suddenness bear the name and the claim, "son of Teófilo Ayala." Teófilo Ayala must have been the centrifical force if one goes by tombstones. The wind, eager and demanding, well agrees.

If nothingness existed, it would exist after nothingness. But this came to be an end to many lives. Thus the mystery and the wonder of man's short existence upon the earth. The suffering and ephemeral condition of human life leaves all this . . . but never a nothingness! Out of something with a pulse came the dead tree stumps,

11

the cracked, pained earth, and the moan. At one time the people were and people did. Here the trees once grew, the stream drank full, and the houses held life. Here, at one time no scattered tombstones existed. The dead were taken to a prescribed cemetery so as not to confuse the living.

What had come upon the day in this town of Quinteco? Wasn't that a famous name? Of course, the Quinteco apples, the famous apple orchards that produced the most unusual apples in the world. Here is where the orchards had once thrived and flourished to give men riches . . . el terreno de manzanas that made the town of Cetna famous all over Mexico. In this semi-tropical climate where the rain found protection in mountains that like a fortress surrounded the town, the famous apple was the opportune fruit of many natural wonders.

It had been a small apple, thin-skinned. Its softness had the quality of mangos in ripeness, and its green sweetness surprised at intervals with streaks of gentle, bitter strains that calmed the fullness of the sugar . . . a bittersweet goodness of surprise. There was no other apple like this one. Long before the planting, long before the harvest, the apples in great demand, were sold to canning industries, fine hotels, and exclusive markets. It was a prosperous valley for apples and people.

Don Teófilo Ayala was sole owner of six hundred fertile acres. He had four sons who worked in love and harmony with him from dawn to dusk to help with the creation of life's fruit. The simple laws amongst them were not vain, or seeking profit for self. It was a wholesome venture of unity, where trust and giving came first. The profit in money was but an aftermath, never the due course or the ultimate incentive. The apple trees came first; they represented a task of God and for God, and in this belief the brothers worked.

It is said that experience is not merely physical, biological or even just human. There is a quality in experience that is very much like the Quinteco apple. It is the quality of creation, of innovation, of that something new. The newness itself, nevertheless, be it creation or destruction, finds its way of changing people, apples, ways. Experience finds expansion in this newness, in this unknown. Even if it becomes the remnants of a dead paradise, it leaves another richness and creation for other men. It becomes a growth into understanding. The story of the Quinteco apple left that to men.

When did the newness come? When did the safety and security of the Ayala family feel the impact of something novel and new? Something exciting and desirous, merely because it was not too well understood? It came with Nina . . . in that long ago. The desolation, then, can be relived, proving the non-existence of a nothingness . . . .

. . . .

Nina married Ismael, the youngest son of Teófilo Ayala, without family approval. The family, with its elementary tie to the earth, had established a working patriarchal order. The father and sons lived for a fraternal cause, the apple orchards. Their women followed in silent steps, fulfilled in their women ways. If ambition or a sense of power touched the feminine heart, it was a silent touch. The lives were well patterned like the rows of apple trees and the trenches that fed them. Men and women had a separate given image until Nina came.

A confident city girl, she showed disdain for submissiveness and the tried patterns. The conversation of the women bored her. Inevitably, she found her way to the men of the family. The men themselves were troubled over the "easy ways" of Ismael's wife. There was too much turbulence under the blush of cheek and coquettish smile. She had ambition and thrilled to the sense of power in interacting. She flaunted; they frowned. She felt herself lucky to have married well into a good family. She had no substantial background in tradition or security. This the family considered as tragic. Ismael did not care. He knew his wife to be intelligent and beautiful. He knew her to be free. What neither Ismael or the family saw was the fear in Nina, a fear that was a sore storm.

A life of alienation and poverty, loneliness and rejection had nurtured this great fear. It was this fear that made her arrogant in self-esteem. She looked down on these high-born, comfortable women who were now her family. There had been few ripples in their lives; their lives of imitated rituals were a dumb-show to Nina. She felt her fire to be unique. She felt a power within herself that well disguised the fear. The sultry power in the half-promise of open lips, a special smile, things unsaid except with eyes became manipulative with the husband and the men of the family. The fear became faint. There would be no more exile.

She was an Eve in a Garden of Eden; her sin was not innocence reaching for "the knowing." No . . . her sin was a violence grown out of the fear of inadequacy. At any cost, she must have power to disguise the knowing of inhumanities and cruelties from the past. She played the game well; chance was on her side for she dared more, knew no qualms, and felt no guilt. In her shining youth and beauty, she was also the snake.

When Teófilo Ayala died, chance was in full force. The apple orchards were willed to the sons who would choose among themselves to jointly own them, or divide them according to their place in the old laws of inheritance. The oldest son received half of the property. The next three sons received an inheritance in proportion to their rank in birth. Ismael, under these conditions would receive the least. Nina felt an anger in the pit of her stomach.

"It's not fair, Ismael. The land should be equally divided."

"It doesn't really matter . . . we may just own it jointly. We may decide that."

But joint ownership was not the decision made. Teófilo Ayala had been the self-sufficiency. Somehow in the patriarchial pattern, he had become the source of existence. Unwittingly, he had willed the lives of his sons who obediently followed his direction. A dependency was left behind with the death of the father. Someone needed to take strong reins. None of the brothers dared. The oldest, Rafael, lacked his father's business sense. His life had been one of Lothario among the village maids. Feminine conquest was his own private proof of masculinity. It was enough for Rafael. Under the will of his father, he had laboured out of duty, not out of ambition. Marcos and Santos, more naturally industrious, could not replace the sagacity of the patriarch now dead. Ismael, as the youngest, was not expected to do so. It seemed much simpler to divide. The younger brothers did not seem to mind. Within themselves, they knew that the pattern of their lives would serve as the cohesion among them. They would labour in harmony and share in harmony as before. Nina condemned, "I don't believe your brothers. They want their larger share. Rafael probably wants it all. You are an Ayala too!"

"Nina, my love . . . don't say things like that. I trust my brothers. You don't understand the closeness."

Nina left the room slamming the door after her. She went to her bedroom and threw herself on the bed. She thought of the other brothers' wives. How they would lord it over her! The insipid, ugly old things! She didn't have to stand for that. She . . . with all she had to offer. Ismael was a coward. She was an Ayala now . . . the name was hers. Suddenly, she remembered the first time when she met Ismael. He had asked, "What is your name?"

"My name isn't important."

"But I want to know who you are . . ."

"I mean my name isn't important like yours . . ."

But now, she was an Ayala. What was fair was fair. She deserved more than those stupid women and their little ways. She heard Ismael's footsteps coming towards the bedroom door. Quickly, she rose, ran to the door and turned the lock. Ismael tried the door and called her name. After the third time, he left. As Nina heard his steps retreating, she observed. "He's so ineffectual . . . he gives in without a fight. But I know how to fight. . . ."

.   .   .   .

Nina waited from a distance until everyone had left the market office. Rafael would be alone now. He was sitting at his desk drinking his favorite brandy.

"You must be tired." She stood in the doorway, an angel dressed in a mist of blue.

"What?" Rafael turned and caught the full impact of her striking beauty. "Nina . . . what on earth are you doing here?"

"I came to town to see my dressmaker. I thought you might drive me home . . . if it's not out of your way." She glided to his side and placed her hand on his shoulder gently. Rafael took another drink. He looked at her searchingly, "I . . . I should have offered you some. . . ."

"I love your brand . . . may I?" She helped herself from the same glass and looked at him over the brim of the glass. "Are you sure you won't mind driving me home?"

"How often do I get the pleasure of your lovely company, my dear sister-in-law?"

She laughed. Rafael swiftly tidied his desk and turned off the lights. He walked towards the door. Nina seemed to remain in the semi-darkness as if waiting for something.

"Is anything the matter, Nina?"

"No . . . no . . . I just felt a current . . ."

"Are you cold. . . ."

"It was a different kind of current." The insinuation was made. Rafael walked back to where she stood. "I always thought you were some kind of witch!" He circled her waist. Nina leaned towards him and laughed again, "I am!" She threw back her head and opened her lips. The kiss was passionate. Rafael's muscles tightened. For a moment, he seemed to hesitate. Nina suggested softly, "Let's go out to the apple orchard. Did you see the full moon against the trees last night? Let's go wait for the moon."

They left the office and drove out to the apple orchards. Nina led the way to a cloistered area under trees in full blossom. She sat on the grass and put out her arms to him. Rafael was a combination of confusion, pain, and desire. Nina was like the Quinteca apple . . . soft, with that special sweetness . . . with that sensuality that spells life . . . she was so special . . . so exciting. Nina was the Quinteca apple in the moonlight.

Afterwards, Rafael felt a remorse. The fabric of brothers' trust had been violated. He dared not think of what had happened. He dared not even look at Nina. Nina was amused by his total suffering. She felt him to be a hypocrite. Just like a man! He took without reserve . . . then, he would justify for conscience's sake. All of them were Pontius Pilates. Rafael talked to her in the darkness.

"Forgive me, Nina . . . Ismael must never know. . . . I don't know what I would do if he ever found out."

Nina's voice was now cold and deliberate. "I am going to tell him."

Rafael's confusion was pitious. "But . . . why?"

"I want Ismael to know that he can not trust you. Why should you be trusted with half of the inheritance?"

"The inheritance. . . . I can't believe you planned all this just to . . . just to. . . ."

"To show you up, my dear, righteous brother-in-law!"

She now stood in front of him . . . a defiant creature. An avenging angel come to the Garden of Eden. Rafael put out his hand in supplication. She violently thrust it aside and ran down the path leading to the main road. She looked back once, to see the dark outline of Rafael still standing where she had left him. She ran and ran down the road that led to the Ayala property. All the brothers' houses were built within walking distance. The orchards were a few miles out. If she were lucky, someone would be driving up the road. As she ran, she began to tear at her clothes. She ripped off a sleeve. With effort, she ripped the front of her bodice, then she stopped and scooped some dirt from the road. She rubbed it on her face and hair. She continued running until she heard a car coming up the road. She stopped and waited breathlessly. She was surprised at her own luck. It was Ismael. It couldn't be better!

Ismael stopped the car and ran towards her with horror on his face. Nina ran to him in tears. He caught her in his arms and she rested there sobbing hysterically.

"What happened? Tell me, are you hurt? What happened?"

She sobbed and shook her head. Ismael looked down the road and saw no one. He quickly led her to the car. She was in need of a doctor. On the way home Nina kept crying softly, but would not speak. When they got home he quickly, helped her off with the torn clothes and got her into bed. She lay there inert. Only a heavy sigh would emerge from her every so often.

"Nina . . . can you tell me what happened?"

Nina began to sob hysterically again. She hid her face on her pillow and her body shook with the crying. Ismael felt helpless. He decided to call the doctor. Then, he went back to the bedside and held Nina's trembling body with great love. His eyes were full of anguish and of questions. Nina still said nothing.

Half an hour later, the doctor had examined her and had deduced what had happened. He spoke to Ismael with kindness. "Apparently she is in shock. That is the reason why she does not speak. I don't know how to tell you this . . . but there are signs of having been ravished. . . . All the evidence. She must have gone through a horrible experience."

Ismael stood there broken. In a world of family pride and honor, this was the worse thing that could have happened. There was now only one course beyond all others. . . . even beyond the cause of apple trees. . . .

The doctor looked anxiously at Ismael. "What you need is a drink. Here . . . let's go into the study. I'll fix you a drink." Ismael followed the doctor into the study for another reason. He went quickly to the gun case and took out a rifle. The doctor, with concern, tried to reason with him. "No . . . Ismael. You don't know who did it. You must wait."

"She was running up the road from the apple orchards . . . he may still be there."

He loaded the rifle quickly and walked out of the study. He got into his car and drove off towards the orchards. Suddenly, he noticed the torn piece of her sleeve on the road. He stopped the car and got out with the rifle in his hand. He looked towards the orchard where silent trees only spoke of peace and magic moonlight. Ismael did not see or hear. He ran towards the orchard and lost himself among the trees. His actions were fruitless. He knew it. He looked in all direction and the memory of his wife overwhelmed him. Suddenly, he shouted in the darkness, "For Christ sake! Where are you. . . . let me see you so I can kill you!" There was only silence. In a burst of new anger, he fired the rifle again, and again. The rifle shots resounded through the apple orchards. In a few minutes, lights from the different houses were turned on. The brothers joined together to see what had happened. With the farm helpers, they began to search the orchards. It was here they found Ismael, kneeling on the ground, covering his face.

. . . .

Nina stood watching the raindrops hit hard against the window pane. She had stayed in her room for several weeks, mostly to find peace within herself. She looked at the raindrops in fascination. She went back in time when she had looked at hard raindrops against a window pane before. She had been six years old. Her dead mother's sister had taken her to live with her father.

"Here, you take her. I can't afford another mouth to feed. Girls are too much trouble. Especially the pretty ones like this one . . . men are all over them before you know it."

The stepmother with thin lips looked at the aunt with hate and suspicion. "She's Juan's brat . . . not mine!"

The aunt was adamant. "You have to take her." With that finality, she walked out. It was raining hard and Nina had stared out into the rain out of fear and bewilderment. Where did she belong? She looked hard at the raindrops trying hard to keep back the tears. The stepmother, as if to get back at life, walked up to Nina and began to hit her . . . again and again. Blows without reason and the rain. There was a knock at the door. Nina shook herself free from the memory and listened.

"Nina. . . . are you going to open the door? Nina . . . for God's sake . . . please let me in." Ismael's voice sounded tired and exhausted. Nina remained silent.

"Nina. . . . you must tell me who did it. For my sanity, Nina." Ismael's voice rose to a desperate shout. "Nina!" There was no response. She knew that he would go away. She began to pace the floor. There were other plans to be made. She knew that her silence was a scream of accusation. Rafael would break soon . . . soon . . . but when?

Every night, she would open the door of her room and walk to the end of the stairway. There she would listen for any conversation from the study that kept her up with the happenings of the day. The evening before she had listened to what had now grown into another plan. The brothers were gathered in Ismael's study.

"For heaven's sake, Rafael . . . you have to stop drinking. We're late on our commitments. The bookkeeper has been having troubles. There were four complaints about shipment schedules from Mexico City. What do you think you're doing?" Marcos's voice was angry.

Rafael's voice sounded bitter. "My little brothers now blame me for the whole mess . . . how convenient. Where's Santos? Why doesn't he help? and you Marcos? what about you?"

"You know that Santos's ulcer was acting up. He took the family to San Luis. He might have to stay in the hospital. I have to supervise the workers in the fields. You know darn well that's my job, and Ismael . . . well, what do you expect him to do after what's happened?"

Rafael's voice suddenly sounded desperate. "Oh, damn the whole business!"

Nina had tiptoed back to her room. She had heard enough. So Santos was away with the family. The idea came during the night. What if Santos's barn and house were to catch fire? What if no one knew who had done it? Yes . . . things were moving too slowly. That would bring things to . . . to . . . well, anything, but this waiting . . . waiting.

. . . .

Nina watched the blaze from a distance. There was a strange excitement in her. The feeling of power was almost orgiastic. She closed her eyes and felt the cool wind against her face. The wind will help the fire spread, she thought. Out of the darkness came a series of screams. . . . The blaze had taken hold. The nightmare began. Out of Santos's house now in full blaze, came two children. "It can't be," Nina felt the panic rise in her. "They went with Santos to San Luis . . . no, no, it couldn't be true!" But it was. She heard Santos's voice screaming for help with the fire. He had started some hose and some men came running to help. He, then, set up a ladder facing the upstairs window. The bedroom! His wife, Irene, was still in there. Nina watched Santos go up the ladder. Suddenly, with a lurch, he fell heavily to the ground. The fire blazed relentlessly now. Men gathered around the prostrate body of Santos.

Nina could hear voices. "Give him air! Don't move him! Call an ambulance!" She ran back to her house and found her way back to the bedroom. No one had missed her. She opened her bedroom door and then closed it quickly behind her. She was safe . . . safe . . . for a little while?

She went to the window and watched the lights cast by the fire against the shape of furniture in the room. There were many sounds now. She tried to drown them out. She remembered a vulgar, tavern song . . . out of the past. Why had she remembered the obscenity? How many years had past since the tune cut anguish in her heart? She covered her ears trying to forget it. It came again and again. She screamed. No . . . she refused to remember. She tightened her body and dug her fingers in her arms. With arms folded, she tried to hold back another scream. The memories came, they came like spurts of blood. There was the stepmother with the cruel mouth. She stood there with some money in her hands. Nina remembered the four drunk men that held her. They had bought her from the stepmother. The room over the tavern . . . the many voices that drowned out her screams. The disgust . . . the long, long vomiting . . . the dark alley . . . the fatigue and numbness of the damned . . . the church door.

She became the scullery maid for the blind old priest. The kind old priest never understood how she came to stay with him, but he needed someone to help. He was so aware of God . . . vainly with blind eyes he reached out for people. There were so many things she remembered after that. The church services, the clean, angelic singing, the bells, all, all were a reinforcement of a worth in life. She learned to sleep again; she learned to awaken happy with the day. Four years, she had scrubbed floors and listened and watched. She said nothing then. She was as voiceless as the priest was blind, except when she felt the loneliness overpower her. She would go into the church when it was empty and try to find God. "Are you there? God! Are you there?" There was a silence. She became bitter. "I don't believe anything, do you hear? I don't believe anything!" She felt better after getting back at God's silence. Now the dirty little song had come back to tear at her. She screamed again and then in a whisper asked the question of long ago, "Are you there?" No one heard. The sounds of tragedy were too many outside the house. Now, she had more reason for never leaving the haven of her bedroom. But where were the churchbells, the burning tapers? the singing voices? She ran to the bed and hid her head under her pillow.

. . . .

The town now spoke of the growing curse. Trees were dying; workers were leaving the Ayala orchards. The assailant of Ismael's wife had not been found. Santos had died of a heart attack trying to save his wife who had died in the fire. Nina was said to be going insane. Rafael was a broken drunk. Ismael was obsessed with the idea of revenge. Marcos was trying hopelessly to save the vestiges of family. Hubris, catastrophic pride . . . avenging furies on the heads of the town's nobility . . . fruit . . . all melting into a great velocity of madness.

In the haze of alcohol, Rafael knew he had to stop it. He must scotch the snake. He must go to Nina and make her confess. That was the only way to stop the madness. She was to blame for everything. He went to the house knowing he must get her out of that bedroom. She must speak. She wasn't mad. She was a spreading Evil that must be destroyed. When he knocked at her door, Nina knew it was not her husband's knock. This knock frightened her. Then she heard Rafael's voice outside the door.

"You bitch, you filthy bitch, open this door this instance. You tell the truth or I'll kill you. Do you hear? Open the door!"

Nina obeyed. She opened the door to the half-crazed man. She looked at him as if she bore no guilt. She, however, observed his drunkenness. He lunged at her and caught her by the shoulders and shook her again and again. There was no response from her. He let her go. She calmly left the room and walked down the stairs. He followed her shouting. "Come back here and tell the truth!" She looked back once as if confused. "How much did you pay her!" Rafael did not understand. He thought he saw through her. "You are very clever . . . pretending to be mad, you bitch . . . you worthless slut!" She repeated the question, "How much did you pay my stepmother!"

"What? What are you saying?"

She walked out of the front door and Rafael came after her. Outside of the door, he caught up with her and slapped her face as if trying to bring her to her senses. At this time Ismael arrived. He was running towards the house as Nina brushed past him walking towards the opened path. Rafael's face, distorted with hate and fear, made things very plain for Ismael. Rafael was not totally aware of Ismael. His eyes were focused on the running figure of Nina. Ismael knew what his brother had done. The mind, nevertheless, can not register well when the heart objects. He stood transfixed as Rafael rushed out after Nina.

Instead of taking the path that led to the orchards, she began to climb a side hill that overlooked the estate. It was steep and rocky, but she made her way steadily upward. She kept climbing without stopping. Rafael followed her, but could not continue. He sat exhausted on a boulder, his breath coming heavy and hard. Marcos, arriving at Ismael's house, caught sight of Rafael sitting on the side of the hill. He also saw a woman's figure slowly climbing up the steep hill. He walked towards his brother to ask what was the matter.

. . . .

Ismael unfroze. Rage consumed him. He turned to see the fleeing figure of Nina climb the hill; he saw Rafael running after her. His brother! His brother! His brother had dishonored his wife. Why? Where was the love of so many years? Where was the oneness? His anger rose again. He ran up the steps into the house and made his way to the study. From the gun case he took out the same rifle that he had shot in the orchards. He loaded it again. Again, he set out towards the hill. From a distance he called out to Nina who did not seem to hear. She never turned as she climbed. Rafael looked up and saw Marcos coming towards him. Not far behind him stood Ismael with the rifle in his hands looking up at the still climbing figure of Nina.

"Nina! Nina! Come back . . . come back! I won't let him harm you!" Ismael's voice was full of love. Marcos looked from Rafael towards Ismael, then he, too, looked up at the climbing figure not sure what to make of it all until he saw Ismael raise his rifle and aim it at Rafael. Rafael just sat there, with tortured eyes, waiting for the inevitable. He did not move. Marcos, moved instinctively between his two brothers to try and stop Ismael. It was too late. Ismael fired his gun hitting Marcos through the heart. His body fell without ceremony at the foot of the hill. With another kind of instinct, Rafael seemed to come to life. He scrambled fearfully to the side of the hill that blocked Ismael's aim if he were to shoot again. When he thought himself safe, Rafael began to run across the open field at the other side of the hill.

Ismael did not fire again. The horror of what he had done grew in him. He ran to the dead body of his brother and lifted the body in his arms. "I'm sorry . . . Marcos . . . I did not mean to shoot you. Why did you get in the way! Marcos . . . my brother . . . Marcos!" The body was limp in his arms. Ismael knew he was dead. Ismael's body became one pulsation of despair. Why? Why? He put the body of Marcos back gently on the ground. Slowly, he looked up to the top of the hill. Nina stood poised on the edge.

. . . .

"How beautiful it is up here!" thought Nina. She looked to the apple orchards. "It will be a good harvest in Paradise." She looked down at Cain standing over the body of Abel. She turned and saw a frightened human being running towards the protection of his home. All this was part of the moving picture of the mind. Again, she looked down at the apple trees. Such a freedom, she thought. Above the world there is peace and an acceptance. After the dark, screaming battles of the spirit, there had been the sweetness. She remembered the hat store where she was an apprentice after she left the blind priest. She had worked hard with her hands and imagination until Ismael came. . . . Ismael came. . . .

He had loved her with a gentle touch. But how could she love? She did not know how. . . . Sooner or later death comes. He had said many things she did not understand because she had never known light and freedom. Sooner or later death comes. All the beautiful things I am . . . the confidence, the power . . . one large frightened sob? Sooner or later death comes. Nina called out, "God, are you there?"

She leaned over simply to be caught by wind and the openness of things. A shower of rocks followed the path of her falling body in full symphony. It sang the praises of a something new in erosive change. Not a nothingness, but a coming desolation. When her body hit the bottom of the hill, the praises still followed like the lingering fullness of one note until her body was covered with debris. She was now part of all . . . sooner or later.

Ismael saw her fall, but his body machine was overcome by folly. It could take no more than bleared, joyless observation, without acceptance, without rejection. What is more compassionate than the numbness after pain? Life-fruitage fallen unsavoured to the ground. He had known its warmth and richness for a little while. Now he watched, with sad separation, the falling body as it gathered momentum and took with it part of the hill to the bottom. After the rocks stopped falling, there was a silence.

The darkness of the spirit kept him away from her body. Death and the darkness did not give her to him. Grass grew above the ledge. The stream spoke in ripples and far off came the distant cry of birds. The land was bright and warm and rain was still a hope. The darkness still kept him away.

Destiny had found a seal. Ismael picked up his rifle and walked towards Rafael's house.

. . . .

Rafael was waiting for Ismael. He too had felt and accepted the seal of falling things. There could be no words now. Too much had happened. Extinction had set in. The hands felt the cold metal of the gun. That was the only surety, and the tiredness . . . that consuming, creeping tiredness. Neither could gladly yield to love because violence had confused that. The only thing possible was the automatic, the next step in inevitable violence that made the seal permanent. It was as if they told each other, "Let's get it over with and die."

They did. The tombstones were now complete.

But still . . . doesn't the universe exist with all it contains to evolve? Is it not true of experience? To find God without question . . . to give to man without question . . . is that not the evolvement? If only this wholeness could piece the Ninas and the Ayalas of the world.

Life was gone now. The orchards followed. The townspeople blamed it on the curse. The curse? Is not all violence . . . silent and corrosive, insidious in its every day ways . . . is that not the curse? More practically minded men blamed the dying of the orchards to a change in climate, to an overworked soil, to a lessening rainfall. Whatever the reasons may be, the Garden of Eden became a desolation. The Eden was only orchard, for its people had brought the confused ways of the world into it. They also brought their basic humanness that was the Quinteca apple in rarety and joy. The tombstones bear the name "Ayala," but where is Nina's grave? Someone forgot.

Perhaps she was never important enough.

PAY THE CRIERS

Rain knows the earth and loves it well, for rain is the passion of the earth. It is tears, joy, hope, melted into cool torrents that fall on the longing and the hunger of the earth in rigorous tenderness to give her life. How well it speaks of senses in its cool excitement. The beginning of passion is a burst of flame. Its culmination speaks of an open door unto light, a lucidity of life, more life, forever life.

The giver, rain, comforts, forgives, understands, as it tells of mountains, oceans, skies, and a breathing consciousness of all things. Earth and rain become dark moisture that finds its brightness of a womb. The first beginning was in rain. After copulation . . . there is a silence. It is similar to the silence that follows love. Like love, it confirms the truth of immortality. Like love, it has the vastness of acceptance. This glorious silence is that open door into a clean, free clarity.

Chucho listened to the silence and watched the water on mud puddles circling for an open way. The smell of rain is rich with life. He, too, was full of the same silence. He stood looking out the door leading to the backyard. The desert had welcomed the rain as Juana had welcomed love. He could hear her soft breathing from the bed. He looked up to see the sky, a cloudless blue. The sun had found its throne again. Juana had gotten up from the bed and was now behind him. The silence was part of her too. His glance now fell upon the jarros full of rain water outside the doorway. The water played with light like singing senses. The rain had given.

Chucho felt Juana's small hands caressing his body. The smell of the clay from the jarros increased the pleasure. The aftermath of love and set earth became the same affirmation. Juana's cheek felt warm and soft on his bare back . . . now her half-opened lips pressed hard, tenacious in their love. The lips held a reverence and a claim. Outside the door there was a newness in the world as if all the ills that fester with droughts had been swept away.

"Will you stay, Chucho?"

"I have things to do."

"You must keep your promise, Chucho."

He shrugged his shoulders indifferently. Droughts lengthen out into interminable desperations for Juana. A time and a place had defined her among the vanquished. This is why inquietude existed within the well-being of love, why melancholy sought a claim. It was now that Chucho became aware of his dead mother-in-law, hidden in the darkness of the room. This was the focus now, the presence of a dead woman who had been a part of them. This was also the reason for Juana's misery.

His thoughts returned to the early afternoon when he had come home after a long absence. Chucho had found Juana, grief-stricken, over the dead body of her mother. The old woman's long drawn-out battle was over. She had given in to death. Juana was clutching the old purse stuffed with bills and coins that the mother had entrusted to her with her last breath. Juana had promised to use the money for a grand funeral. When life left the body, Juana, lost in her despair, let it fall to the floor. She clung to the dead mother with a lostness.

A clap of thunder and lightning broke the heaviness of death. It was at this moment that Chucho had arrived as if he had brought the welcomed rain. She now turned from the dead mother to the live haven of his arms. He gave comfort simply and silently. Waiting for Chucho to come home had been long and frugal for Juana. Now in the realness of his compassion, Juana felt the body hunger, tormented and bursting into flame.

As he made love to Juana, his glance fell upon the purse fallen to the floor. He knew what it contained. For many years, he had fought with his mother-in-law and with his wife over the use of this money. The old mother, Refugio, had worked hard for it. She had saved it religiously for her funeral for a long time. "A waste!" Chucho had screamed. Refugio was their only means of support. She meted out the necessary money for frugal survival. The purse had grown fat with time. "I wonder how much?" Chucho asked himself as he caressed his weeping wife.

"Oh, Chucho, it was a bad time . . . I've been so alone."

"Hush, don't cry; I'm back."

Another clap of thunder brought Juana closer to him. The natural shocks of the body found their end. It was enough. Chucho whispered in Juana's ear, "I will take care of everything. I'll see about the funeral." He felt the sudden tenseness of her body. She held her breath. She knew too well her husband's ways. The fear, however, was secondary to her husband's arms. He was here; he could do as he wished. The gentle rain soon became heavy storm; with it, ascended the heartbeats of the living, a symphony of open doors, the light of life, more life, forever life.

In the shadows of the room, the old cot with the body of the dead woman served as a counterpoint, now lost, as Juana and Chucho swam the colors of the struggle. At one time, the now dead woman had known a struggle too. When youth had passed, the colors of struggle became greys in black descents of tragic things. The colors, the greys, even the black descent had ended for Refugio. Was there some kind of open door in death?

In life, Refugio had been a lusty warrior full of battle cry. The ready passion, the ready appetite, the way out of things, all had been her banner. Her crude grasp had been bloody and her blow heavy. This was her kind of grandeur. In the midst of her poor, monotonous greys, the armed savage had many times touched, harshly and with numbness, the consequence of rainbow spectrums so delicate they had made her fear a shattering of spirit. Perhaps this was why she had scorned impracticality, dream, illusion. But she had walked stoutly across the actuality of things. Her vision had small radius outside the slavish ways in the life struggle. The focus had always been to keep fighting, to keep abreast. If there was rest she reached for greys, for her eyes were now unaccustomed to the colors of the youthful dream or hope. She was earth with its tenacity, its instinctual freedom, and its voracity. The roughness of Refugio gave way only to a simple faith, a childish belief in the ritual wonders of her church. Its pageantry made her one with God, the master in the center of the ring. She had wanted a warrior's funeral when her time came with all its mummery and the jugglers of immortal hope. A fiery skyrocket must streak the heavens with her names for one last time to make up for shackles and for colors lost. A feast in her honor where tears would be wept in ceremonious grace. This had been the wish of the dead woman on the cot.

This was the woman that Chucho and Juana had forgotten when the flame had burst the glory—affirmation of the seed denying death in the dark corner. Now in the silence and the calm, her deadness became real to those well satisfied with love. Juana could not stand the thought of what she had done. Anxiety, too, suffocated her with doubt.

"You must take the money into town and pay the criers, Chucho." Now Chucho stood looking out the door. His wife's anxiety had made him rise impatiently from her side to seek a cleaner refuge with the rain. He reached down and picked up the old worn purse full of money. He put it in the pocket of the coat lying on a chair and returned to watch the rain. Suddenly, he turned and began to dress.

Juana sensed herself alone again. She looked towards the cot apprehensively and shivered with guilt. A horror began to grow. She had proved herself faithless to her mother. The money was now in Chucho's hands, easily taken. When she had come up behind him at the door, she was still warm with love, but guilt was taking hold. Chucho sensed it. Now that the rain had stopped, the jolt of life sounds from the barrio made his blood race. He must go. He walked away from the door to finish dressing. Juana's hold on him had been broken without ceremony. Juana felt the consequence of her stupidity. "Oh, God . . . I wish I could trust him . . . I wish I could erase the fears." But there had been so many times before when he had used her for his ends. The money is for the funeral; he must use it for that . . . he must. Her voice was thick with anxiety:

"You must pay the criers." He dared not look her in the face.

"Yes, yes . . . now leave me alone." He finished dressing hurriedly. He was alone in his pride and his plans. The shadows grew and made her cringe against her own weakness. This was the stamp long ago given to her by her dead mother and a disgusted husband when they had shared the wine. This creaturè well accepted condemnation as the measure of her life. The pain of loss found pulse again. "My mother's dead . . . my mother's dead . . . what can I do?" The weakness was a falling . . . a fearful falling. . . .

The dark hysteria grew. There will be no funeral. He will spend the money. In sudden desperation, she reached for Chucho's coat before he picked it up and fumbled through the pockets. He was beside her with a curse. He hit her and the blow erased the world for a second as she fell backwards against a chair. Again, she had done the wrong thing. He would leave her now. In desperate defeat, she had tried and failed.

"You must keep your promise, Chucho."

No! He was gone. The money was gone; her mother was gone. Her sobs came slow at first; soon they were hard and painful. Instinct took its course. The blind child from the womb went to her mother. She dragged herself across the floor to the cot where her dead mother lay. Her arms reached out to touch a stiffness; it was little comfort. "Mamacita . . . que voy a hacer? What is there without you? Without him?" She laid her head on the bosom of the dead woman, cradling her non-existing safeness, a nipple of security with no nourishment but touch. . . . Where? How?

. . . .

Chucho walked out of the two room hut he had helped Refugio build. The old bitch was dead! He touched the pocket of his coat where the money was. He had got the best of her after all.

He quickened his steps when he reached the bottom of the hill. The smell of food for evening meals mixed strangely with the fragrance of wet earth. Yes . . . the first thing he would buy would be a good supper for his best friend Chapo and himself. The best in the house . . . he could afford it. The anticipation made him rather light-headed. He felt joy rising to the throat, escaping into a shout of joy. All the things that would be his in the next few hours! The lighting of lamps in the houses that he passed reminded him of the people of the world. They had all the meaning for the time he touched them, talked to them, shared with them. He would treat everyone tonight. It was a beautiful thought. He would be the giver . . . he, Chucho! Never before could he give so much. He was always broke. Tonight he had much money. The glory of the feeling filled him.

He would tell Chapo about the money and then he would buy a full tank of gas for Chapo's old car. Tonight he would try his luck at the gambling table. Tonight he would visit Adela's girls . . . yes, this would be a night to remember. He reached the bottom of the hill and turned towards Chapo's house. Chapo washed cars all day long with a trance-like vigor. This was the pattern of his day. Soap, mop, hose, car after car. Chapo was a machine, numb to the soul, grateful for the pittance to buy existence for another day. He had to close his eyes against himself as a man to give his life away for a few centavos. He had lost the freedom, poor Chapo! Chucho knew deep down in himself he would never give up the freedom. He was condemned by everyone as shiftless, worthless, no-account, but he would never give up the freedom.

The old dead bitch had been the worst one. He remembered her wild roars and accusations. Why tell him what he already knew? He drank too much and played the fool too often. The old woman's venom had been a fearsome thing. But, then, he curiously remembered times when they had laughed together. There was always relief in the eyes of his simple wife when he was friends with his mother-in-law. It meant peace for a little while. But the old woman had never understood his need for the freedom . . . perhaps because she had never had it herself.

One time he had seen some ice-skaters in the city. He had watched their graceful, skillful skating with great wonderment. Such a difficult thing looked so easy, so effortless. That was beauty. Somehow he felt it had something to do with the freedom he loved so well, but he could not explain it. The skaters must work hard for that beauty . . . very hard. The easy, swift, graceful gliding was the work conquered and transformed into a freedom now a part of them. Yes, yes . . . that was it . . . ease came with becoming a something in action. That is what he wanted to do in life . . . find an ease of action. Now, he was only a spectator of a great number of confusions and fears. But he was also a spectator and he shared the freedom with others.

There were glimpses of many kinds of beauties that went beyond the traps of every day. Each man must be involved in his destiny, but first he must recognize the part he plays, and the ease behind the play. Otherwise, the skill that brought the freedom would never be found. He remembered watching the skaters and remarking to Chapo:

"I want a skill like that, Chapo."

"You want to be a skater?" Chapo was never too surprised at Chucho's remarks.

"I want a skill for life, a smooth running to a freedom to make people see that I can see."

"Oh, you have a skill for life, Chucho. You can drink more, fight harder . . . you have been in jail more often than anyone I know . . . why I remember. . . .."

"Never mind, Chapo, I mean . . . never mind."

"I know what you mean, Chucho, it doesn't buy you any bread. What do you care? You have a mother-in-law with a good job."

"Oh, shut up, Chapo!"

"You play with many blows for the freedom, Chucho, but at least you still have the freedom. Look at me! That bastard without balls pays me like a slave because I need the money for food for my little ones. I would like to spit in his face . . . but I don't think about it. I just wash cars until they shine. Pretty soon, I get my centavos and I go home . . . we eat one more day."

"I find a skill . . . a good skill . . . then I will skate through life like a god." Chucho reached Chapo's shack. Next to it stood Chapo's bright green car like a sentinel against total decay. The oil lamps were lit. Chapo must be sitting down to supper.

Chucho let out a shrill whistle; then, he called out, "Chapo!" The door opened and Chapo came out hurriedly, closing the door behind him. Chucho was not welcomed at Chapo's house. All the neighborhood women considered him a bad influence.

"Hey, Chapo . . . let's fill the car tank with gas . . . and maybe you would like some new tires?"

"You joking?"

"The old woman died today. I got the money."

"May she rest in peace . . . all the money?"

"All the money. . . ."

"Ah . . . jaaaaaaaa!" Chapo grabbed Chucho and happily began to wrestle like a bear. They fell to the ground with much laughter and rolled around in happy jest. Finally they lay there looking up at the first stars of evening.

"It's going to be quite a night, eh, Chapo?"

"Hey, let's get going." Chapo jumped to his feet and kicked Chucho who was still looking at the stars.

"You see something special, you old dog?"

"A bigness. . . ."

"Let's go!"

A moment later the old green car was rattling off towards town where city lights spoke of temporary lightning dreams.

. . . .

"I am waiting for Chucho," Juana's voice was tired. She sat in her neighbor's kitchen. She had waited for Chucho to come back two nights now, waited with the growing stench of death. It did not change the indecisions in her life. She just waited for Chucho until the neighbor found her. It was now two days since the afternoon of life and death. The days had divided themselves in Juana's mind into convulsive terrors, where the chasms with no anchors whirled into a darkness. Memories were a surer stronghold. Then, the neighbor had come to warn her.

"Someone told the authorities about your mother. They're coming today to take her to the crematory if she is not buried right away."

Juana began to cry softly. "I can do nothing until Chucho comes."

"He will not come. He is passed out somewhere. Why wait for the scoundrel?"

"But what can I do? I have no money. No one can help."

"They are going to take her to the crematory today, just wait and see."

"When he feels guilty, he always comes back; he spent all my mother's money, so he will be back."

"Chucho . . . feel guilty? The devil he does!"

"Not guilty . . . it is more of a remorse, after he drinks too much . . . there is always the remorse." Juana remembered well her mother and her husband in the aftermath of drink. The tears for tears' sake, open memories like wet catacombs of sorrows that echoed a burning. Yes, there would be remorse when Chucho came back.

"The crematory will test its new efficiency if your mother is not buried by this afternoon."

"No . . . it is against our religion. My mother's body cannot be burned."

"If there is no money to bury her, she will be burned."

Juana began to weep again. "Mamacita . . . forgive me . . . what did I do to you?" It was a piteous crying of self-accusation. The neighbor stroked the disheveled head of the poor girl in sympathy. Such a soft, helpless thing. That brute of a Chucho should be flogged!

They both heard the car stop at the bottom of the hill. The voices of Chucho and Chapo were heavy with happy memories.

"Oh, Chucho, thank you for the beautiful tires. You are a good friend. Was that a good time or was that a good time?"

There was a short silence as they heard the men go into the house. Suddenly, a long, drawn-out bellow filled the air. Both women ran outside. Chucho was standing at the door looking like a wild man. He shook his head in disbelief and let out another bellow like a wounded animal. He fell to his knees and began to pound the wooden planks of the porch. Chapo stood by helpless and greatly distressed by Chucho's agony.

Chucho moaned, "She's still here. Oh, God . . . the rot! the rot!"

"We'll do something, Chucho," Chapo clumsily reassured, walking nervously around Chucho's kneeling body.

"It's not fair! It's not fair! Life should not rot!" Again he hit his fists against the planked floor.

Juana had run across to him to comfort. He needed her. She went on her knees to take his head in her hands and kiss his forehead as if to stop the suffering. She knew the heights and depths of her husband as she knew the old surface freedoms of his ways. She must tell him right away. "Chucho, the authorities are coming to take her away because there is no money to bury her."

Chucho looked into her face in bewilderment. "I cannot believe the stench . . . but her face, it is the young face of a virgin . . . God forgive me!"

"They will burn her body, Chucho."

He put his arms around her body as if to ask forgiveness. "I won't let them, Juana."

"You have some money left?" There was a ray of hope in Juana's voice. Chucho shook his head in utter despair, not because of the money, but because he could not imagine the body being burned. It was against God . . . never! never!

He raised himself to his feet and picked up his clinging wife. He turned to Chapo.

"She must not be burned, Chapo."

"What can we do?"

"Get some money somehow."

"Let's take the tires back, Chucho." Juana looked from one to the other, hoping.

Chucho said nothing for he was thinking hard. "The money from the tires will not be enough. We must go to our friends, to our many friends. We can take the body with us, so the authorities will not find it. We can tie it to the trunk of the car." He turned to Juana. "Get some saffron."

The neighbor shook her head in disapproval. Juana stood by helplessly and asked blankly, "Saffron?"

"Yes . . . it will stop the smell. Get as much as you can."

She seemed unable to move. She had no certainties in her experience bank. The neighbor took Juana's arm gently. "Come, I'll go with you." As she led the girl away, she turned to the two men. "You're a couple of fools if you think they are going to let you drive around with a dead body that should have been buried a long time ago."

"They'll have to catch us first . . . go . . . get the stuff."

Half an hour later a mummy-like body was being carried from the house into the trunk of the car. The saffron had been found; sheets had been used to wrap the body carefully. Chucho and Chapo then tied the body to the trunk securely. Juana and the neighbor watched in quiet disbelief. The trunk door remained half-way open when the job was done. It could not be helped. Chapo seemed skeptical.

"You sure it will work, Chucho?"

"Of course I'm not sure, but something has to be done. I'm not going to leave her for the authorities to burn. She was a very brave woman."

"You hated her guts, Chucho."

Chucho did not answer. He got into the car and turned on the ignition. "Get in." Chapo jumped in beside Chucho murmuring, "¡Que Dios nos bendiga!" As the car started off, Chucho called out of the window, "Don't tell the authorities anything. You know nothing." The car rattled down the road in a cloud of dust.

When the car had disappeared, the neighbor turned to Juana, "Stay with me if you want."

"No . . . thank you. I have many things to do before Chucho comes back. He will come back soon."

The neighbor walked away shaking her head. Juana sat down on the porch steps to watch the dying afternoon glorious in color. All traces of the rain were gone. The land had settled down to wait for the long drought. Gravely, her eyes looked out to the familiar desert, waiting too. She imagined an apricot tree fully in bloom. She never had seen one; she looked out into the glare of the sun and her mind's eye saw the apricot tree. There was no mother now, no weekly ritual of expectation, no stories from her mother so full of the outside world. The apricot tree grew in beauty with the mounting loneliness. What was she to do? Tears came to her eyes. She opened the palm of her hand to catch the tears. They glistened in the reflection on the sun. Colors could be found in slight whispers. She looked for a jewel in the wetness. Soon . . . she lost the world around.

. . . .

Chapo's face was fiercely red. He shook his fists in the air, "Thieves . . . they would not even give me a part of the price we paid for them. We can twist the tires around their necks . . . we have to take the money."

Chucho shrugged his shoulders. "Never mind . . . that small amount won't help . . . and we need the tires to get around."

"Where you wanna go now?"

"Let's try La Sevilla. The sun has set; our night friends will be there." La Sevilla was the favorite bar among the poor, for the owner Mando would many times forget an old bill. Here Chucho had spent money two nights before. Chucho was right; there were many people as Chucho and Chapo went in. Here were the faces of night friends wiped free of fear; this was the place to grapple with the honest fear and the

honest hope. Eyes were the full story, here, past the neon lights. The
nuances and puppet strings simply did not belong where eyes spoke
truth. How well loneliness speaks; it has no cotton mouth or twisted
word; tried lies have no place where men go to seek themselves.

Outside, the red neon cast a fierceness on the exposed dead body in
the trunk of the car. On and off . . . on and off; the vigil yet was young,
a reversion of destiny where one dead woman waited for the living to
find life. Inside, the place was filled with tourists and Mando worked
feverishly for a "good" night, wiping clean the altar full with communal
warmth. The welcomes, too, were warm for Chucho and Chapo. The
current carried them towards the usual rectitude that built, slowing to a
common human victory.

"Have a drink, Chucho. This is for you, Chapo."

"Listen, the gypsy is still here, Chucho, the one that found the spirit
of the mountain in you the other night. Hey, Gitano, look who just
came in."

The gypsy saw Chucho and rushed to him with arms outstretched.
"You have come back . . . to share the spirit . . . ah! what a night it
was! My music and you, the bull, in the arena."

"Not tonight, Gitano . . . I have a mission."

"We all have a mission . . . there will be tears and joy this night." He
began a lament on his guitar that extended itself to find the sad waiting
in all who heard. Waiting for what? No one really knew. Chucho gulped
his drink and slammed his glass upon the bar. "There is something
much sadder than your music . . . it is a sadness of the world. If you
only knew!"

Chucho put his head down on the bar feeling the weight of Refugio's
death. "I did a terrible thing, muchachos . . . a terrible thing."

"What's the matter with him, Chapo?"

"He did a terrible thing."

Chucho raised his head and wiped his eyes with his sleeve
unashamedly. "All that money I spent the other night . . . it was the
money to pay for a fine funeral for my mother-in-law. Now the
authorities will cremate her if we don't find the money to bury her."

"We need the money for the living, Chucho; the dead don't care
about their funeral."

Gitano's wailing song rose to torture in sound. Chucho's voice was
earnest: "You don't understand. This was no ordinary woman. She was
a beautiful fighter. She spat on misfortune and dug her heels for a fight
because life was a grand thing to her. There are a few women like her."

"Is that the mother-in-law that had you thrown in jail so often . . .
eh, Chucho . . . here have another drink; you can't think straight."

"The fights . . . it was because we cared as human beings, muchachos.
Listen, this is no joke. I will not let the authorities cremate her."

Gitano's song began to gather wisps of growing frenzy. It was a happy frenzy that well belonged to the snapping of fingers and the flame tapping of feet.

"Hey, Chucho . . . toro! toro!" The boys began to jostle him. "Dance . . . fight the bull as you did the other night . . . come on, Chucho . . . Ole!"

Chucho was determined to convince them of his plight; Chapo, on the other hand, had been caught up with the music and the mood. Refugio was a far-away thought when someone put another drink in his hand. Chucho screamed "She deserves a burial . . . you understand . . . she deserves it!"

The boys laughed and continued their chant: "Ola . . . toro! Dance for her, Chucho . . . she would like for you to dance for her. . . . Dance for her . . . dance for her. . . ."

Chucho looked into their faces in half-denial, "But she is. . . ." Suddenly he jumped up on the table next to Gitano. "I dance for her!" He exclaimed to the world. "I dance for Refugio! You understand, I dance for Refugio." The frenzy grew as Chucho dared life and pain and fear with his feet and the furious movements of his body. "She felt life like this!" The dance became hard and unrelenting until both Gitano and Chucho were spent. There was no clapping. Only a silence. The toro now sat as clown upon the table to make things tolerable.

"That was a good thing to do for her, Chucho . . . a good thing." Voices rose in agreement. Chucho looked at them like a prince of sadness and confided, "You know what? She liked autumns best because it was a time of realness when the fruits were gathered and the flowers had given of their bloom to all. She used to say dreams were cruel because the waiting sometimes has no end. But autumn . . . ah! It gives men heart, the golden things that are . . . you think I'm crazy . . . eh?"

"You talk as if you loved her . . . who loves his mother-in-law?"

"One who remembers long after . . . long after the things of heart . . . that's who!"

Chucho took another drink from an outstretched hand and gulped it down. Then he took another and another. "Hey, look at Chucho go . . . more! more! more!"

Chucho fell back upon the table like one dead; his eyes were closed. Everybody stared in silence. He spoke slowly and deliberately. "We have the body tied to the back of the car. Just go out the door and see for yourselves; she is waiting . . . how can I go to her without help . . . she is waiting." The crowd mumbled disbelief, but almost all of them hurried out to see. The commotion grew; so did the crowd until Mando went out himself to look. He ran back into the bar and shouted at Chucho, "You crazy fool. You have a dead body outside my

place. You know what the authorities will do to me? I'll lose my
license. Get her out of here . . . do you hear?" Chucho, still lying on the
table, sat up and saw his friends too lost in the circus of things. He
knew he could ask no more. He spotted Chapo looking anxiously at the
crowd. "Hey, Chapo . . . let's go!"

Outside the neon lights still claimed the body. Chucho and Chapo
got into the car without a word. They drove off with the crowd still
looking on. They drove down the street drowned in the neon promises
of desires, eerie in their brightness. After a while, Chapo asked, "Where
to?"

"Adela's place." Chucho leaned back thinking of the woman in the
trunk.

"Chucho, she's stinking terrible. Did you see the dogs sniff and run?"

"Shut up. Let's find some money."

"They were right back there. You talk as if you love her."

"I loved her. That is why I hated her so much. But when she bought
wine . . . those were very warm times. She used to tell me about her
man. He was shot mysteriously. She never found out who did it; she
had to bury him by herself. She lost four children in the epidemic. She
survived everything. When we drank too much wine we understood
things without saying."

"What did you understand, Chucho?"

"Life . . . and each other."

"That's a lot."

"That way we could hold on tight."

"She used to call you a coward."

"She called me everything. She had a big mouth. She was just jealous
of my freedom. She worked hard; she had a right to resent me, I
suppose."

"Remember when she cracked your skull?"

"What's the matter with you? You bring up all the bad things. Drive
and don't talk. The silence was brief for they soon arrived at Adela's.
Her place was a dilapidated two story building that seemed almost
deserted except for lamp-light and shadows that escaped through drawn
shades. Most of the windows were dark. The place did not wear a sign.
In earlier days, Adela had catered to the best clientele. The police
commissioner had been her confidant and protector. But all good things
had come to an end. Both Adela and the establishment had resigned
themselves to second-rate flurries.

Chapo parked the car as Chucho hurried to the door of the
establishment. Chapo soon caught up with him. One of the girls opened
the door, then silently disappeared. They entered a small foyer dimly
lighted and filled with artificial palms weighed down with dust. Beyond
was the sitting room. Behind an old, flowered, satin sofa was a beaded

curtain, covering the stairway leading to the rooms. As usual, Adela came into the room with her greeting for customers. Chucho and Chapo had been there a few nights ago. They had been most splendid and companionable. They seemed to be sober tonight.

She gave Chucho a hug. "Still sporting?" She then kissed him fondly.

"Not tonight, Adela. We have a mission."

The middle-aged madam took his arm and led him to the sofa. "A mission?"

Chapo followed doggedly behind. Chucho asked right out, "Adela, we need some money."

Instinctively, Adela straightened her back and her tone became business-like. "You came to ask me for money?"

"It is to bury my mother-in-law. It was her money I spent the other night. If I don't raise the money, the authorities will burn her."

"You get your wish then. You were always damning her to hell." She was both amused and cautious.

"You and your girls . . . everybody says you have the biggest hearts."

"No!"

"No." echoed Chapo.

"NO!" repeated the madam. She stood up and looked at them. Then she began to pace the floor up and down as she explained. "You say this is a good cause. Every time an old customer asks for help, they all have good causes. Believe me, we have heard stories of real distress. But, if I am not around, my poor girls are fleeced. They give all . . . foolish, foolish creatures! They cannot afford the luxury of helping everybody who asks. They have next to nothing. Only I stand between them and the world. I sympathize with you. I like you, but they are little sheep . . . little sheep."

"This one exception, Adela."

"If I make one exception, I will have to make many. That is the way. I cannot do it. However, I shall make a small personal contribution." She lifted her skirt and pulled out some money from the fold of her garter. "Here . . . I know it is not much, but I hope it helps." Chucho took the money, graciously accepting her generosity. He thanked her and kissed her before departing. Adela begged him to come back again. Out in the street, Chucho put up the collar of his old, worn coat. The wind was now raw. Chapo followed behind him. They got into the car without saying a word. They drove around a while and then decided to go to Kiko's. There would be winners there tonight. When they came to Kiko's place, they found it in total darkness. Chucho jumped out of the car and went to inquire next door. In a little while he was back.

"The place was raided. Everybody's in jail." They both stared out into the darkness.

"There will be no criers, Chucho. You cannot pay the criers."

"To hell with the criers, those wailing banshees, fakes!" Laughter spilled from opened doorways. Far off in the distance, the howl of a coyote could be heard. They continued staring into the darkness. "The criers are not good enough, Chapo."

"What are we going to do with the body, Chucho. We are going to land in jail."

"We are going to bury her ourselves, Chapo, out there where the coyote cries."

"You are crazy. We are going to dig a grave in this freezing weather? With what shovel?"

"We shall go to the undertaker and borrow a shovel."

"He's asleep."

"We'll borrow it anyway. It's justice since he refused to bury her just because we had no money."

"Now, Chucho?"

"Yes . . . but first we buy a couple of bottles with Adela's money. It will keep us warm."

. . . .

It was well past midnight when they got to the outskirts of the city. The climb up the hill and the biting wind had been torturous. The weight of the body and the overpowering stench made the bitter wind welcome. The heat of over-exertion mixed in with the smell of rotting flesh would have been intolerable if it had not been for the cold. Nevertheless, their fingers and faces were half-frozen. Chucho climbed the hill first, carrying the greater part of the weight. Chapo held the lower part of the body. Around his waist he had tied a rope that dragged the shovel after him. Twice they stopped to rest, but not for long, for too many stops meant wasted effort.

When they finally reached the top, they did not know how much time had passed, but the lights of the city still blinked back in reassurance. Distant and much smaller, they had lost their glaring vulgarity. They were now clear lights in sympathy with the night. The men began to feel the cold.

"Let us build a fire, Chapo."

They began to gather sagebrush and dead pieces of wood. It was hard to start the fire without protection from the wind. In time, they managed to start one behind a huge boulder that broke the wind. Soon it was blazing bright.

"I think I am freezing to death, Chucho."

Chucho began to scan the area for the proper burial ground. He finally pointed to a high spot next to a dead clump of trees. The spot was close to the edge of the hill with a full view of the town . . . her town, thought Chucho. He walked over to the spot and dug his foot on the soft earth. "We'll dig the grave here." They took turns with the shovel. Every so often, Chucho would take out a bottle and drink, then he would hand it to Chapo who did the same. In the midst of the warm glow, they looked down into the town that spoke of lifetimes. Then, one would resume the digging while the other scooped the earth out of the shallow grave. They had laid the body next to the boulder where they had built the fire. It was hardly discernible from where they were digging. Finally, the grave was ready. Chucho went back to where Refugio's body lay. "Come, help me carry it to the grave. Careful! Be gentle!" Chapo did as he was told. When they reached the grave, Chucho laid it down close to the edge of the grave almost reverently. "Now we wait."

"Wait?"

"For the sunrise. I want her to see it one more time." Chapo did not answer. He took out the bottle in his pocket and offered it to Chucho. They drank in silence. Chucho asked Chapo for his knife.

"What are you going to do, Chucho?" It was something crazy; Chapo was sure. Chucho took the knife that Chapo offered him and sat down on the ground next to the body. He picked up its head and held it on his lap. Then, he carefully cut into the cloth that covered the face of the dead woman. He stopped when the face was fully exposed. "There, she will be able to see."

They watched the lights from the town gradually disappear as they waited for the sunrise. The fire, too, was dying. Chapo decided to look for more firewood. Chucho sat watching with the head of the dead woman still on his lap. From time to time, he would look down at the face as if trying to understand something on the other side of life . . . past death.

"Do you suppose, Chucho, that where she is now there are city lights? Chapo was now warming himself in the replenished fire. The town was now in almost total darkness. The friends of night had given up the quest.

The first light rose in the East. It took the darkness gently like a lover. The city did not have long to sleep. The mingling of lives with chance would have another day to try. Chucho was holding the head of the dead woman high as they faced the East. "Look at the sunrise, Refugio. It is like the sunrise already in your face. Chapo, look . . . what beautiful peace, look! All the strength of life is in her face. Are all faces beautiful in death?"

Chapo left the fire and looked at the face. "She was a fine looking woman." Chucho felt the stiff, dead weight in his arms. As he watched the coming of the morning, tears filled his eyes. "Refugio, I didn't give you fancy criers. I, the poor fool, found my own way. I hope it is good enough. You deserved a grand funeral."

"She cannot hear you, Chucho."

"But I am listening now, Chapo, to all the sounds she left, good and bad. You are clear to me now, Refugio." He bent his head and kissed her fully on the lips.

"I love you, Refugio, for having lived." With care, he laid the body down on the ground. Then he jumped into the shallow grave. He took off his coat and made a pillow for Refugio's head.

"That is your only coat, Chucho."

"Here, help me lower the body." With great effort they lowered it until Refugio's head rested on Chucho's coat. Chucho scuttled out of the grave. Both men, dirty, tired, and half-frozen, looked down at the body, and suddenly became very conscious of death. The silence of the two men expected something more than finality. There was the morning and the sunrise unexplained, like the life of days; then, there was the still, white form deep in the earth. Both spoke of something more . . . but what?

Chucho found his way out of the mystery. The grave had to be covered. Then there were the coyotes.

"Let's fill the grave . . . then, we must find the rocks to cover it." They took different paths to find the rocks. Each one would come back with some and he would put them beside the grave. It was a long tedious job, but the rocks were gathered. The sun was high when they finally filled the grave and then sat down to fit the rocks into the mound.

In the atmosphere that diffuses light, there is celestial song of currents and a higher mathematics. There is the push and flux of life that finds its way to man. Man tastes it as a freedom, a way of depths, a way of new life. If the skill lies in the freedom, thought Chucho, then it belongs to death as well as life. The sunrise became part of the "not enough." Refugio has sufficed. Clowns must be because the world sometimes does not see. The task was done; the moment of somber thought passed. They were filled with a great relief and a great joy. They began to laugh. Then, they clapped each other on the back. There was an intensity in their horseplay; there was a realness in their jest. Chucho took out his bottle and peered into it. "Look . . . there is still some left." He took two gulps and handed the bottle to Chapo. A thought came to Chucho, "A plain cross with two good pieces of wood and her name on it. It would please her."

They found the wood. They sat down near the grave again to make a cross, sharing the rest of the drink.

PILGRIMAGE

Nan had come back in the middle of the night from New York and awakened the tenants living in her house. She demanded on the spot that they vacate the premises, lease or no lease. A week later, the tenants were gone, convinced they wanted nothing to do with a mad woman, much less live in her house. So Nan was back home in the great, big, empty house. She preferred it that way. Why clutter it with furniture again? All she needed was the four-poster bed in the master bedroom. The electric kitchen provided everything for civilized survival. There was time, now, to work things out. How do you work things out when your husband of sixteen years leaves you for a syphilitic bitch? Well, she was glad she had carpets on the floor, since she had given up wearing shoes, too. Carpets can be kind.

Dave and she had spent a fortune on the carpets. So much of the enthusiasm of those sixteen years had been spent planning and getting things, like the carpets. Life had been a mad song of possession-gathering after the first initial success. One status victory after another . . . busy with things outside the self with self-made hungers. So the roller coaster ride turns out to be no more than a roller coaster ride . . . how can it possibly be the summation of a marriage? It wasn't fair . . . no, it wasn't fair! Damn it! She had given all from the beginning. It had been the simple human faith of really loving. How long did it last before the roller coaster ride? She felt a dryness in the throat.

She went into the kitchen reminding herself it was time for the green pills. She opened the cupboard . . . green pills, red pills, yellow pills . . . hell! What's the use? She slammed the cupboard door. Pills . . . regulators of life in the metallics of ownership among beautiful, competitive people! Who knows what?

She went into the huge, empty living room and flopped down in the middle of the carpet. She sat with legs crossed as if in a yoga stance with only half effort. She focused her eyes on her pajama's design for the want of something to do. It was a pretty design of a Bodhi tree with tiny slant-eyed creatures around it. Pink, pink, pink people with

41

Buddha love. Buddha love? She laughed. The selfless Buddha love that killed . . . what else? She felt the bitterness in the pit of her stomach. She thought, "Maybe it's just hunger."

There had been another kind of violent hunger in the marriage. After the happy time of faith, something had happened to the core ego of the male and female bound by matrimony. It demanded constant feeding. Cyclonically, the feeding urge was a demonic pattern for the chic and the fashionable, the striving for eternal youth, the healthy nonchalant look of the solvent and socially accepted. The easy life just wasn't that easy. It tied one up into a self-knot that heard no one and saw no one except the striving demons in the superdandy of one's guts! To hell with everything!

She felt the need for a cigarette. She went into the master bedroom and fell into the bed, reaching underneath the pillow for a cigarette. She found one. She fumbled again for the lighter. Her hand found the cold, hard metal. She eased herself up to her pillow and lay there for some time with the cigarette in her mouth unlighted. The sins of ego-food will out! will out! How deep does one go in despair? Deeper than in hate? No . . . no . . . hate is a bright thing that stays and gashes on the surface. It has no depth . . . it is a thing of claws and teeth. There she was again . . . another lapse into . . . into what?

"A creature of little ways, I now light my cigarette," she thought. She lighted the cigarette with mock deliberation. Then in sudden rage, she threw the lighter against the wall as if to hit life itself.

"I humiliated myself following him and the tramp all the way to New York. He wasn't even guilty . . . and she, with that pumped up stomach . . . looking innocent, the filthy . . ." she fumed as if she had a joy for the masochistic knife. "What a fool, what a stupid, desperate, vengeful fool I must have seemed. At my age, to play the heroine!" She saw the cigarette ash fall upon the cover and watched it burn a small jagged hole. To destroy . . . that was a hunger now too. She would bleed them dry; she would make them pay. She would think up a thousand ways to kill. . . .

The doorbell rang. Who on earth? She had frightened everybody away. She got up and went to the door. It was only Cuca, the cleaning woman. She stood there smiling at her, this heavy, brown lump with Indian features. It was Cuca's day.

"Oh, it's you."

"Good morning, Miss Fletcher; the bus was late."

"Come in." Nan walked back into the bedroom and sat on the bed. Cuca followed her, taking off her old worn sweater. Nan watched her curiously. Was the enigma deliberate on the part of the numb creature? To chase your tail all day long for a few dollars. How did they withstand? What did they withstand? How much did the mind dispel to save the body? The life style of servitude found cheerfulness in the very unimportance of things. Mexican Cuca with her Mexican moods. Nan felt Cuca's eyes on her. How funny! She too is wondering. . . .

Cuca looked at "mad Miss Fletcher" and wondered if the nervous energy was just the cause of idleness. One cigarette after another . . . poor thing! She should find something to do besides smoke, pop the pill and lie on that bed. What the neighbors said was not true. Miss Fletcher was harmless. It was easy to clean her house. She never bothered anyone. Sometimes she threw things . . . but never at her. These American women were such cold, nervous things . . . always with the shifting eyes. Relax . . . relax . . . they do not relax. But Miss Fletcher would sometimes take a bottle of brandy from the kitchen and invite her to drink. "Here's mud in your eye!" Whatever that means, it was still good brandy. From the corner of her eye Cuca watched Miss Fletcher pace the floor. Suddenly, she remembered what she had to tell the gringa.

"I will not be here next week."

"You quitting?"

"No, Miss. I am going to San Juan de Los lagos to pay a manda."

"What's that?"

"Una peregrinación . . . people from all over go to make an offering to the Virgin."

"Shades of Chaucer! You mean a pilgrimage? A religious pilgrimage?"

"Yes, a manda paid by the faithful."

"You go to ask for something?" The faith struck Nan as funny.

"The asking is not important."

"Why do you go then?"

Cuca's face lighted up strangely. "To be reborn."

Nan looked at her with disbelief. Here was this illiterate Indian talking philosophy. The instinct at work. She had never given credit to Cuca for a single thought. Come to think of it, she had never given Cuca a thought. "You walk to . . . San . . . to that place?"

"I ride the bus to León . . . that is my home town. From there I walk with many, many others to San Juan. It is a three day's walk."

"That's how you get your kicks."

"What?"

"You enjoy doing this?"

"It is a satisfaction that leaves no hunger."

Again! That blind knack for hitting the nail on the head. No hunger! Nan looked puzzled as she lighted another cigarette. How far away were the religious rituals of her childhood. They had been a part of the young faith. Orthodoxy had been a hard prison to break away from during her college days. She had finally learned that the higher power of things was in the innards. Was it so different from the old Israelites, before Constantine blew his mind with pagan ritual and glorified the church with it? glorified . . . stupefied? Perhaps, one and the same! The "God" so high simply did not relate with man. So god had become a talking friend to Nan. Not now . . . not now. . . . He had forsaken . . . she had forsaken? Nothing made sense anymore.

The sudden light in Cuca's face when she had admitted rebirth came back to Nan's mind. She watched Cuca take out the vacuum cleaner from a closet. Her movements were quick and deft from long training. Cuca's variety of faith was as old as the hills, but there was something about the simple trust, that holding on to the unseen and not too well understood. Without words . . . without words. "Maybe that's better," thought Nan. "Words were hard to communicate with . . . but that simple, shining light from within . . . that's different! No muddle there! Words snuff out being . . . being. Have I forgotten?"

Critical detachment spells a doom. She remembered words analyzing the actions of Prince Hamlet in an English class. Detachment from people is a death . . . . one can only be to love . . . even among murderers. How strange is insanity mixed with the sane. She watched Cuca again attempting to find the woman inside the maid. "I must have a drink!" She went into the kitchen and took the brandy bottle from the cupboard. She poured herself a drink and scolded herself, "You know what you are? You're drinking too early in the day! Who do you think you're kidding?" She took the drink in one gulp then refilled the glass. She looked at it thoughtfully. The sound of the vacuum in the living room recalled the fascination with Cuca and her faith. She went into the living room and watched Cuca vacuum. Her eyes roamed around the room.

"You know what I am going to do, Cuca? I'm going to paint this room black. I'll change the carpets to black. Only the ceiling will be orange. I'll call it my 'passion room.' I'll come in here and have orgiastic rages. You don't know what I'm talking about, do you?"

Cuca shook her head and went on with her cleaning. Nan continued. "I'll paint my bedroom a sea-green. I hear it is very calming. I'll just lie there and float. To float through life . . . isn't that nice, Cuca?"

Cuca shook her head again. Nan sighed.

"I can't talk to you, Cuca . . . words again!"

Cuca looked at her in puzzlement. Nan suddenly asked, "When do you leave on your so-called pilgrimage?"

"Tomorrow morning I take the bus to León. Next morning I start with the people from my town."

Cuca would go on her pilgrimage and find the light she saved deep in herself. She would stay lying on her bed and plan revenge. Something was wrong. "How many did you say go on that pilgrimage?"

"Many from León and many from towns all over Méjico . . . I say, thousands. The people go together from their town and all meet at the same time to go into the Basílica at San Juan on the saint's day. All wait at La Puerta del Llano until then."

"Puerta del Llano . . . what does that mean?"

"It means the door of the desert."

Nan was amused. "How appropriate . . . door of the desert, door to faith!"

Cuca agreed very seriously, "It is in the desert one finds faith."

"Why not?" thought Nan. She remembered the long desert faiths of the Bible, the isolation of Zarathustra, the lonely track of Odysseus, Moses, Lao-tzu . . . who knows? In the desert there is the bloom. . . . The paradox had purpose. Somehow the depth of Cuca's wisdom stirred something in her. So long ago . . . she and Dave, like children . . . so long ago. She looked at the cleaning woman as if looking for an answer. She sensed an answer.

"Cuca, may I go with you on your pilgrimage?"

Cuca was silent. It was an unheard of request from a "gringa" without the fear of God. Yes, maybe Miss Fletcher was crazy. . . . Nan repeated sincerely, "May I go with you, Cuca?"

"Why do you want to go?"

"Maybe, I want to find . . . What you find in the desert."

"You have yourself, Miss."

"It's not enough now, Cuca."

"Each person finds his own, Miss Fletcher."

"I know . . . but I want to look . . . not out of curiosity. It's more than that."

There was a silence as if both were considering it very seriously. "If you wish . . . I suppose it would be nice."

"It's all settled then. I'll lock up the house, take a knapsack, and I'm ready to go."

Cuca nodded her head and went back to her cleaning.

Next morning, Cuca waited for Nan to cross the border into México. She easily spotted the blond head. Cuca felt somewhat self conscious to be seen with the gringa among her own kind. Heads were already turning in observation. Nan, however, was unconscious of the incongruity. Other times, she might have noticed. But not now. She only felt an exhilaration. There was a newness to this adventure, a certain difference that made her feel new. This Nan was a different one than the one that stared at the ceiling planning revenge.

"I need a cup of coffee, Cuca . . . I left so early."

"You want to eat in a restaurant?" Cuca's voice was hesitant. Nan felt the awkwardness. "Oh, any place you like . . . where they will give us a cup of coffee."

Cuca was relieved. "I have a friend who has a bakery close to the bus station. We can go there. She will give us coffee. We buy some sweet bread for along the way. There are no stops between here and León."

"That is a good idea, Cuca."

Still that eager feeling of lightness. "What on earth is the matter with me," thought Nan, "I feel like a girl finding." She walked alongside Cuca keeping up the fast pace of one used to walking. The bus depot was several blocks away from the border, but Nan was not tired by the walk although the sun was hot. The small shop with cotton curtains had a faded blue sign "Panadería" on its white-washed walls. It was a small shop with a heavenly smell. Nan had forgotten the smell of baking, fresh bread. Again, the lightness.

They went in and Cuca greeted a woman wearing a large white apron. The woman smiled at Nan when Cuca told her why they were there. They were invited to go behind the shop to have their coffee. A long curtain divided the back room from the bakery. The back room was dark. It was a narrow kitchen partitioned off from the bakery ovens. It had a kitchen table and chairs and a window that looked out into a small patio full of bird cages, cobble stone, and potted plants. The air was a mixture of wet clay and baking bread. The birds were in full chorus; the cobbled stones glimmered gladly in their wetness. "How old world . . . how peaceful!" Nan's heart gladdened again.

All three women sat down for a cup of coffee. Cuca and the bakery owner began to talk in Spanish. Nan did not mind being left to herself. She was too happy in absorbing the world around her. There was an ease here that had nothing to do with wealth or success; it was a richness close to nature and to the realness of people. Nan took a piece of the sweet bread that was offered her. It was the most delicious bread she had tasted. She sat silently munching and looking with the peace of a child. She looked into the eyes of the other women who seemed to understand and accept. Afterwards they walked three more blocks to the bus station. Cuca warned, "We may have to stand on the bus, Miss Fletcher. It is always crowded and the ride is a long ride."

Nan said simply, "That's all right with me. Everything's just fine." Cuca smiled. The bus was crowded and they had to stand. The air was heavy with human smells and the sounds of many conversations, but Nan was listening to rhythms and looking at the expressive eyes of the people on the bus. They would stare curiously and she stared back with a smile. That made all the difference. Cuca, nevertheless, warned her in a whisper that she had better hold her handbag tight for there were many thieves on buses. Nan tightened her hold on the handbag as Cuca told her to do. She felt the closeness of so many human bodies as part of the new excitement. How long ago was it when a similar closeness would have been repugnant? It was midday when they arrived at León.

Cuca seemed tired. Nan was glad to get off the bus into open space.

"It is a mile to my home, Miss Fletcher." She led the way. Nan silently followed.

They spent the night in Cuca's house. Next morning, Nan awakened pleasantly remembering where she was. The family had insisted that Nan sleep in the only bed in the house. It seemed like an imposition to Nan when she saw the many people that slept in that one room. But the gracious offer was so golden, so sincere, Nan could not refuse. Now, she was awake; for a moment, she looked at the many children of mother, sister, cousins, huddled in worn old blankets on the floor. In the only other room, Cuca was making coffee. Nan smelled it. She quietly dressed. Still in bare feet, holding her shoes in her hand, she made her way through the sleeping bodies into the kitchen. Cuca looked up and smiled. "We start in half an hour. Sit down and drink your coffee."

Both women sat down and drank in silence until Nan suggested, not without embarrassment, "Listen, Cuca . . . don't prepare too much food for the journey. I have enough money for every thing along the way."

Cuca nodded her head. "Yes, there are many booths along the way. I am taking canteens with water and some oranges. We buy the rest along the way."

Nan was glad she accepted the offer. "Good!" There was a mutual contentment. Nan became very much aware of a strange metamorphosis of spirit that had begun when she had crossed the border and recognized the freedom. Freedom? Freedom from what? Nan could not yet tell. . . . But she was shedding old, sad, frightening things. It was a new perception with sun, wind, and desert yet unclear except in sense.

"This is the best coffee I have drunk in a long time," she told Cuca. Before the family had risen for the day, the two women were on their way. They set out for the highway leading out of León to San Juan de Los Lagos. Nan watched the crowd multiply as they progressed on the journey. People seemed to come from nowhere; in silence, they would join the others. All would converge to find a similar destination . . . a reassurance in the existence of a God. The small group of the first few miles was now a large crowd, but it was a hushed, determined crowd with a purpose that lent individuality to each; each world was still personal in its seeking. Booths were already lined along the way. They were located on the outskirts of the town. In one of these booths Nan bought two straw hats and she handed one to Cuca. "This will make the sun less terrible," observed Cuca. The further the crowd walked into the open desert, the fewer the booths became, as if they ended with the safety of the town. At the beginning of the journey there were no forces of dialogue holding people together; it was still a silent trudge to faith and promise. The sun was an ocean now that covered the challenge of wide desert. There was nothing visible at the distance except horizon.

There was no visible Moses, either. But there was the element of Moses in each of them. This was the new point of evolutionary history. This was no exodus, but the finding of a regenerative power to help each of them live among Egyptians.

Each would return to the Egyptian pyramid, to a slavish struggle and a suffering. The promised land was no more than the spark of hope to withstand the already known. After two hours walk, Cuca made no attempt to hide her fatigue. Her breathing was hard, and large drops of perspiration shone on her forehead. She wiped it with her sleeve and stopped to rest for a moment. Nan stopped with her. People continued their way and passed alongside the two women. Nan watched their faces, trying to find the hope she so badly came to find. Their faces were an enigma. Only the signs of tiredness and heat showed. Perhaps it was too soon. After a moment, Cuca and Nan followed those who had already passed them.

Nan felt as if the desert had swallowed her. Sand invaded her pores, her eyes, and her every breath. Cuca saw the fatigue in Nan's face and felt a burst of liking for the "gringa." She was human after all. "She behaves more like a child lost in a wilderness." She pushed Nan ahead of her as if to carry part of the weight. Nan turned and smiled and stood next to Cuca, wanting to seem as capable, as able of taking the discomfort. Cuca understood. She let Nan walk alone.

The rest spot proved to be a pasture. On this pasture was a giant cottonwood tree. The herculean size of the tree had been obvious for miles before they reached the pasture. It was like a citadel at a distance awaiting them. Once they reached it, its shade proved itself a citadel in the burning sun. It covered dozens of people. Under its shade, people would look up trying to see the top of the tree. But it was well lost in the sky. The rest of the crowd dispersed to find shelter in an old farmhouse. Nan was curious about the tree that did not cease to amaze her.

Cuca explained. "This land used to be a cattle ranch. The cattle were slaughtered under this very tree. It was fed on blood; that is why it is a giant." Nan thought of the old Celtic druids with bodies painted blue, offering the blood sacrifices to the oak tree. Cattle blood or human blood . . . and giants grow!

Cuca pointed to the abandoned farmhouse. "Before this land became a slaughterhouse, that farmhouse was used by Pancho Villa's men as a stronghold. Like all men of war, one night they surprised the sleeping family. They killed the men whom they knew to be sympathizers of Orozco; then, they raped the women. There was one fifteen year old girl who resisted. She stabbed a colonel who swore to hang her. The next morning they hung her right on this tree. The body remained on the tree for a long time. By the time it was found, it was a skeleton wearing a blue, print dress. It is a sad story." Cuca sighed profusely.

Rebellion and death . . . resistance and death . . . how many forms did it take? Nan wondered if men truly found raptures in the sorrow of others. And is it that way with women? She read the truth in herself. She remembered the plans for revenge against her husband and his new found love. To make them suffer had been her only pleasurable thought for a long time. Was that not a resistance and a death? Was it not a rebellion? She looked up at the peaceful branches that swam in sun and living breeze. She visualized the skeleton in the blue, print dress . . . for all time?

"Would you like a drink of water?" Cuca offered her the canteen.

"Yes, thank you," Nan took it and drank deeply. The parchness gave way. She wet her hands and put their coolness against her face. How sweet the end of any agony be it big or small. She gave the canteen back to Cuca who also drank with relish. They found a place under the tree. Here they sat and stretched out their legs and drank afresh. The gratitude of tired limbs and dry throats gave a new dimension to body pleasure. Sweet, sweet rest.

Four hundred people camped that night in another pasture a few miles away which was crossed by lines of dark trees merging with the hills. There was the sound of a river nearby that reminded Nan of a life-giving force that could not be explained, the sound of life immemorial. The pasture was a few miles in from any vital crossways. Still observable in the growing dusk were farmhouses scattered along the hills. The lighted windows were legends of hidden hearts.

The two women exchanged some of their oranges for beans wrapped in wheat tortillas. Never had Nan tasted anything as delicious as this wanted food in the desert. Cuca commented, "We will sleep here for the night."

She then unrolled two blankets. Taking one, she draped it around herself and told Nan to do the same with her blanket. "This way," she told Nan, "We shall not freeze to death." Nan followed suit. Before sleep came with the whispering of trees, Nan looked up and saw the many stars that spoke of a long lost hope now to be found. New life . . . new life . . . new life! With half-closed lids, she prayed for the first time since she was a little girl. "Thank you, God, for letting me come." Sleep came.

At breakfast, Cuca told Nan that the local priest of the town would now join the group all the way to San Juan. "He will lead the way like a shepherd," Cuca accepted the idea of being a sheep. Nan looked at the people preparing for the journey and somehow she could not see them as sheep waiting for their shepherd. No . . . it was a healthy situation with reality; it was people going with people, each with a Moses in the self. Yes, this is how it is, all part of the quest and the equality. Is this what happens in the desert? Cuca pointed to the top of a hill.

"Up there is a shrine of the Lady of Guadalupe. The priest will offer confession and communion to the faithful this morning at the shrine."

"I am not Catholic," explained Nan.

"Then eat your breakfast, for confession will take a while; after that you can come and watch the communion service . . . if you wish."

"Oh, I want to very much!"

"Then eat your breakfast."

"And you?"

"I am fasting before communion."

Cuca rolled up the blankets while Nan ate her breakfast of orange and tortilla. Other people were doing the same. The priest came into sight. He approached the hill where the shrine was. People followed him to the foot of the hill. Cuca joined the group. Before they climbed to the site of the shrine, the priest explained to those who were going to confession. "We shall have a group confession for there is lack of time. Your day's journey speaks of sincere repentance . . . so your sins no longer are. You are forgiven. Now join me in an act of contrition and three Our Fathers."

After the prayers, the priest led the way to the top of the hill where the shrine was. It was half-hidden in overgrown foliage. Within a recess was a small figure of Our Lady in a niche surrounded by a bower of old artificial flowers. Here the Mass was celebrated.

Nan watched from a distance. She had a deep desire to join the spirit of the Mass. The waves of something singing inside were carrying her to the same God. In her silence, she felt one of them. The composite of Man's singing good was here full, strong; it was a part of her too. Good . . . good . . . good was everywhere. She remembered the words of St. Augustine before he became a Christian. "I tried to find the source of Evil and got nowhere." Neither could she . . . not anywhere. If evil were negligible, so was hate? despair? Salvation, then, became the positive force of Man.

The priest ended the Mass with a reading from the Exodus. "My presence will go with thee, and I will give thee rest." How true! how true! sang the spirit. Nan looked at the faces around her to find the same glory that she felt. Did she see it . . . it seemed to shine in their eyes . . . or was she imagining what she wanted to believe? The singing must be in them too. They must hear the same night-river that speaks of life immemorial, the sound of immortality through the sameness of all. Nan took Cuca's hand in happiness as they went down the hill. Cuca understood.

Cuca warned that the second day was to be an ordeal for they would travel through open desert without a single stop until night-fall. People filled their canteens for the crossing of the desert. By late afternoon, eyes were caste to sandled feet and staff and never-ending desert sand. Twisting, moaning whirlwinds hid the red of the sun. But there was no atomization within the group there was no separateness, for the faith of Moses was within the heart and very step of Man. They clung together in common feel and the amethyst of light in a distant mountain gave a stamp to the truth of God. The night-river sound was now a far-off memory to Nan, caught in a drowning of heat and exhaustion.

They stopped to pray and to rest for a while in the insolence of the sand-storm. A short while after, a mystery fell. Perhaps out of exhaustion, perhaps of overexposure, an old man died. Perhaps he died because the struggle was no longer his after many pilgrimages. They buried him beside the gorge where they had stopped to rest. When night fell, there was a clean soundlessness that give them hope. The coming dusk made the next few hours' walk more bearable. Finally when the land began to slope to a serrated ridge, the people knew the campside was near. There were shouts of exaltation. The murmur of the people became the night-river sound. The death of the old man made each man conscious of his own breath, the long-extended promise of a hope for more than journey's end. Here they made camp. Nan and Cuca rolled themselves up in their blankets again. The wind told stories of the long, long wait, but the stars spoke of a brightness in the heartbeat, in the understanding of life. Sleep came again.

. . . .

The greens of dawn swept all desolation away. Nan opened her eyes to fluffy clouds in the sky. The priest offered the Mass for the soul of the dead man who had died looking for God. It was a solemn, happy moment when they set off on their journey again. The heroic scale of horizons were still too intangible, too unreal. There was to be a greater satisfaction, a greater happiness not yet understood by Nan. If the people were aware of indelible shadows, they were also aware of indelible suns. The far away never belongs to Man, but the near is part of his heartbeat, so it was the awareness of the people who had shared the same experience before that brought the journey's end much closer. Shadows and suns mixed with the excitement of arrival. People began to talk of friends and the fare of the coming carnival; they talked of the miracle of San Juan and the understanding Virgin; they talked of the high Mass, of food, of drink, of women; they talked about real things, the shadows and the suns as one. There was no talk of heaven. Who wants "vales of lilies and flowers of bliss?" The need was for common pleasures and common needs; there God would be, the night-river sound.

Was the faith in full bloom? Nan was not sure. She felt the faith as a growing thing in sharing of common experience . . . in search for something in themselves. Nan thought of her husband and the girl. Did she hate them now? No . . . she was sure she did not. They had become like all these people, searchers of the night-river sound. Somehow in his own way, Dave was searching; so was the girl. It was their privilege. Suddenly Nan felt very happy with herself. She was free from the hate. By early afternoon, the group had reached La puerta del Llano. Everywhere was a sea of people. They had come from other towns to meet at La Puerta del Llano. Groups seemed to emerge from every direction. The emotional key of the journey had had its profound effect. There were reunions and new friends were made. The intimacy was a warm glow among the people. The love and laughter found this night would always be a happy memory without taint; it would be a good part of the journey.

Bright booths were set up along the way. The air was festive and full of expectation. Nan and Cuca explored the wares with excitement. Nan wanted to do something special for Cuca. She reached into her purse as she watched Cuca's happy eyes.

"I want you to buy any thing you want, Cuca."

Cuca looked at Nan and hesitated for a moment. "Anything?"

"Yes. . . ."

"Well . . . there is so much, I am not sure. . . ."

Suddenly, they both burst out laughing. Nan felt she wanted to buy things too. With the happiness of children, they bought ears of corn and beads; they bought rosaries and blouses. With arms full they went back to camp. They joined a group of people who were already celebrating the tomorrow. The happiness of things made them warm and safe. Past midnight, drowsiness set in. Nan and Cuca took their blankets. Sleep came.

.   .   .   .

They had gathered from many towns. From San Miguel, San Luis Potosi, from Aguas-calientes, from many places far and near. From La Puerta del Llano they started a procession to El Encabezado for a special blessing from a bishop. Long queues formed the lines that led to the shrine of La Virgin de Guadalupe in the basílica. Choirs led in music and penitent believers went the long way on their knees; people from all walks of life walked the long way to the Virgin. The walk to the shrine was slow, for the people were many. Nan observed the lightness in the voices of the people. No one minded waiting. All were shining with the faith. By the time Nan reached the Virgin it had been a long eight hours walk from El Encabezado to the basílica. It was well worth it. She knew that the Virgin was a symbol to these people, but now before the shrine, the vagueness of the freedom, of the not yet realized, cast off its mists. She understood now why people came; why the faith was strong. She stood before the Virgin. How strong The Lady was in this great cathedral with its campaniles and cupolas, with its slanted light in full color, sifting through stained-glass windows, mixing with long profound shadows. In the eyes of the Virgin was the knowing of the centuries. She was Nature with its fertile womb of compassion; she was the cool recess of something beyond hurt and pain that is within the life of everyone. Her eyes spoke to Nan, "All the love there is . . . IS YOU." The eyes pleaded with Nan to see this truth; they pleaded with Nan not to waste a life in searching outside of herself. "All in you . . . all in you," the eyes said. Her eyes were the night-river sound.

This was the rebirth. Nan knew her life had not stopped; now it would have a greater essence, a certain surety of how much she had to give . . . because she was love. The Virgin had told her so. She left the cathedral in full joy. All the people she met were as beautiful as the Virgin. She had found the faith in the desert. She would take it back home and grow with it. She would open her heart and arms to whatever came to enrich the life, to give it the worth it should have. It was God's gift because it was God. She would go back with the night-river sound, knowing a part of her immortality. But now, people beckoned.

DUENDE

Names were not necessary. The street and its people were very much a part of Triano. Many years ago he had come across the ocean from his Mountain of Sadness in Andalucía with his gypsy family. The street had been his education and the assurance of human things. Patterns existed as elsewhere, but they were a wandering caught in days seemingly without purpose. But they were Days. Triano smiled. Purpose? What greater purpose than Mama Tante making coffee? The constant song of the hills in her throat? The shuffle earnest and sure? The senses added the silent shadows of afternoon. Marusha would be home soon wearing a serious, troubled face. Poor little sister! He felt deeply the hurt in her eyes as she looked at the ugliness of the room that was home to the family. Always, he would watch her swallow her despair. She would lift her soft, white throat with its living pulse and close her eyes to erase what was. The ugliness did not go away. Did she expect it to go away? Triano loved her, but he knew he could not comfort. He was silent. Marusha alone would have to learn how to accept.

One day, perhaps, Marusha would look out into the street without anger, without disdain. One day, the web of the street would be bright and beautiful because it was alive with doings and attempts at an endurance. The endurance was honest and brave. Some live from scraps and others call them fools. Existences, nonetheless, differ little, and scraps have their dimensions. Life comes in little pieces, in short, warm instances and familiar acts. When would Marusha see beyond the ugliness? When would she hear the deep, deep song of the beautiful life on the street? Triano looked out the window and what he saw was the street singing.

"Triano!" Mama Tante's voice was impatient. "You left your cart in the hall. You want the super to complain . . . eh?"

"All right, I'll put it away." Triano walked out into the dark passage that led to the street and wheeled the small cart into the room . . . a burdened room. The cart was his livelihood. All day Triano would venture out into neighborhoods, trails of proven ground for human nesting, where worn-faced women with fringes and traces of dreams

would welcome any piece of promise. He would journey during the day
into the dark corridors in tenement houses. The many cubicles had
their women busy at some order. There was the ordering of self in little
ways and with little hopes, and there was the ordering of daily duties as
a meaning to things without. Man is a funny thing. By ancient instinct
he ritualizes life to spell out purpose. Men in poverty flounder in the
outside world. When the order is gone, they flee or find escape into a
realness all their own. The woman ritual stays within a cubicle that
makes small demands, but that kills with that same smallness. They are
women alone. It is a hard battle.

Triano sharpened knives. He found work in restaurants, but mostly
among the housewives. He could ask the question, "What can I do for
you? Any dull things that need sharpening?" A new, small, shiny edge
in the lonely lives of long, lost waiting. The restaurants were better at
paying Triano for his services. Among the housewives, it became more
of a play on life to cut clean a reaching out to fill the loneliness for a
little while. Triano loved his work. Its monetary reward was a pittance,
but the days were rich with common sharing. The adventure of faces,
the roar of dreams and fears, the many colors of sorrow and joy, all
were a richness, a belief.

Everyone knew the gypsy was a good listener. He melted well into
life. He mended things and people. He was full of the duende spirit
from the mountains of the old country where survival was a precipice
giving the gift of sky and barren earth. That is why the passion was the
main artery to the feel and the freedom of the day.

One seasoned woman would complain, "You know what that
good-for-nothing did to me? Look at my face! He came home drunk
and beat me. Look at my face!" Triano would flash his gypsy smile.
"It's a beautiful face. A man beats a woman because he loves her."

"You men are all alike. You stick together. I wish he would not love
me so much."

"How can he help it? You keep his bed warm and make food for his
belly. You are the best in a man's life."

"Mentiroso, you make the truth of a lie."

There was the too young mother surrounded by a swarm of little
children. Her eyes told him she did not know a safe direction. She
would apologize, "I cannot pay you now."

"That's all right . . . another time." He would hand out nickels to the
older children wanting to take away the mists from the young mother's
face. He didn't know how. What do we do, he asked himself. We run, or
stand still, or strike out . . . but we are . . . that is the important thing.

Now in his own home, Triano pushed his cart into a corner of the
room at the end of the Day. He now remembered the many faces
finding an instant light. It would not last for too long, but it made the

realness. Marusha came into the room. Today was Tuesday, thought Triano. Marusha would not go to business school tonight. He felt the fluttering of her usual impatience with coming home. She was always too tired to talk. She sat on the edge of her bed in silence and began to unbutton her blouse. Her beautiful dark eyes told of centuries of lost struggle. There was a waiting with a hurt and a small flicker of hope. Triano lit a cigarette and watched his sister through half-closed lids. Stay! Stay! little sister . . . don't strain so . . . don't tear at yourself. He said nothing, but wanted so much to smooth out the torture. Little Marusha had learned to read well and did fine in school . . . poor little Marusha.

Marusha, free from the buttons of the blouse, fell back on the bed and closed her eyes. She did this often to think or to talk of "ifs."

There was always the old world she had left when still a child. She remembered poverty differently. The child had seen good strong things. They were still there, but the eyes of the young girl saw other things now. The "ifs" started.

"Sometimes I wish we had stayed. Many people left the mountain to find jobs in Madrid. Why did we have to come across the ocean just to live in this sewer?"

She knew Triano would not answer her. He was like that. She opened her eyes to the familiar, tormented ceiling . . . faded, peeling . . . aimless. Canals and tributaries of artless cracks, a dedication to an emptiness. She continued her desperate wondering. . . .

"Remember Lila? She wrote me that she was working for her aunt in the pastry shop. She said she is the only living relative and will inherit it one day." Triano tried to make things light, "She'll be plump in no time."

"Be serious, Triano. She has security now."

People find paths like cracks in the ceiling, and the same artlessness makes monuments of aimless dreams, desires, and all the "ifs" that fill the gaps. It was almost mysterious, this exploration of decay, of broken plaster and the persistence of a rain. The ceiling spoke of the Mountain of Sadness. It was a vague stirring in Marusha.

"Triano, was it this bad on the mountain?"

"How do you remember it?"

"I remember being hungry. One time I was very hungry . . . my stomach hurt so!" She smiled. "You came in with a rabbit. Remember?"

"I remember."

"And that old coat you found. It must have belonged to a giant of a man. I remember the sleeves dragging on the floor, but it kept me warm all winter. Funny, I don't feel sad about those things."

"Angry now?"

For a moment Marusha looked at him with puzzled eyes. "Anger?" She thought about it. "I keep thinking it is sadness."

"It's whatever you feel, Marusha. I don't know how to wish very well . . . but if I would wish, it would be one thing . . . that you could be happy."

Marusha felt the love. It was a second of safety, but only a second. She smiled softly, but the current of her torment took the second and rushed into a tumult, "You and Mama Tante, both of you take this terrible existence so calmly. All the ugliness and defeat . . . can't you see it? Doesn't it touch you?" Triano spoke gently. "I know what you want, Marusha. You are like a child looking through a window at beautiful things that you can't have. But, Marusha, they are only things."

Marusha became impatient. "It's just an excuse. Everybody wants things." Triano was silent. Marusha continued. "People in this country are so active, so full of ambition; they want to succeed. Don't you want the same things? I do!"

"I want to be happy with other people. Maybe that is not enough to you, Marusha. But Mama Tante and me . . . we tasted, heard, and captured the spirit of the mountain; the spirit asks for little beyond a personal freedom. I think that is what it is."

"Spirit! Oh, Triano, you don't make sense!"

"People feel differently, Marusha. I can't feel as you feel. It is good for people to be different. You like books; you want to get ahead. You'll do it. You'll find what you want. That is your kind of freedom."

Marusha did not answer. She stared at the cracks that now wore a pained expression of futility. She bit her lip. She felt a sob deep in her. "By myself?" The thought drowned her.

Mama Tante entered the room wiping her hands on an old apron. Her face marked the seasons of a long life. Time and passions well spent had left their lovely message of a living fierceness. She held tightly to things that spelled life. Mama Tante was a mountain, a barren earth, a sky, a precipice. Her big body was now cumbersome and slow, but the hands were still quick lightning. The fierceness was in the doing and the reaching out in good, strong simplicity. The eyes reflected a history caught deep and pure in the story of the heart. The voice was matter-of-fact.

"Are you two going to eat your supper? There's soup on the stove, and a tomato for you, Marusha."

Triano sniffed the cabbage smell, pungent and heavy, in the room. Too often it was cabbage soup, but the stomach stirred expectantly. It wanted to be filled. Mama Tante encouraged. "There's a good soup bone. It's a stuffed tomato, Marusha. It is in the ice bowl on the window sill. There is some meat on the bone, Triano."

Triano went to the stove and looked into the pot. Marusha buttoned her blouse neatly up to the neck and washed her hands as Triano filled a plate with the soup. Marusha took the stuffed tomato from the ice bowl and set it down on the kitchen table beside Triano. Mama Tante sat down to enjoy her children. Marusha was not really hungry, but she knew Mama Tante put much store in feeding her children. Mama Tante had prepared the stuffed tomato to please her, to spell out the love of mother for child. She would eat her tomato and please dear, fierce Mama Tante. Triano was already tasting and feeling the warm liquid with hunger. He would enjoy. The world was for a little while focused on soup. Mama Tante watched her children eat in silence, and the treasured chore of feeding was a peace. To be eager and intent and to know peace . . . Mama Tante was safe with God and life. At the supper table Mama Tante would find her dead husband el Gran Vulbo in the gestures and the smiles of her children. Memories would flow into the yesterdays that had left a beauty etched in her life. These were implements in the basic design of a today that dipped and swayed in a long loneliness . . . until supper time. Mama Tante reached out and stroked Marusha's hair. Marusha looked up, saw the liquid fierceness in Mama Tante's eyes, then caught her mother's hand and kissed it. It was all good, deep feeling. Triano watched and loved them with his eyes.

· · · · · · · · · · ·

Dusk . . . a new dimension. Outside there was the squeak of an iron door and voices in choral expansion that exclaimed and claimed the passions of a day now gone. Laughter tumbled and rolled and found its place between the shouts and in the serious overtones. Frayed discordances of daily deed found focus in angry words or wordless lassitude. If the day had been disheveled, it was now given some seeming order to rest the soul. Dusk now brought the night. Like the day, it would be unkempt and muddled, but there would be a difference. The night would play with dreams and hope would blossom magnificently. Ramshackled truths and aimless acts found their own fanfare in the night. The taste of the night is not the taste of cabbage, thought Triano. It is more a mixture of sweet blood . . . perhaps it was mixed with wine. The night is a center arena with a man and a bull and cheering passions and a death . . . "Triano, look!" Kata, long and dark, stood in the doorway holding a bright bundle of flowers in her hands. They were hued too brightly to be real. Kata lived on the second floor of the same tenement building. Her splashy beauty still had the grace of youth. Still, the total aspect of her person showed she was a weary, lusty warrior of many battles. Marusha stiffened and became a stone. Triano smiled a welcome, "Hey, Kata, those are some flowers!"

"I made them. They came out nice . . . eh?"

Mama Tante agreed the flowers were beautiful. Kata awkwardly handed them to Triano. "They're for you."

Triano was grateful. "For me . . . well . . . well."

Kata suddenly kissed Triano unashamedly on the lips. It was a long arduous kiss. Marusha felt the rising storm of anger. Mama Tante watched with the memory of el Gran Vulbo in her eyes. Triano had not risen from the kitchen chair. Now he fingered the plastic flowers curiously. "You made beauty, Kata."

"I learned from the old folks at the church. You made beauty too, Triano . . . for Tati and me. I don't wish him dead anymore. Thank you, Triano." She had knelt next to where Triano was sitting and was now looking up seriously into his face. There was a quiet happiness in Triano's eyes as he looked into Kata's eyes now brimming with tears.

"And the spirit of God moved upon the face of the waters."

Tati was Kata's little boy. Seven years before he had been born blind because she was syphilitic. It had been the height of stupidity for her to have had a child. In her profession children were a tragedy. Medusa-like torments to conscience and fear tore Kata to shreds. The body followed the regular routine pattern of survival. The inside was a holocaust. She wished the child dead and had left him in his crib for two days alone so he would die. She had stayed drunk the whole time wishing to die within the stupors of pain. Triano heard the baby cry and had brought him down to Mama Tante who cared for him with effusive love. Four months later Kata had come downstairs to tell them to mind their own business. Nevertheless, she had taken the baby with her. Kata's misshapened life led to more abandonment and hunger, so Triano had taken the baby to Sister Mary at the orphanage. There was no more room at the orphanage, so Triano had walked sixteen miles to a clinic where handicapped children found a refuge if they had no one to care for them. He agreed to do odd jobs around the clinic to pay for the boy's keep. Triano had watched the baby grow into a boy. On Saturdays Triano would take him to the park and would describe the world to Tati. They would listen to the sounds of the world and give shape to a confidence of all things living. What were the birds feeding on the grass like? What did faces look like? Did the world look as beautiful as it smelled after rain? And cars . . . were they as powerful as their sound? Triano would describe with love and a depth of excitement that left the boy with wonder, happy to be alive. Triano would arrive at the clinic early on Saturday mornings with a lunch of sardines and bananas; then, both of them would set out to make adventure of ordinary things. They became a part of other lives parading in lovely pieces to grow on.

"And God saw the light and that it was good."

This sobered Kata. She went to the clinic and claimed her boy. She

was trying her best now. Kata began to see a strange kind of vigor and
confidence in her blind child. She was awed, subdued and happy by the
gladness he exuded. One day, she woke up and knew she was glad to be
alive, for the first time in her life it seemed to her. This was the day she
had decided to make the flowers for Triano. For many days she had
watched the old folks in the church making the flowers out of old
nylon stockings and dyes. Many times she had wanted to ask if she
might learn. Kata was a religious person. She never missed Mass on
Sunday mornings. She would take communion wearing a small bright
cross around her neck. After mass, one day, she asked if she might learn
to make flowers herself. She was welcomed and she worked with
dexterity and brightness to make her flowers for Triano.

Triano was stroking her cheek. The noises of the night came through
the window. By instinct, Kata rose to the usual occasion of a livelihood.
There was night, pawing men, and the money that made the difference
between starvation and a mute survival. She would cruise the streets for
customers making the night do for one more day. Sunlight would find
her looking and sharing with her boy. That was enough.

"Well, I'm off." She looked Triano in the eyes telling more than
words. Then, she turned and left. Triano watched her go. Mama Tante
understood the symphony of pain and courage and the rages of a life
that sometimes takes without giving too much in return. She also
understood that small flickers of pain spell a strength and a hold.
Triano felt Mama Tante feeling. He turned and handed her Kata's
flowers. Mama Tante saw the face of the world in the flowers. She
touched them gently remembering the long tempers of her youth. The
storm within Marusha broke.

"How can both of you . . . sit there . . . and listen to her. . . . She's
a . . . she's a. . . ."

It was all a blindness without an opening. "Don't you care about me?
I hate the people around here! I hate this life! I hate you both! I hate
everything!" She sobbed hysterically. She prayed frantically, "Oh, God,
help me out of this . . . out of here."

> *"And the earth was without form, and void,*
> *and darkness was upon the face of the deep."*

Triano felt a helplessness and a resentment against the helplessness.
Mama Tante took her child in her arms and felt the torment of the
young, slight body. Marusha pushed her away and ran to her bed where
she hid her face and cried out all the dark despair. There was no
distance between Mama Tante and her child, but there was a
separateness as if one soul could take in all the world finding place for a
grotesqueness that was part of truth and beauty, and the other . . . poor
Marusha! One day she would be fine; she would be complete after

many storms had passed to give new life, new seed. Triano put his
fingers to his lips and nodded towards the door. Mama Tante
understood. They walked out and left Marusha to herself. A walk
around the block would clear things for everyone. Mama Tante would
meet old friends and put the pieces back into the spirit of her design.
The evening was cool. Triano put his arm around his mother and guided
her steps. She was sure of her ground but she enjoyed the solicitude of
her boy. They strolled leisurely in silence, once in a while stopping to
look at the stars. The same heaven was over their old home, the
Mountain of Sadness.

Marusha found a calm. After the anguish, there was a new grasp. She
turned around on the bed and stretched her body. It felt good. She
stared at the cracks on the ceiling, little by little losing all the pain in
many "ifs." The cracks became a map of her life, one drop at a time.
There was the other side of town where she worked. Over there was the
street leading to the bus stop where she took the bus to the public
library every day. One crack outlined a face she recognized. It was Miss
Marsh's face. She remembered the first time she went looking for a job.
Miss Marsh had tightened her lips and narrowed her eyes when Marusha
told her who she was and where she lived. Marusha had admitted almost
in the same breath her hate for the things of her life. Words tumbled
out wishing for self improvement, hard work, education, a future. Miss
Marsh's mouth had softened. There was approval in the eyes of the
head librarian. She hired Marusha on probation. That had been three
years ago. Someday . . . someday, Marusha would be another Miss
Marsh. That was her dream. She was only an assistant working in the
catacombs of the library. In the bottom, cement room of the old
building she would repair old books and check on accession numbers.
Marusha lived with mountains of books that surrounded her. She
worked alone in the room. In her silent tomb Marusha would dream at
leisure. There were always the intervals between routine. She was going
to business school so that she would someday become Miss Marsh's
secretary. Carpets on the floor and all things in order . . . one day soon.
The cracks were now swirls of happy feeling, each one a step up into a
clean successful world of efficiency and good manners. She emulated. . . .
She would belong some day. The cracks were now swirls of cool,
delicate, fragile flowings into soft voices, smiles, and ways of
confidence . . . swirls, swirls . . . all her feeling was caught up in her
dream. A rudeness came in the form of the iron gate and coarse
laughter. She was back in the ugliness. She steeled herself. It was time
to concentrate on things to be done before the morrow. She would
wash out some things, fix her hair, and work on her shorthand.
Yes . . . it was good to be alone with earnestness, with a plan for
tomorrow. She got up from the bed and began to gather the clothing

that needed washing. With quick movements she put the clothing to soak in a small basin. She put the kettle on for some hot water. Her concentration was broken when she heard Jacobo's car pulling up on the curb. Another encounter. Her nerves taut again. A coldness. Jacobo came into the room without ceremony. "Marusha?"

Marusha did not turn from the stove. She watched the kettle as she answered, "Yes?" There was an awkwardness. Marusha made Jacobo uneasy. Her icy superiority scattered him, but he was so full of liking, he would try, "Would you like to go riding?"

No. Jacobo, her silence told him, I don't want to go riding. I want you to go away. He tried again. "I got the new car all gassed up."

The kettle began to boil. Marusha took it off the stove. "I have many things to do, Jacobo."

Jacobo coaxed, "I'll take you where the big houses are . . . the ones you like. I got money."

She poured some of the hot water in the basin where her things were soaking. "Not tonight." She went to get her hairbrush. Jacobo followed her every movement with his eyes. What was the matter with her anyway? She was a gypsy. His father was "king" of the gypsies. He felt an old embarrassment. Marusha did not approve of the new car or the money. She had contempt for the whole thing. He could not forget this. The "king" of the gypsies and his family had had some television appearances. They had been paid. Marusha had been furious when she heard his family had accepted. Marusha had accused, "You'll be a circus!" Oddities in a side show . . . differences to be laughed at . . . a condensation. She had almost screamed, "Do you think they respect us as people? They want to see freaks! Freaks!" Jacobo had been ashamed of his father and mother for appearing on the television show. But now he had a new car and could find justifications. When he had come to show Marusha the new car, he defended the family standing. "It's only freaks who want to see freaks . . . so the whole thing doesn't matter." Marusha simply refused to see. She would not forgive. Now, here she was, arrogant and distant. Jacobo tried again.

"You need to relax . . . you're all up tight."

"Leave me alone."

"What do I have to do to please you?"

Marusha's voice was deliberately tolerant. "I don't want you to please me. You don't have to come around trying to please me. You have other friends."

Jacobo became tender. "I like you best, Marusha . . . ever since you were a little girl, I liked you best of all."

"That's ridiculous! I just want you to leave me alone. If I go riding with you, you'll spend the evening getting drunk, trying to get me drunk, pawing me . . . it's sickening."

Jacobo's eyes showed a mixture of hurt and anger. "What makes you so special? You have no father and your brother is a bum."

Marusha sat down and covered her face with her hands. She was holding on . . . holding on. Jacobo felt uneasy. She whispered: "Go, Jacobo, go."

Jacobo looked down at her still figure. She was almost a shadow in the growing darkness of the room. There was a lot happening outside of that dismal room . . . there were lots of broads. . . . "See you around, Marusha." He was gone. She was alone again. She sighed in relief and sat in stillness feeling the darkness. There are things to do, she told herself. There are things of order that keep a sanity. The hairbrush was in her hand. She began to brush her hair in the darkness. She thought . . . the waiting princess combing her hair . . . waiting . . . waiting. . . . The strokes were slow and careful, each an affirmation, "I'll never give up . . . I'll never give up." She began to brush her hair with great vigor almost in defiance. Her scalp tingled with a warmth. She put down the hairbrush and went over to test the soaking water. It was not too hot now. She could hardly see in the dark. She turned on the one small ceiling light that made shadows in the room. When she had finished the wash, she put it out from the kitchen window onto the clotheslines. The night air cooled her face and felt a wistfulness for something she did not understand. She went back into the room and took out her schoolbooks. In a few moments she had found a new salvation, a far-away light.

> *". . . to rule over the day and over the night,*
> *and to divide the light from the darkness."*

· · · · · · · · · · ·

The sounds on the street were not deep sounds; they were sounds that floated on the surface of a breathing darkness. The timbre was unhurried, spreading out to what man calls chance. Chance has little conscious deliberation though experts claim man never reacts to chance. Chance, they say, is a subterranean calculation that adds and subtracts from any human decision. Spontaneity, then, has its own rigidity. Somehow the sounds of the street were not aware of this. The sounds did not admit adherences to ready-made patterns, ready-made "ways out." All was random. People believed this at night on the street. Random thoughts and deeds add to individual blitheness, so who will admit that random living is a part of a tried pattern? That chance in its substrata is a careful calculation? The pieces that come together to make the puzzle whole should be verities of some kind of freedom. A man will not be denied this much. The day of work and obligation has taken enough from him, so let him have his night.

All the people Triano and Mana Tante saw on their walk around the block, friends sitting on the stoops, the women of "business" filling out a place in "time," the men on their way to the corner bar or talking earnestly by lamp post, all were part of structured motion. Because the mind was not at work, because the night is given up to human feel, the usual things to do at night are better thought of as a haphazard act to recapitulate. . . . There must be a beginning and a middle of life, a continuation of their own making. This is the method in the direction of a stability. Melodic shapes, like stars, seem without sequence; but all are an ultimate progression that confirm life. Envisaged goals belong to the limits of the mind, but human feeling is a universal thing. . . . What happens, happens. Give it to Chance, that wild free man that follows his instinct to an end. He defies and defies the root and is arbitrary to only a part focus. He prefers to be blind and thus see. What does he see? That each man stands alone, and that *that* in itself is a good. And woman? Each woman sadly waits.

Mama Tante was out of breath when they had finished their round. Triano held her by the elbow as he helped her up the stoop. He was about to open the door for her, but she touched his arm.

"No, wait, Triano. I want to sit out here a little while. Such a nice walk." They both sat down. Mama Tante's breath came heavy, Triano noticed as he lighted a cigarette. He also knew it was time for Mama Tante to gather the blood-wine of memory, the spilling brightness of a happiness still there. The memories were of her husband, el Gran Vulbo. It was incandescent fruit that mellowed life. Triano would listen, not only to please his mother, but because the spirit of the duende became alive. The duende was the spirit of Chance, doing for freedom what he had to do. It was a magic immeasurable in its embrace. Tonight Mama Tante did not start with the memories of the Mountain of Sadness. She was still distressed by Marusha's unhappiness.

"I do not understand, Triano . . . I do not understand the hate inside of her."

"Don't worry, Mama Tante, she will find her way out of things."

"She frightens me sometimes. I try to remember myself at her age. . . . I can remember. Mine was the eager body. El Gran Vulbo would play the flamenco guitar and I danced. It was a world of the eager body . . . there was a power in me." Mama Tante sighed. She continued, "El Gran Vulbo would tell me, 'you are a tide . . . you know your ebb and flow.' That big voice of his took command of all I was. . . ." Her voice trailed off, but her eyes were full freedoms now, like stars. She remembered the passions bursting into a million pieces as they lighted up the sky. The face had softened to a clear love. She asked Triano, "Remember your papa, Triano?"

"Yes, I remember him."

Marusha was still on her mind. "How can we help her? I have found

the heart to be big because my world has been small. Her world grows
and grows and her mind grows and grows. I cannot read. I know of
things like sorrow and the doing together in gladness. I built fires in the
desert of the mountain and milked the goats and bore thirteen
children . . . but that does not help my Marusha who believes in words
and the shiny new things of this world. I am ashamed, Triano."

"It is nobody's fault, Mama Tante. Don't feel that way. You love all
things."

"You're a good son, Triano. You listen and understand."

"I learned that from you, Mama Tante."

>   *"And God said, Let the earth bring forth grass,*
>   *the herb yielding seed,*
>   *and the fruit tree yielding fruit after his kind."*

They were back on the mountain, the Andalucian road. There, in the
barren mountain, the gypsy people had been a clear affirmation of life.
El cante hondo, the deep song of human roots springing forth to claim
human things. If pain had depth so did joy and each single daily act
that builds a fire. All was fire. The sun, the song, the fiery earth, the
dance, the struggle for life, the facing of the brave bull . . . all was fire,
and that was the spirit of the duende. It is loud, happy declaration; it is
a burning intensity of acceptance; it is a consummating need. That was
the inheritance left to the gypsies by a barren mountain so rich it
glowed with its wine-blood. A figuration of freedom? Ineffable,
indefinable spirit offering life. . . .

Mama Tante took up the thread of memories again. "We have been
campesinos for centuries; your father was a great shepherd. He knew
the wiles of the mountain like the back of his hand. He knew how the
mountain gave and how it took away. He faced the brave bulls in his
youth because they were like the mountain. The mountain taught him
that one must dare death to gain life. He spilled his blood many
times . . . on the arena . . . on the mountain. He loved me, Triano. He
loved many women and I waited because he loved me as a strength. I
have been so fortunate, so blessed. I want Marusha to have such a
thing." Mama Tante looked at Triano almost beseeching.

Triano was certain, "She'll have such a thing." His eyes gazed off into
a distance trusting. Mama Tante believed, but there was still a puzzle.

"Tell me, son, are the things of the mind always so full of anger?"

"Not always."

Mama Tante sighed again. She rose with difficulty. She wanted sleep.
The day would come again. Together the mother and son walked into
the tenement building. The room was quiet. Marusha was already
asleep. Mama Tante made ready for bed.

"Are you going out, Triano?"

"Yes, Mama Tante."

She kissed him fiercely on the head. "Go on! Go on!"

Triano walked out the door full of the fantasy of his mother. His was now the fluid power of the duende. Someone had said that feeling was the tremble of the mind? Triano was struck by another thought. Perhaps, maybe, only perhaps, the mind, when all words had been erased to become a light, a wordless sound, was a feeling. Because he believed this, he had to find people now; he had to drink with friends and listen to dreams. He hurried down the stoop into the striving night. I'm out there somewhere, he thought. The night is the total of the day; it is necessary for the full creation.

"So God created Man in his own image."

RECAST

When life came out of the sea, when the process of persistent survival found the earth, there was a great diversity. Arthropods, great in numbers, came to swim, to hope, to crawl, to burrow, to fly and make all space their own. Most of them set out as predators. But before setting out, they waited for a time in dark, damp corners. Here an armor grew to keep the soft body parts safe. The armor covered the soft body parts, but it too was soft. It needed the sun to dry and harden. So, they came out to find the sun.

It is believed that the beetle's armor has a dazzling array of colors . . . soft, delicate, rich, and glittering. The shimmering colors dazzle the eye. Yet, in reality these colors on the surface of the beetle's armor do not exist. They are an illusion, like the rainbow. Further study of the beetle's armor reveals the substance of the illusion. It is the manner in which the strong plate of armor grows. The body covering consists of many layers, one upon the other, in various thicknesses. It is the layers that break up light to create a bright glitter . . . thus the brilliant color. The refraction . . . reflection . . . inflection of light interferences are the magic. Magic is needed to protect vulnerability. Whether the soft parts are of the body or the heart, the magic color and the hardness of an armor protect and build . . . for good and for bad.

There are many soft parts in the human self, and the self is a construction in space and time taking from the world around to make its color and its shell. To grow with a common world is to find resilience, a bouncing way of life. But if the resiliency does not come about, then, the reliance is on the hardness of the armour. For after all, the thing to do is to protect the soft spots. Resiliency builds upon an inner skeleton of spirit that makes of mind and heart a loving thing. The hardness of the armor is another situation. If soft parts find themselves in circumstances alien to their nature, the shell becomes a perpetuating destruction that can explode the very soul. What then? It is important that the human self find a damp, dark corner to find the inner skeleton of resilience to change its color with the time and space and movement of the world. If the human self builds only an armor of illusion because the soft parts fear . . . then:

Manolo remembered that at fifteen a girl, sitting up all the way close, teasingly had asked, "Why don't you teach me how to kiss?"

"Close your eyes and open your lips."

"Like this?" She sat there waiting with a softness of a mouth. He had kissed her using all his knowledge of seduction, rolling his tongue in her mouth and pressing her against his thin body. He opened one eye in his feverish labor to catch her looking at him. He sprang away from her.

"What's the matter? Don't you like that?" He saw the laughter rise in her body before it became a spilling, shrill sound.

He was angry. "What's the matter?"

"You're so funny looking!"

It stayed all his life . . . it stayed! It was a clamor and a braying that would repeat itself time and time again. "You're so funny looking!" Manolo took this to his own dark loneliness and grew a hardness. Loneliness became an intolerable thing to Manolo, for all there was to loneliness . . . the building of a shell. Loneliness and suffering, to resilient people, can become a challenge to beauty and to self discovery. There is no need for shell, for an autonomy is found . . . a trust, an initiative to reach out and to do. The sun becomes humanity, a generativity, an integrity. This kind of loneliness has no fear of darkness. Darkness is a hope of a wider radius of light to be discovered.

Manolo found only fear in loneliness. He built a beetle's armor. The interplay of his life was similar to that of beetles found under rocks. When disturbed by the removal of the rock under which they live, they eject a drop of volatile fluid from the anus, an audible explosion in a jet of smoke, acidic, caustic, destructive. Manolo had built a shell that was the emblem of what he would like to be . . . a heroic, handsome image; a template of the virile man of power found in slick magazine advertisements or television commercials. It shone above the ordinariness of people. It buried the old fear of "You're so funny looking!" that followed lurking in the background of his life. When people endangered the image of his armor, Manolo's actions would become acidic, caustic, destructive. He was a blind beetle who could not see beyond surfaces. He became an expulsive character . . . cruel, possessive, argumentative.

Poor Manolo. If only he had known that to be funny-looking did not matter. That deep in him was the beauty that existed in all humanity, the capacity to love. Because he feared there was no emancipation, so love was thwarted. There was only mistrust and doubt. There was a guilt turned into a condemnation of the world. There was an inferiority that repudiated the identity of others by making-believe, a spotlight lighting up only the magic false image of himself. It was all an isolation and self-absorption that turned his life into a despair he would not admit. The caustic explosions of defense became a hero's way of life from his perspective. It was all, all a game of comparison and competition. The spotlight belonged to him. The darkness and the loneliness still screamed, "You're so funny looking!"

The world and its absurdity was ugly to Manolo. No one and no situation was worthy of serious consideration. All feeling became a caricature. This gave him a safety. No one could touch beyond the shell. It was his own mutation to save the heart. He had a talent for mimicry that he used to advantage. He discovered theater. Graceful, extroverted, with a talent for mimicry, Manolo worked hard to build up the magic heroic colors of a beetle's armor. There were no hero parts in the theater for him. His facility ran to character parts. He lacked the heroic charisma even for the make-believe of theater. There were few incidents where Manolo had the authority to command a situation, a girl, or power over others even in the role of actor. He did not let this bother him too much. After all, he had a spotlight and the attention of hushed audiences even in lesser parts. But it gnawed and gnawed, the constant wish to be on top. There was no deepening process in Manolo. In time, he discovered a way of beetles that allowed him the feel of power . . . to feel the power! The power! This took the place of human feeling and satiated the gnawing. Power! Power! A brutish cadence . . . a sad song.

A way of beetles had been found in theater politics. For centuries the ancient Pharoahs worshiped the scarab beetle as a supernatural phenomenon. It's mode of life had a puzzling, sophisticated politics. The scarab lives on dung. The scarab gathers in a slanting burrow. The procedure, however, changes when it is preparing food for its offspring. Then, the dung is made into a small ball the size of a nut and it is rolled again and again until it reaches the size of an orange. A danger game. A passing scarab who sees another scarab working laboriously with his ball will immediately offer his help. The one offering help gets on the other end of the ball and both get to the job at hand. The ball grows larger. The owner, thoroughly absorbed in his work, becomes lax. The helping scarab has been waiting for just that moment. The helping scarab steals the ball. The owner then sets out to catch the thief. When he catches up with the runaway, he, too, pretends to want to help save the ball from running away because it is getting so big. So he places himself on the opposite side of the ball and starts to work. At the first opportunity, the original owner steals the ball back. The scarabs show no displeasure during this duplicity. It is a tactical stroke of cautious cunning . . . cautious cunning . . . a delicious thing in theater politics. It had the type of undiscernible violence that Manolo enjoyed. Small town theater is usually one of pretenders composed of the beginners and the forgotten ones. As a beginner, Manolo learned early the way to cut a throat and the way to please the existing power. The artful game of duplicity, the way of beetles, came easy to Manolo.

"Darling, bring me that comfortable chair over there," the old actress abandoned by a husband would order. She always patted Manolo on the arm as she commanded him. Manolo hovered over the power with proper humility, mincing admiration. After he got her the chair, he would light her cigarette.

"Mano, don't you agree with me that the upstart is simply a 'no talent'?"

"Right, Jo, right . . . you should know talent."

"You see, Mano agrees with me." She patted him again. Manolo smiled as his insides wished her dead. But she was an instrument in theater and she could open doors as decrepit as she was. He kowtowed with a finesse unbelievably artistic. There was always the imaginary spotlight on the duplicity as he played at life. His parasitic instinct shone with sophisticated brilliance. He was the perfect villain off-stage as well as on-stage. There was no feel, only the power orgasm.

Now, many years later, he was one of the forgotten ones. He was still not top man at any thing, but his long experience and exposure in theater had taught him well the role of manipulator. He had stolen the dung ball, but he was very wary that someone would take it from him. The power in his instances as manipulator on stage and with theater people was all he had. He had never made the hero roles, so he enjoyed torturing the young beginners who coveted such parts. The handsome actor, the beautiful young ingenue, had to be manipulated to their knees . . . ridiculed in every way, and kept down so that they might cater to him, the manipulator. This was his definition of "hero" now. Somewhere, the depth of human emotion was lost under the hardness of the colorful armor caste in many layers of fearful illusions and a killing sense. The shell had hardened in the spotlight.

Only yesterday he had proved himself a conqueror. He remembered Chita's big breasts, fluid and firm, as she danced on stage. His eyes caught the triumph of his manipulation in the pink nipples that swayed before him. The cast, composed of beginners, was helping him with his dung ball. He was the star in this production. The young dancers were the background. He had made them a promise to prove to them that he was a hero on-stage as well as off-stage.

"I'll have her dance for you without any top." Manolo had promised the boys in the cast. They looked at him with youthful admiration. "When?" "Anytime." Manolo felt the glow of power. It had not been difficult to convince her with threats and promises. Chita was ambitious and gullible. This was prime victim material for the likes of Manolo. Her contortions told a heroic story of Manolo, the easing, the pulling, the beckoning . . . Ah! All for him . . . no more "You're so funny looking!"

. . . .

El Soldado had just returned from Viet Nam. He had opened fire among the people in a small village at the command of his superior officer. He had no sense of who he was or what he was since his return. Those tyranosauri had discharged him from their service. All things were scattered, for the elements of his life were hazy workings beyond him. But even before he had gone to fight in Viet Nam, in a war commanded by tyranosauri, he had had no real focus in his life. Stumblings and failings had been a regular diet. This was the pattern of his common world. He was a part of its confusions and its hungers. He, too, feared loneliness and darkness; but had not grown a shell. His was the lowly ground, the ground of snake. His lowly state was decided by the king of beasts, the tyranny, the material men. He had been born earth and did not understand the actions of such men. Lowly snakes survive, no more, and hope not to be victims. The activity of the money world of tyranosauri was not of his rhythm. The earth world was honest and simple, but akimbo. Akimbo, snakes crawl, belly on the ground. The venom is one simple defense in their legless helplessness among tyranosauri.

El Soldado had belonged to a gang. Gang dreams, gang codes, gang violences shaped the little world of the barrio. Gangs outdid the loneliness and the fears. As a teen-ager, however, he had misgivings about using the knife. To the other boys it was a phallic, gleaming symbol of a power they did not have. The knife in their hand gave them a sense of tyranosauri. In the rumbles where blood was spilled, El Soldado had stayed in the background.

Barrio boys went to war to fight the money battles of the tyranosauri. When a person is hungry and there are no jobs, the army is one form of security. El Soldado was sent to Viet Nam. There he had killed for the tyranosauri. He remembered his own helplessness on the faces of the children he had shot down. The old men and the old women looked unbelievingly . . . the old women . . . an old woman . . . the mother of his life. It could have been her.

His mother. She had wiped the world clean in her stale one room darkness. She had clawed at life with the softness of angry syrup, this spoil of a woman who lived by sweet ironed shirts and God. She had found both of these in her son, El Soldado. Her fierce desire for human terrain for the son and herself held on and on. She, of shapeless body and careless heart, lived in a twilight of one day upon another. El Soldado still remembered his mother's eyes, wearing the long, lonely fears. They would make him wince, but he would instinctively recoil from them. They said too much. They wanted too much that could not be had. He had refused to feed on her defeat. So, she was left alone to praying beads and sorrow. He narrowed his own life to the single moment. This kept out the truths that haunted her. The mother became a vaguery to him . . . shut out. She would put a plate of earth-beans for him to eat. She hovered, cajoled, and pampered with bird-like overtones. The father had deserted long ago. She, somehow, managed with her fatal tenderness. He would sit there and wolf his earth-beans and wear the shirts of love . . . but he locked his mother out. It was the only way. He would sit at the kitchen table and eat in silence. His half-opened lids would no longer claim her existence. He had a sense that he would die in short, swift chapters. But the day would drift into an afternoon . . . then night, when his friends, the gang, would give him drink, plan a strategy for excitement around a few blocks bleary in their poverty, and look for woman-softness or lie about it. El Soldado would sit there and think about these things as he finished his beans, eating the warm, soupy life to fill the yawn of hunger.

Woman-softness he had with Chita, venomous and beautiful. She belonged to the barrio and to him. Chita had accepted El Soldado's claim on her automatically, for the want of a better thing. She was ambitious and fashioned her own escape from the barrio with a ruthlessness that would in time forsake El Soldado and others like him, those who crawled akimbo. She wanted to be a tyranosaurus.

El Soldado had gone off to war and the face of the barrio had changed. The gang element on the street disappeared. The old codes of territorial rights, the forbidden ground for coveting, the settling of grievances with knife fights between gangs from different barrios, all these were gone. New codes had taken their place. There was a new militancy. The snake circumstance was disappearing. There was a changing mixture of knowledge and of feeling that strove for the good of a people. There was a real, common purpose compared to the gang ground of snakes. There was a renewed sense of lions.

When El Soldado returned from Viet Nam, he found these changes and was glad. He became a part of the new militant movement with its brown berets and its sense of dignity. Grievance upon grievance was aired against the tyranosauri. They were confronted, and the militants made demands. The tyranosauri listened with patience and tolerance and the well mannered duplicity of the "god" business man. The tyranosauri were not giving up their dung ball to honest demands. It was not the game. Nothing came of the militants' plans. Their anger and the city tyranosauri's indomitable stand created little outside the realm of idle promises and confused attempts. There is no instant process to correct the wrongs of centuries. The tyranosauri hemmed and hawed and played their cards close to their chest. The militants built a life around grievances without the realization that change must come from within the human imitator and the human initiator. It would take the same centuries to undo. . . .

The militants were angry with gradualism. Their efforts had little precision and too much of the duplicity of making dung balls. The earth honesty was lost in a struggle over the glitter of things. The die-hards among the militants continued the struggle to build some kind of a violent impact. Many were disillusioned with rejection of a new kind and reconsidered the way of snakes again. It was a pattern of centuries carved into the spirit. El Soldado still had his knife from the old days in a drawer at home. The gang ways were well remembered. Then, there was the great injustice . . . he had killed for the tyranosauri. He had the memory to live with. He had kept the tyranosauri safe. The fuel was added to the fire. The tyranosauri had made a fool of him. He had lost his girl to a foreign element . . . one that smelled like tyranosauri. He heard what they had made her do in public. The world of the tyranosauri was screwing him again . . . the rage grew.

. . . .

Manolo had grown a beard. It was thick and bushy, a dark shiny black. He was pleased. He stepped back from his four-view mirror and posed theatrically. He liked the effect. The stance was perfect! From the part-turn to the pointed toe, the stance was perfect! His beard gave him a look of intrigue, he thought. The cunning face behind the beard now became a new mystery. He noticed that his eyes looked more dangerous than ever. As he scrutinized his face, he drew his lips tightly into a cruel line to get the effect of toughness. His myopic eyes under the thick black brows were full of admiration for this new personality. He began to prance and pirouette before the mirror with growing addiction. The long, thin legs and arms flurried in graceful, feminine gestures. A few turns . . . a little fandango . . . a little vicious heel work . . . there! He, then, extended his arms to pose dramatically and his eyes caught the little finger of the right hand. Pride swelled in his little thin chest. It was beautiful! Beautiful! Such grace! Almost simultaneously an uneasiness grew. The word "Joto! joto!" resounded in his mind. It didn't matter to him, but those Chicano bastards with their ignorance. Oh, well, I can handle them . . . they're nobody, he thought.

He remembered asking Babs, "Look!" He had posed his hands, bending the beautiful little finger. "Do you see anything wrong with that?" Babs was slightly amused with the old actor's question. "They think I'm a fag because of that." Babs wasn't interested. She had been waiting for friends to pick her up. She gave Manolo a blank stare with a dead, set smile. Her friends had come. "See you at rehearsal, Mano!"

He was playing and dancing the part of a gang leader involved in a rumble. He won out in the end. He killed the other gang leader. He loved the new look of power, the beard, the role of the killer. It was a hero's part. One of the best he had ever had. His many years of experience as a dancer had gotten him the part. He was not the image of a macho, but as the lead dancer, he had worked hard at the part. He was well content with himself.

Now in the mirror Manolo studied his graceful movements with relish. Deliberately, he began to mime obscenities with his hands, wiggling his little finger with delight. Then, there was the annihilating laugh, like dry wood burning, a rasping sonorous hollowness. He became obsessed with himself. He could feel the power rising in the groins. Spit! Spit! Spit! He felt a hunger to destroy. The feeling was a delicious, burning thing. Manolo and four mirror images . . . the explosive, acidic anus.

An outside observer might have spuriously noted his similarity to a black beetle. He and his reflected myrmidons with elongated heads and small, beady eyes, clawed the air in an orgiastic frenzy. The shortage of appendages and missing antennae gave it no direction. The myrmidons suddenly disappeared as Manolo danced away from the mirror. Long steps and swaying hips took him to an open area where he did a long series of *grande jetes*. Movement is a vitally important factor for many beetles. It has been proved that insects have powerful muscles and that many beetles are "strong men." With concentrated precision, Manolo practiced his *tour en l'air*. Up! Up! Up! to the top. The ego was at his throat. At long last he stopped and threw himself into a chair. There was a smile on his face. He heard a knock at the door. It opened and Chita stood there.

"I got a bone to pick with you, Buster!" Manolo took in her anger like wine. He just looked. Chita went to the bed and sprawled out. She lighted a cigarette and decided to dig at Manolo's guts at his leisure. "El Soldado is going to cut your throat. He found out what I did."

"You're a liar. He's probably out to get your fat tits and cut them off."

"You fag . . . you made a bet with the boys and picked up money. How much?"

"My business, baby."

"You fucking son of a bitch. You better watch yourself. El Soldado's too crazy about me. But you . . . you're nothing!"

She was before him with her hands on her hips. He grabbed her by the hair and viciously pulled her down against him. He whispered hoarsely, "You're nothing . . . you're nothing . . . and you've had it. You're out of the play." She dug her nails on his arm and pulled herself free. She made her way to the door and opened it. She turned before leaving and sneered. "You think you're so big. . . . He'll cut your throat."

"Up yours, Baby!"

Manolo felt somewhat shaken after she left. The lying slut. She was out. He would make sure the director would kick her out that very night. She was lying about El Soldado. All those Chicano militants were too wrapped up in their marches and their meetings. The old gang revenge was gone. Who did she think she was? "You are nothing!" was still ringing in Manolo's ears.

. . . .

Babs did exactly what Manolo had asked. Manolo had promised her Chita's part. Over the phone they had discussed his plan for having Chita kicked out by the director. Chita had been late a couple of times and the director had warned her that one more time would be the last.

"What do you want me to do, Mano?"

"Call her up and offer her a ride to the theater. On the way to rehearsal pretend something's wrong with the car . . . anything . . . you can manage it. You're a good actress. Stall and make her late. I'll tell the director I'll coach you for the part."

Babs had done as she was told. Chita was duly kicked out and Manolo felt the power. He enjoyed watching her leave the theater. "Drag your tail, Baby, drag your tail, Baby," he murmured to himself between his teeth. When she was gone, Manolo got up and clapped his hands and took command of the situation. He worked the cast up to a good show. The rumble came out a showy, professional job. The fight was perfect. The jumps, the kicks, the blows . . . the kill was smooth like fire. The whole world was in tune with Manolo. They tried the kill one more time. The dancers came to a standstill. The lights turned red. Manolo's sinuous heat followed the drum beats. The spotlight caught the contortions of the sinister face. This was an offering to his god . . . Destruction. He flashed the knife dramatically not wishing to lose the message of death. His whole body became one violent, graceful swirl as he pointed the knife straight at his victim. The other arm was extended in a triumphal pose, the little finger curled in grandeur. Two graceful steps towards his victim with a slight bend and then fully . . . one thrust . . . two thrusts . . . three thrusts . . . the other actor fell, huddled on his knees, and then lay prone on the floor. Manolo thrust out his chest, lifted himself in full pride and stood priming his full profile . . . the pose of the conqueror. Manolo had the full feel of the kill. He was a tyranosaurus. Such a beautiful indelible impression. The armor shone in the illusion.

Manolo suddenly realized he had no audience. It was only a rehearsal and rehearsal was over. Oh, well, the opening would be glorious. Thousands of eyes would see him as a symbol of power. He would feel the waves of power sweep him again; it would set him on fire again. . . . He came back to the present and realized that he was the only one on stage. Everyone had left. The last ones were going out the door. He was the last one to leave. His convertible was the one lone car parked in front of the theater. He stopped outside the door to light a cigarette. The night was cool and invigorating. Manolo took a deep breath. As he did so, the corner of his eye caught a figure lurking in the darkness of the side alley. He froze. The nail of the little finger was digging at his flesh. He had recognized the figure of El Soldado.

"Oye, Joto! Desgraciado!"

Manolo did not answer. The mind, the body, the spirit, suddenly felt the impact of his nothingness. The swirling spotlight was leaving him . . . leaving him . . . the darkness overwhelmed him. Who had taken away the chitin? He became very conscious of the soft spots. Love, for a moment, became visible to the mind and the emotions that now fluttered without armor. El Soldado's voice said everything.

"Maldito . . . you think you can make fun of my girl?"

El Soldado was now in front of him. His eyes were glazed and wild. He was one long fury against the world. He slithered out and gave his warning. The venom was the fear and Manolo saw both, each one distinct like the opening of a flower. Manolo also saw the knife. Somehow he did not feel anything. His eyes curiously caught the glint of the knife as it reflected the neon colors. Colors . . . colors . . . melting into black. The glint was still . . . grasped tightly in El Soldado's hand. No more scrimmage . . . only the glint that found the guts with a flash. Manolo photographed the coldness of the thing without understanding. When he felt the opened guts, and the blood ran, Manolo's eyes betrayed surprise. One thrust . . . two thrusts . . . three thrusts. . . . Nothingness took over. How funny the world looked as the snake scurried to a dark hiding place and the tyranosauri in steel structures, moving vehicles, and split level homes felt no pain. Only a funny, dying beetle. The soft spots were heroic and brimming with life's last breath.

THE SECRET ROOM

His name was Julio. That is what he preferred to be called. His full name was Julius Otto Vass Schleifer, sole heir to a now dangerously dwindling fortune. He stood in the walled garden of the Schlass built by his father on a high mountain in the mining area of Chihuahua. Since his father's death, he had felt like the keeper of a monstrous museum that flaunted the violence of earlier ages. No . . . he must be fair. His father's mementoes were proof that the Aryans were masters of the world. Primordial greed made masters! He frowned, thinking of a greater catalyst for masterdom . . . the masses, whether they be proletariat, Indian labor, or city worker. Where would masterdom be without them? This garden was not a memento . . . it was the gift of earth cared for by those who loved the earth. To Julio, it was part of the realness in every man. No master, no mass in this garden!

The garden was not German; it was Mexican. It was an opened surprise of patio encircled by profuse foliage. Tall umbrella pines rose far above the wall. Earthen jars in all colors served as holders for colorful semi-tropical plants. It had a natural opulence . . . orange trees, laurels, willow trees, and a multitude of water lilies floating on a mosaic fountain. Nothing was bordered or trimmed. The only apparent, planned sections were rows of willow trees that led to the garden gates, and out beyond the gates into a willow grove. These were Canadian willows planted by his father a long time ago. Part of the garden had steps that led to an open terrace that overlooked the valley and the mountains beyond. Julio climbed to the top and looked down at the land that was his inheritance. People were working in the field. *People*, not masses. He knew each one by name. They had been his father's workers for many years. They had worked the land for his father. After Julio inherited the estate, he divided the farm sections among them. He gave them individual deeds to the property. He remembered the puzzlement and the wonder in their eyes. He also remembered the hordes of relatives who protested and called him a madman who was throwing away what his father had earned. Where was their sense for people? They still computed the masses. The animal mass under the

Aryan rule. Was this a dictum of the gods? But the gods had fallen . . . the gods had fallen! The idea of a god, like anything else, does not die a quick death. The historical pull of things shapes the mind and creates the action. The gods had fallen, but their patterns were still very much with the world. Why are the masses a shapeless substance to the masters? Why must they be used as instruments? Julio had heard his father say many times, "This is the destiny of the German race, to direct the minds of the masses. Believe me, the people are grateful for direction. We were born to lead . . . it is a heavy burden." His father believed it.

Julio saw Mando's figure coming from the main house. The brown-skinned servant had a message for him. "Your uncle Anton will come this evening."

"What time is it, Mando?"

"Two in the afternoon." Mando quietly departed through the willow trees. A time for rest . . . a time for rest . . . the burning point of soul. Anton wanted a decision. He had none yet. There was a center to be found. His sister Wilma many times had accused him of lacking a center. He could not be his father's son. His father, the hero, the fighting man. How does one qualify "hero"? How does one qualify "fighting man"? There is no constancy in qualification. The only thing he felt sure about was the waiting . . . waiting for what?

Julio walked back into the house through a long, dark hall leading to the trophy room. He threw open the double door and stood there very much aware of something dying. The sun touched the room in sympathy of many empty years. The walls were covered with the mounted heads of animals. Their eyes spoke of triumph; they were still there, very dead, but eyes looked out as if to see. But where was the hunter? Buried and his eyes did not pretend to see. All these animals had been his father's prey. In the room was the famous gun case holding every conceivable kind of death instrument. A proud collection, another proof of his father's masterdom.

When Julio had been a child, he had come into this room to find his father always with the guns. The pattern with guns was to hold, manipulate, caress, until the cold metal became the thought. There was that inner glow of power polished to a metal sheen. The father was always totally aware of the boy. There was nothing living between them; they were two worlds harshly alien.

Many times this room had been full with his father's friends. There was the reminiscing interludes where Islandic legends of Nordic grandeur were the topic of conversation. Interludes . . . repeat . . . repeat . . . the Aryan masterdom. Nostalgia about the "intelligent dawning" among the Germans. The Nietzsche philosophy distorted in the small box of self-greatness. Julio had not understood then what the masters had done to Nietzsche to justify their cult. Years later, when he had come to know the lonely philosopher's ideas, Julio had seen him as a humanist whose Superman was not the nationalistic, super, tyrant, but he who put all things of violence away. When he had been a boy, how many times had he heard his father's friends talk about the men with the castiron souls! Far above the herd were the soaring German masters who would not allow themselves to be stamped into shape. But they shaped and stamped others for control. This was their interpretation of their Superman. They would raise their steins in blind pride. As a boy he had felt a wonder and sometimes considered himself very lucky because his father's blood ran in his veins. There was an awesomeness, a reverence. But now the childish things were far behind. There was a pity now . . . no, no, of course not! There was a regret, a regret for little worlds, for Lilliputian struggles. Whether it be a man of industry, a fighting man, a leader and his herd, it was all a Lilliputian struggle.

Julio took off his shirt and shoes. Then, he lighted a cigarette. He wore the "pantalones" of the peon. His brown skin glistened. The moustache was the same as many of those worn by the farm people. He had become of the earth by choice. Or at least, he thought he had . . . up to now. Tonight, he would tell Anton . . . what? Anton would insist on some kind of decision. He would confront Julio with an ultimatum. Julio could no longer afford time. His father's mining interests needed a transfusion . . . good, strong, blood money to resurrect. This could be possible if Julio married Helga Kleist. Two German families would unite fortunes to strengthen the now dying dynasty built by his father. Beautiful Helga. Why not? She was the most desirous of women. So strong . . . so principled in German ways. The Schleifer cult would be continued. Little German children would play in the garden and sulphur fumes would curl in the sky from the mines' smokestacks. Ores would be gathered from the earth. He could be his father's son. Yes, why not?

The Rhine maiden, Helga, by his side would demand her own ring of fire. She would keep supreme the German culture and prove the masterdom. Julio could fall in step. Was it so hard to fall in step with machine, industry, war? Helga had been corresponding with Julio from Germany since their first meeting before the outbreak of World War II. She had well documented a bad marriage, a divorce, and the new need for a good German husband, an epic of the Aryan race. The ring of fire would gather strength in iron and copper riches. For some unknown reason, Julio felt vaguely dissatisfied. There was a greater hunger in him; one he could not pinpoint. The goose-stepping gait of masterdom was not enough. He could not be a warrior of war and business like his father.

His father with a frontline biography. Herr Schleifer had come to Mexico commissioned by the German government to obtain mining concessions from Mexico. He had stayed to become a mining magnate. He had taught Villa's men the use of modern weaponry.

His father had refused to give up his German citizenship during World War II. He made the dramatic choice of imprisonment. The Mexican authorities had pleaded with him. After all, he was an influential man; he did not have to go to jail. All he had to do was accept Mexican citizenship. Never! He was a German. In jail, with his ways and means, he shaped his own life style bringing into the prison the luxuries and pleasures of the outside world. He became a hero to many. His code of masterdom was not interrupted. He had merely given it a flavor of martyrdom. As a young man, Julio had gone with his father to visit Germany during the rise of Hitler before he overran the German people with race passion. Hitler was building this tidal wave when Herr Schleifer and Julio arrived in Germany. His father was caught in its momentum. Hitler's storm troopers were learning terror as the main control of the masses.

It was during this time Julio met Helga. Too young to understand the machinery of power, the young people had spent their time discovering each other. They spent every day together and made love in small canoes. Julio still remembered the golden youth untouched by a world that didn't know love. Lying on the grass, Julio plied Helga for a sign of knowing love, for a sign of free giving. But Helga only seemed to make pronouncements:

"Heute Deutschland, morgen die ganza Weit!"

Julio felt a slight repulsion. "Why do you say that, Helga?"

"Because Germany and the Germans are the superior race."

Julio jumped up and began tossing stones savagely into the park lake. "Do you have any ideas that are your own . . . just your own?"

Helga pouted. "You're not a good German, Julius." Julio silently agreed. He was not a good German. He didn't know what he was.

Julio and his father attended a Nazi rally in Frankfurt. His father was entranced with the philosophy of the Third Reich. Hitler was most successful in pressing his will on those around him. In the hall, Julio watched Hitler, who, to him, seemed like an ineffectual little man, go through a well calculated, passionate process. With the cleverness of a Mark Anthony who changed a thousand enemies into a thousand friends, Hitler used the passionate word. He divided; he accused; he titillated. The enemy was kept in the minds of the people at all times. He compared to create opposites; he united the elite against the "scum." The mania floated in its magnitude. Julio's father was transfixed . . . Heil! Heil! . . . Heil!

Now, Julio sat in a large oak armchair and remembered vividly the process he had not understood so well at the time. He understood it to be a sham. Why had his father, the hero, believed? The repetition of phrases, the calculated sighs, the pauses, the orgiastic arousals of hate and egotism. The Hitler salute was a power orgasm. The gradual building up with the songs, slogans, insignias, anthems, and the marching . . . the tread of the enslaved . . . the marching . . . the, Ah! Heil! Heil! Heil!

The room seemed very depressing now. The depression was part of the weight of self-search. He must make a decision. This room of weapons and dead animals. But then . . . his father had built a heaven! Julio felt the sudden urge to laugh. He hurried on to the adjoining room. His father's Valhalla! It was really a banquet hall oval in shape, curiously surrounded by a series of doors that seemed to circumflect in all directions. Here, Herr Schleifer had reproduced a piece of the Rhineland. The center of the room held a massive round table made of oak. This was surrounded by massive oak chairs holding the coat-of-arms of various German noble houses. Between the numerous doors there were busts of the great . . . Wagner, Schopenhauer, Bach, Neitzsche. Where there were no busts, there were huge sideboards holding goblets bearing the various coat-of-arms. A huge French window led out into the garden. The relief! On the walls hung shields, spears, and swords.

In this room, his father and his friends had had their feasts after the hunt, after the kill. To Julio's mind came the memory of another Valhalla. During his trip to Germany, he and his father had gone to Passau. He saw in his mind's eye the sanctuary like a Grecian palace on the side of the Alps. Outside, the moon was cool and impervious to any victory celebration. But inside the Valhalla at Passau, Hitler's SS troopers celebrated after the hunt, after the kill. With swastika mentality, they raised their steins to toast the master race. Am I right in thinking, wondered Julio, that Valhalla is the false flooring of the gods? The domination, the prey, the hunt, the war, these things never seemed to disappear, but the Valhallas sank into the twilight. Today, now, this moment, questioned Julio, how many white sons of the gods want to be gods? If he decided to marry Helga, she would be the Valkerie gift to the god-man . . . Helga. . . .

Mando came into the room to tell him a young lady was coming up the willow walk. Girl? Julio looked out of the french window and saw her approaching. She came towards him. Elsa! When she caught sight of Julio, she extended her arms. Julio remained at the door. Elsa's arms came down to her side, but still came up to him and silently raised her lips to his. He kissed her.

He seemed somewhat puzzled, so she explained, "I saw your castle from a distance. In fact, it is the first thing we saw on the main

highway. We were sitting there on the bus, and one of the kids pointed
at it. . . ."

"Kids? Bus?"

"Oh! I'm traveling as an artist-teacher this spring. I ran out of
money, so I took this job. The young people are very nice. I do not
teach them much art. But we have an interesting experiment looking. . . . We are learning to see." She said it like a child; she meant it like
a child; she looked at Julio who still seemed unsure of her presence.

"I am here, Julio."

Julio smiled at her, "Of course you are! And I am glad to see you."

"Hey . . . lover, remember me? I'm the girl you can be honest
with. . . ."

"I am glad to see you."

"I believe you." She began to stroke his bare skin. "I also came to
tell you, I'm getting the cottage ready as soon as this trip is over.
Almost a month early . . . can you come early to Vera Cruz?"

"I might get married." He knew it was cruel, but he also knew this
was the way she would want to be told. The palms of her hands lay still
on his body. With the innocence of a child, she now folded her hands
and moved away. She sat down and silently looked up at his face. Her
eyes asked much, but she was silent. Somehow he could not speak
either. Damn her! If only she would accuse, demand . . . not she! She
now spoke to make it easier for him. He was aware of that. "Well, I'm
going around the country place looking. There's so much to look at. It's
hard to learn to see . . . one can so easily miss something . . . something
that puts all things in their place."

Julio listened. Learn what she already knew so well. She could be
happy in gazing without the greed of egotism, with a zest for just being,
without the clutter of the mind. He had seen her do this so many times.
Elsa was still talking. "I decided to paint the bedroom . . . the color of
the sea. The trouble is, the sea is all colors, how can I mix so well. It is a
problem. Remember the old mattress with the broken springs? It's
beautiful now. You should bounce on that bed now." She looked at his
half-naked body and decided she needed to be comfortable like him.
With great pre-occupation, she began to take off her stockings, after
kicking off her shoes. When she finished, she rolled them neatly into a
ball and stuffed them in her purse. She looked outside the window.
"Your water from the fountain was glorious. I was dying of thirst
coming up to your castle."

"Would you like something to drink?"

"No . . . the water was enough." She got up from the chair and began
to look around the room with the grace and curiosity of a little child.
When she came to one of the many doors, she would turn the handle
and look inside. Satisfied, she would then close the door and continue

looking at things. Julio watched her, and remembered so many things about her. She was fine and sweet and created the joy of lovers. The child was wise, but she was far from a child. She knew the body well with the sweet lust of earth.

The summers at the beach of Vera Cruz outside the cottage, she had painted, and he? He had been happy. She would cook some special dish for him, and would insist on spooning the first morsel into his mouth. Then, she would watch for his reaction with delight. In the afternoons, they would look for firewood along the beach, and when the moon rose, they would build a fire. She would race him to the sea. Their bare bodies would float and find their way to shore again. They would run back to the fire and wrap themselves up in one blanket. She would lie there with her heart beating fast. Seriously, she would look up into his face and ask, "Did you like the pastrami sandwich?" He would laugh and kiss her behind the ear. Then, the fire ran. Her tongue far into his throat . . . yes, she knew the body well; she loved it, sensed its life, and gave all things for the body. Savage in her gentleness, she belonged to him for two whole summers.

"Where's Wotan?" She was still opening doors.

"What?" He was somewhat startled by her question.

"I want to find out where you keep the gods." She had reached a locked door. She turned the handle. When it didn't open, she looked at Julio. After a moment, she knew he would not satisfy her curiosity. She wrinkled up her nose. "So that's where you keep the gods!"

Julio kept his voice casual. "Sh-h-h! Don't tell anyone."

With the same suddenness she had come in, she decided to go. "I fear I have stayed too long. My little ones are probably starving at the local hotel wondering where their errant teacher has gone." She picked up her purse and her shoes and walked towards the opened french window. There was a struggle from within. She stood there poised and started to speak, "I. . . ." She changed her mind. She simply smiled and looked at him with love. She turned to go and over her shoulders she waved the shoes as a goodbye. Down the willow walk. . . . He did not follow her. She would be all right. She knew who she was. "But when will I know?" he asked himself. He watched until she had disappeared from sight. She seemed to have no need of end, but if she ever had one, it would be merry; it would let go with laughter and joy. That was the way of the real gods. The real gods had a merry, divine ending. The real gods were of the earth. They were never solemn in a man-made Valhalla. He remembered the locked door Elsa had found. An inspiration came. He rang the bell for Mando and called out impatiently, "Mando, where in the hell are you?"

Shortly, Mando came. "What do you want?"

"The key, Mando. The key to the room." Mando knew what room Julio meant.

"Your father wanted it to stay locked, Julio." Mando did not move.

"My father's dead and I'm alive. I want the key."

Mando had the key always with him. Now he did not argue, but silently removed it from a key chain and gave it to Julio. He had been entrusted with the key. A dying man had left it with a faithful servant. But then, a servant serves the living, so Julio wanted it. He complied.

Julio took the key and looked at it. Then, he began to pace the floor in excitement. Real gods were never solemn, he kept telling himself, over and over again. The old wrath-beard of a god, the jealous god, the fearful god, the demanding god, they were only temporary creations of men's minds. The real gods laughed at little men's ways; the gods laughed at themselves. Somewhere in the tangle of old dead values was the sign of earth among the man-made gods of fear.

Mando watched Julio's excitement for a while, then shaking his head departed. He would leave Julio by himself. It was better that way. Julio put the key in the lock and turned the knob. Slowly, he opened the door of his father's secret room. What betrays a man? Things? Words? Deeds? The sad, wrong dream? Julio had been in that room as a child. He had watched them put up the first mural, the second, and then, after they had returned from Germany, the third mural. The three murals covered the walls. They took the room and the minds of the people in the room. The murals were the sad, wrong dream of his father. Tears came unashamedly into his eyes. His father had been so much more than this dream that had possessed him. Julio looked up at the murals. They were three portraits. One was of Bismarck, one of Porfirio Díaz, and one of Adolf Hitler. Their faces were set and hard over all the impressive insignia. The mouths were the tattle-tale proof of their brittleness. Theirs were the faces of masters beaten down by power. They were tired slaves. Only the eyes, faintly, from a distance, showed the hope of the earth they had once been. The mutation of the hard-line mouth and iron jaw were the battlescars. Poor men! The din of Valhalla resounded in his ears. . . . What is war? What is power? It is a necessity of Fate . . . for the . . . for the? Control the masses . . . use them . . . twist them . . . turn them . . . mold them to the gods . . . they are brutes . . . the noble of the earth . . . count them . . . count them with guns and death . . . victory . . . conquest . . . gods die . . . and mediocrity survives to make new gods . . . because it doesn't know any better. . . .

Laughter rang in Julio's ears. This was the clear, free laughter of real gods. The ones that only knew love. They must take men for fools! Somehow the memory of his father's servile following, the believers of false gods, could not escape. But didn't they? They were still so much of the earth, these slaves! He remembered the long line of Indians transporting equipment over hard mountains. The long train of human beings enslaved to another man's mad obsession with power. They were the same slaves as those who died building pyramids, the useless, useless pyramids! But all these slaves, in spite of chains, kept part of the earth; much more than the men on the murals. Their dependency, their vulnerability spoke of something pliable and soft; something very human. The men on the murals had lost that. The slaves had mastered the earth qualities. The masters are chained to sad, false violent dreams. They have killed the earth. They die hard and their dragon of riches with the values of riches glitter for thousands of years confusing man.

A light began to dawn in Julio. He murmured to himself. "No . . . no . . . I can't do that! How can I go out and create new values in the world? Who me? One man? It is impossible . . . but he could attempt creating some kind of freedom out of masterdom . . . then, *that* could find its own creation. Yes, there would be no fear with the inner freedom. The conqueror and the conquered both had lost their freedom long ago.

Twilight of the gods? The first arm that raised a weapon to control, then the true man died . . . and wasn't he the god? The dragon had never been killed. It was too well fed. The only way to kill it is to refuse the slavery of power. Julio knew now what he must do.

"Mando! Mando!" He looked at the murals one last time while waiting for Mando to answer. When Mando came, Julio pointed to the murals. "Let's take those things down and give some life to this room."

"But your father. . . ."

"Get me a ladder." Four hours later the murals were down. They had been neatly rolled and relegated to the attic. Tired, but excited, Julio stood looking at the empty walls of the secret room. The purge was over. He noticed the struggling light through closed shutters. Julio went to the window and let in the falling sun. There! The sun was something else. It sang about the earth, its constancy and neverending creations. Julio felt very, very Mexican. The earth people could more easily find a freedom from the center of being for their chains were from without. It is the masters who wear the chains from within. There was still time to escape that kind of mutation.

Julio felt whole. He also felt a deep yearning for the impetus of earth that had visited him that afternoon. That crazy Elsa with her Zen and her Tibetan ways didn't have to wave the goddess of equality under his nose! He smiled. He knew now what she meant when she talked about turning the separateness inside out to find love. Yes, he suddenly felt he needed the cottage; he needed Elsa. Julio caught sight of Mando who was still uneasy about what they had done. He was looking at the empty walls. The old world had been betrayed in his eyes. Julio wished Mando could understand. But in many ways he was like the men assigned to the attic. He had to hurry.

"Mando, I want you to give a message to Anton when he comes this evening."

"But he wants to see you."

"I won't be here, Mando. I have to go away. Tell him to give my regrets to Helga and her family. Tell him to do whatever he wishes with this place. Tell him that I'll write from Vera Cruz. I got to get myself down to the local hotel and take in some lessons."

"Lessons?"

"Yes . . . on how to see."

THE BURNING

The women of the barrio, the ones pock-marked by life, sat in council. Existence in dark cubicles of wounds had withered the spirit. Now, all as one, had found a heath. One tried soul stood up to speak, "Many times I see the light she makes of darkness, and that light is a greater blackness, still."

There was some skepticism from the timid, "Are you sure?"

"In those caves outside the town, she lives for days away from everybody. At night, when she is in the caves, small blinking lights appear, like fireflies. Where do they come from? I say, the blackness of her drowns the life in me."

Another woman with a strange wildness in her eyes nodded her head in affirmation, "Yes, she drinks the bitterness of good and swallows, like the devil-wolf, the red honey milk of evil."

A cadaverous one looked up into a darkened sky, "I hear thunder; lightning is not far." In unison they agreed, "We could use some rain."

The oldest one among them, one with dirty claws, stood up with arms outstretched and stood menacingly against the first lightning bolt that cleaved the darkness. Her voice was harsh and came from ages past, "She must burn!"

The finality was a cloud, black and tortured. Each looked into another's eyes to find assent or protest. There was only frenzy, tight and straining. The thunder was riding the lightning now, directly over their heads. It was a blazing canopy that urged them on to deeds of fear. There was still no rain. They found blistering words to justify the deed to come. One woman, heavy with anger, crouched to pour out further accusations, "She is the devil's pawn. On nights like this, when the air is heavy like thick blood, she sings among the dead, preferring them to the living. You know why she does it . . . eh? I'll tell you! She chases the dead back to their graves."

"Yes, yes. She stays and stays when death comes. Never a whimper, nor a tear, but I sense she feels the death as life like one possessed. They say she catches the flitting souls of the dead and turns them into flies. That way the soul never finds heaven."

"Flies! Flies! She is a plague!"

A clap of thunder reaffirmed. The old one with nervous, clutching claws, made the most grievous charge, the cause for this meeting of the judgment. She shaped with bony gestures the anger of the heart, "She is the enemy of God! She put obscenities on our doorsteps to make us her accomplices. Sacrilege against the holy church!"

There was a fervor now, rising like a tide. They were for her burning now. All the council howled that Lela must burn that night. The sentence belonged to night alone. The hurricane could feed in darkness. Fear could be disguised as outrage at night. There were currents now that wanted sacrifice. Sacrifice is the umbilical cord of superstition. It would devastate before finding a calm. Lela was the eye of the storm, the artery that must flow to make them whole when the earth turned to light. To catch an evil when it bounced as shadow in their lives, to find it trapped in human body, this was an effective stimulant to some; to others it was a natural depressant to cut the fear, the dam of frustration. This would be their method of revelation. The doubt of themselves would dissolve.

But women know mercy! Mercy? It was swallowed whole by chasms of desire and fear of the unknown. Tempests grow in narrow margins that want a freedom they don't understand. Slaves always punish the free.

But who was Lela? She had come across the mountain to their pueblo many years before. She had crossed la Barranca del Cobre alone. She had walked into the pueblo one day, a bloody, ragged, half-starved young girl. In an apron she carried some shining sand. She stood there, like a frightened fawn, at the edge of the village. As the people of the pueblo gathered around her strangeness, she smiled putting out her hand for touch. They drew back, and she fell to the ground in exhaustion.

They took her in, but she remained a stranger the rest of her life in the pueblo upon which she had stumbled. At the beginning, she seemed but a harmless child. But, as time passed and she resisted their pattern of life, she was left alone. The people knew she was a Tarahumara from Batopilas. Part of her strangeness was the rooted depth of her own religion. She did not convert to Christianity. People grew hostile and suspicious of her.

But she had also brought with her the miracle sand. It had strange curative powers. In no time, she began to cure those in the pueblo who suffered from skin disease, from sores, or open wounds.

"Is it the magic of her devil gods?" the people asked themselves. Still, they came for the miracle cure that was swift and clean. She became their *curandera* outside their Christian faith.

The people in her new home needed her, and she loved them in silence and from a distance. She forgave them for not accepting her strangeness and learned to find adventure in the Oneness of herself.

Many times she wanted to go back to Batopilas, but too many people needed her here. She learned the use of medicinal herbs and learned to set broken bones. This was what she was meant to do in life. This purpose would not let her return to Batopilas. Still, she did not convert to Christianity. The people, begrudgingly, believed in her curative powers, but did not believe in her. Many years had passed and Lela was now an old woman, and the council of women this night of impending storm had decided her fate.

Lela lay dying in her one room hut. There was a fire with teeth that consumed her body. She only knew that her time was near an end as she lay in her small cot. Above the bed was a long shelf she had built herself that held rows of clay figurines. These were painted in gay colors and the expression on the tiny faces measured the seasons of the heart. They were live little faces showing the full circle of human joy and pain, doubt and fear, humor and sobriety. In all expressions there was a fierceness for life.

Lela had molded them through the years, and now they stood over her head like guardians over their maker. . . . Clay figurines, an act of love learned early in her childhood of long ago. In Batopilas, each home had its own rural god. He was a friend and a comforter. The little rural gods were like any other people. They did not rule or demand allegiance. The little rural gods of river, sky, fire, seed, birds, all were chosen members of each family. Because they sanctified all human acts, they were the actions of the living, like an aura. They were a shrine to creation.

Lela's mother had taught the little girl to mold the clay figures that represented the rural gods. This was her work and that of Lela's in the village, to provide clay little gods for each home and for festive occasions. This is why Lela never gave them up in her new home. She had molded them with her hands, but they dwelled boundless in the center of her being. The little gods had always been very real, very important, in her reverence for life.

There had been in Batopilas a stone image of the greater god, Tecuat. He was an impressive god of power that commanded silence and obedience. People did not get close to Tecuat except in ritual. As a girl, Lela would tiptoe respectfully around the figure of Tecuat, then she would breathe a sigh of relief and run off to find the little gods.

This was her game, god-hunting. One day, she had walked too far towards the pines, too far towards a roar that spoke of rushing life. She followed a yellow butterfly that also heard a command of dreams. She followed the butterfly that flitted towards a lake. As she followed, she looked for little gods in the glint of the sun, and in the open branches that pierced the absoluteness of the sky. The soft breath of wind was the breath of little gods, and the crystal shine of rocks close to the lake were a winking language that spoke of peace and the wildness of all joy.

When she had reached the lake, she stepped into the water without hesitation. She felt the cool wet mud against her open toes. She walked into the water, touching the ripple of its broken surface with her finger tips. After a while, there was no more bottom. She began to cut the water with smooth, clean strokes, swimming out towards the pearl-green rocks that hid the roar. She floated for a while looking up at the light filtering through eternal trees. The silence spoke of something other than itself. It spoke in colors born of water and sun. She began to swim more rapidly towards the turn that led to the cradle of the roar, the waterfall. . . .

This is what Lela, the old Lela dying on her bed, was remembering . . . the waterfall. It helped to ease the pain that came in waves that broke against her soul and blackened the world. Then, there was the calm, the calm into which the experience machine brought back the yesterdays that were now soft, kind memories. She opened her eyes and looked up at the row of clay figures. She was not alone. "The waterfall . . . " she whispered to herself. She remembered the grotto behind the waterfall. It had been her hermitage of dreams, of wonder. Here her Oneness had knitted all the little gods unto herself until she felt the whole of earth—things within her being. Suddenly, the pain cut her body in two. She gripped the edge of the cot. There were blurs of throbbing white that whirled into black, and all her body trembled until another interval of peace returned for a little while.

There was no thought; there was no dream in the quiet body. She was a simple calm that would not last. The calm was a gift from the little gods. She slept. It was a fitful, brief sleep that ended with the next crash of pain. The pain found gradual absorption. She could feel the bed sheet clinging to her body, wet with perspiration. She asked herself in a half-moan, "When will the body give way?" Give way . . . give way, for so long, Lela had given way and had found ways to open herself and the world she understood. It had been a vital force in her. She could have been content in Batopilas. The simple truths of Nature might have fulfilled her to the end of her days if she had remained in Batopilas. But there was always that reach in her for a larger self. Nature was a greatness, but she felt a different hunger and a different thirst.

There was a world beyond Batopilas; there were people beyond Batopilas. She was no longer a child. It was easy to find little gods in Nature, but as she grew older, it became a child's game. There was time to be a child, but there was now time for something more. That is why, one day, she had walked away from Batopilas.

Beyond the desert, she would find another pueblo. She knew there were many pueblos and many deserts. There was nothing to fear because her little gods were with her. On the first day of her journey, she walked all day. The piercing sun beat down on her and the world, as she scanned the horizon for signs of a way. Something at a distance would be a hope, would be a way to something new, a way to the larger self. At dusk, she felt great hunger and great thirst. Her body ached and her skin felt parched and dry. The night wind felt cold, so she looked for a shelter against the wind. She found a clump of mesquite behind some giant sahuaros. This was not the greenness she knew so well, but a garden of stars in the night sky comforted her until she fell asleep.

At first light she awakened refreshed and quickly resumed her journey. She knew she must make the best out of the early hours before the sun rose. By late morning, the desert yielded a mountain at a distance. She reached the mountain in time to rest from the sun and the physical effort of her journey. When the sun began to fall, she started up a path made narrow by a blanket of desert brush. It tore the flesh of her feet and legs as she made her way up the path. In a little while, it was hard to find sure footing. The path had lost itself in a cleavage of rocks. Night had fallen. She was not afraid, for the night sky, again, was full of blinking little gods.

Then it happened. She lost her footing and fell down, down over a crevice between two huge boulders. As she fell, her lungs filled with air. Her body hit soft sand, but the edge of her foot felt the sharpness of a stone. She lay there stunned for a few minutes until she felt a sharp pain at the side of her foot. Somewhat dizzy, she sat up and noticed that the side of her foot was bleeding profusely. She sat there and watched the blood-flow that found its way into the soft sand. She looked up at the boulders that silently rebuked her helplessness; then, she began to cry softly. She had to stanch the blood. She wiped away her tears with the side of her sleeve and tore off a piece of skirt to use as a bandage. As she looked down at the wound again, she noticed that the sand where she had fallen was extremely crystaline and loose. It shone against a rising moon. She scooped up a handful and looked at it with fascination. "The sand of little gods," she whispered to herself. She took some sand and rubbed it on the wound before she applied the bandage. By now, she felt a burning fever. She wrapped the strip of skirt around the wound now covered with the fine, shining sand. Then she slept. But it was a fitful sleep, for her body burned with fever. Half awake and half in a dream, she saw the sands take the shapes of happy, little gods. Then, at other times, the pain told her she was going to die. After a long time, her exhausted body slept until the dawn passed over her head.

When she finally awakened, she felt extremely well. Her body was rested and her temperature, to her great surprise, was normal. She looked down at the wound. The blood was caked on the bandage. She took it off to look at the wound. She could hardly believe her eyes. There was no longer any open wound. There was a healthy scab, and the area around the wound had no infection. It was a healing that normally would have taken weeks. She stood on her foot and felt no pain. "My little gods!" she thought. She fell down on her knees and kissed the shining sand. After a while, she removed her apron and filled it with the shining sand. She secured it carefully before she set off on her climb. As she made her way out of the crevice, she marked the path leading to the shining sand to find her way to it again. It was hard making marks with a sharp stone, and it seemed to take forever. At last, she reached the top of the crevice and noticed, to her great joy, that it led down to a pueblo at a distance. She made her way to strangers that day. Now, at the end of a lifetime, Lela felt the pain roll, roll, roll, roll itself into a blindness. She struggled through the blackness until she gasped back the beginning of the calm. With the new calm came a ringing memory from her childhood. She saw the kindly face of the goddess, Ta Te. She, who was born of the union of clean rock, she who was eternal. Yes, Ta Te understood all the verdant things . . . the verdant things.

. . . .

And who were these women who sat in council? They were one full sweep of hate; they were one full wave of fear. Now these village women were outlined against a greyish sky where a storm refused to break. Spiderlike, apelike, toadlike was the ferocity of their deadness. These were creatures of the earth who mingled with mankind. But they were minions to torture because the twist of littleness bound them to condemn all things unknown, all things untried. The infernal army could not be stopped now. The scurrying creatures began to gather firewood in the gloom. With antlike obedience they hurried back and forth carrying wood to Lela's hut. They piled it in a circle around her little house. The rhythm of their feet sang, "We'll do! We'll do!"

"The circle of fire will drain her powers!" claimed the old one with claws.

"Show me! Show me! Show me!" Voices lost as one.

As the old one with claws ordered more wood, the parish priest came running from his church. With raised arms he shouted as he ran, "Stop! Do you hear? Stop this madness!"

It can be argued that evil is not the reversal of good, but the vacuum of good. Thus, the emptiness is a standing still, a being dead, an infinite pain . . . like dead wood. No one listened to him.

"Burn! Burn! Burn!"

Life? The wood? The emptiness? The labor pains were that of something already lost, something left to the indefinite in life. The priest went from one woman to another begging, pleading, taking the wood from their hands.

"Burn! Burn! Burn!"

The old priest reasoned, "All is forgiven, my children. She only made some figurines of clay!"

There was a hush. The one woman with the claws approached the priest and spit out the condemnation, "She took our holy saints, Mary, Joseph, and many others and made them obscene. How can you defend the right hand of the devil? Drinking saints! Winking saints! Who can forgive the hideous suggestions of her clay devils? Who?"

The priest said simply, "You."

But if there is only darkness in a narrow belief, who can believe beyond the belief, or even understand the belief itself? The women could not forgive because they did not believe beyond a belief that did not go beyond symbol and law. Somehow, symbol and law, without love, leaves no opening. The clay figures in the church with sweet, painted faces lifted to heaven were much more than figures of clay to these women. Their still postures with praying hands were a security. Now, the priest who had blessed them with holy water said they were not a sanctuary of God. Why did he contradict himself?

The old one with the claws felt triumphant, "She has made our saints into pagan gods!"

The priest shook his head sadly, "It is not a sin, what she did!"

No one listened. The piling of wood continued until the match was lit. Happy. . . . Happy fire . . . it would burn the sin and the sinner.

. . . .

Something in Lela told her this was the last struggle now. She looked up at her clay figurines one last time. Her eyes had lost their focus. The little gods had melted into one another; all colors were mixed. They grew into silver strands of light that crossed and mingled and found new forms that pulled away from one center. In half consciousness, she whispered, "Yes, yes, pull away. Find other ways, other selves, grow. . . ."

She smiled; the last calm had taken her back to the caves outside the pueblo. The caves were not like the grotto behind the waterfall, but they were a place for Oneness, where one could look for the larger self. Here the solitude of the heart was a bird in space. Here, in the silence of aloneness, she had looked for the little gods in the townspeople. In her mind, she had molded their smiles, their tears, their embraces, their seeking, their *just being*. Her larger self told her that the miracle of the living act was supreme, the giving, the receiving, the stumbling, and the getting up.

In the caves she had sadly thought of how she had failed to reach them as a friend. Her silences and her strangeness had kept them apart.

But, she would find a way of communicating, a way of letting them know that she loved them. "If I give shape and form to their beauty," she thought. "If I cannot tell them I love them with words. . . ."

The lights of the moving, mixing little gods was becoming a darkness. Her body would give in now. Yet, she still wished for Batopilas and the old ways with her last breath, "If only . . . if only, I could be buried in the tradition of my fathers . . . a clean burning for new life . . . but here, here, there is a dark hole for the dead body. . . . Oh, little gods, take me back to my fathers. . . ."

The little gods were racing to the waterfall.

"IF IT WEREN'T FOR THE HONEYSUCKLE...."

There was one huge white church towering high over the village. It seemed to stand alone, for the mud huts that surrounded it gave the appearance of growing out of the mountain, like its fruit. Down, down the mountain, like dust colored stubble, the scattered huts continued until they came to the low ground of an old river bed. Here things were green. There were cottonwood trees, deep-rooted weeds of a primitive human life. They were staunch and demanded little other than their subterranean sustenance. The source of life reached down to far depths. In one of the huts surrounded by trees, the one covered by honeysuckle, Beatriz dug in the garden.

A slender, small woman with wisps of brown hair and watery blue eye, her lineage was dubious. She was one of ten illegitimate children perhaps sired by a passing German or a wandering gachupín . . . it didn't matter, she was part of the construction of a wayward destiny. She was past her youth now, and she had found roots, perfumed coronets of pink, yellow, and white honeysuckle. It had grown all around the hut because of careful care; it had also become the Dionysian covering of a soul.

Beatriz was at this moment working around her tomato plants. She gently broke the soil around the plants with a rusty spade. She had a good, thriving vegetable garden. The earth was moist and its fragrance smacked deep upon a good contentment. The air was cool this time of morning. It was time to exercise her own refinement of passions at leisure. They were cool passions that blended well with the climbing sweetness of her honeysuckle vines.

In the dark, rich soil, Beatriz's eyes caught sight of a fat worm burrowing with careful deliberation. She had exposed it to the sun. The crumpled earth around it formed new worlds for the tiny creature of the earth. Beatriz spoke to it in a soothing voice, "Chiquitito . . . dig . . . dig . . . a cradle." It will find a new paradise, she thought. She had touched upon its design and now she shared. When it had disappeared, she sat flatly on ground and leaned her body back, her arms holding the body taut and straight. Squinting, she looked out into a distance towards the steeple of the church. Somehow, the whiteness rising above everything spoke a language she alone understood. Contours were a safety . . . a pristine castle-building neatness with little things . . . *if the garden does well . . . there will be a few more centavos. . . . I will buy a pane for the broken window . . . some brown sugar for melcochas . . . sell them at five centavos apiece. . . .*

The smell of coffee reminded her the morning must now take on serious intent. There were many things to do to keep the order of things. She got up and shook out her skirt and tidied her hair as she walked towards the door leading into the kitchen. Always, before going indoors, she would stop for a moment to glance around, looking at the wide, profuse tendrils of honeysuckle that had formed their own geography, growing in all directions. The tendrils crept in and out of the trellises Beatriz had made for their support.

It had rained for three days and nights. The greenness was bright and now had a sweet heaviness. She looked up to watch the cloud movement with its secret of raindrops. The tapestry of the earth she knew well and loved because she saw an order. She loved order above all things.

She had clipped and trimmed the honeysuckle so that it would not choke itself. Its berth was free to reach the sun. She noticed, however, that she had neglected the bottom growth close to the ground. Here, the honeysuckle had grown profuse and chaotic. There were no ins and outs, but an overlapping and an entanglement that made her decide to clip and trim it later that morning. First, however, she had to help with the house chores. Also, the problem of Lucretia was heavy on her mind. For the moment she left her green triumph and went into the house.

Sofa was moving in the kitchen area of the one room hut and Lucretia was still asleep on an iron cot in one corner of the room. Over the cot was a gaudy calendar picture of the Virgin. Her painted smile and a saintly bright yellow aura gave the wholeness of the picture an absurd passivity. On the cot, Lucretia's face was pure and sweet in sleep. So young, thought Beatriz, so very young. . . .

Sofa was pouring water from a bucket into a pan for cereal. The buckets had been full for several days since it had rained so much. She had not had to walk up the hill to where the huge city water trucks would distribute water for the neighborhood. She put the rainwater to heat for the cereal. She muttered to herself as she worked, "Mofi . . . Mofi . . . he'll come back this morning." It came like a moan from deep in the throat. She felt the steam from the boiling water on her face. She poured in the dry cereal and began to stir the contents in the pan. Her face and body wore the tension of waiting. A tug . . . a bafflement . . . the steam that softened pores. There was an affliction that Beatriz understood. She looked kindly at Sofa and reassured: "He'll come back, Sofa. Mofi will come back."

Sofa's face brightened with hope. She would believe. Her life dangled on belief . . . there was little else. Mofi had been Sofa's cat. Beatriz knew it would never come back. Robles had dashed Mofi against the wall in a rage and had broken its body. Sofa didn't know and Beatriz did not have the heart to tell her. It was a common thing for Robles to do . . . to translate vindictiveness into maiming, killing, displacing . . . always displacing the order of things. Beatriz watched Sofa limp from the stove to the table and knew that Sofa had to hope for a little while longer.

Beatriz, on the other hand, did not rely on hope. She was a realist bent on making do with what there was. She made herself a part of things around her in a clean dispassion, a calculated, simple order of a sanity all her own. She had brought her simple kind of order to the jumble that was Robles's life. There was much to regret about her union with Robles, but she did not. She made the best of a mistake. When she was fourteen she had met Robles, a middle-aged man, violent in his ways with women. At fourteen, she could not see this. Riding her trembling little donkey to the feria, she had hoped for no more than time off from the common slavery at home where she spent her days doing the family wash at the river. She had nine brothers who demanded herculean servial attentions from an overworked mother and Beatriz. The ferias were once-a-year affairs. Her brothers always built a booth to sell to the crowd. They had made headdresses out of turkey feathers. Beatriz had spent many extra hours dyeing feathers for her brothers' booth. When she reached the booth, she dug her heels against the donkey's side and touched his head to make him stop. The first time Robles saw her was when she rode in on her little donkey. He was drinking with her brothers.

"So this is your little sister, eh?"

"She's a good worker; has a strong back."

"Maybe I'll steal her. You don't feed her enough . . . all bones."

"Apestoso . . . you got a wife and six children . . . and how many other women . . . eh?" Robles laughed. Beatriz had run away with Robles in his vegetable truck. He had bought her a new dress and she was tired of slavery. She felt the idiocy in the predicament of being a woman. She had no illusions. But washing for one man was better than washing for nine. Robles had promised her a house of her own. She was curious to see how he would provide. Robles had bought a piece of land on the river bed. There was no house. He had other women and children to support. They were scattered in the little towns through which his vegetable truck traveled. For this same reason, he saw Beatriz only once in a while.

In the strange town where Robles had bought the land, Beatriz found odd jobs and set about to building a house on her own, little by little. The house had taken twelve years to build. She had gone hungry to save enough money for nails. She would buy a handful of adobes at a time. She watched men build houses and learned, and wherever a big building was being dismantled to give place to a new construction, she would beg, buy, or steal materials to build her house. This became the design of her life, the realization of an order more important to her than anything else.

Beatriz was happy Robles came to town only once in a while, for living with him was like living with a pig who insisted upon a sty. He was dirty, destructive and greedy. He looked like a pig. She hated the touch of his thick, heavy hands and the rotten smell of his mouth. She tolerated him, looking forward to the times he wasn't around. Sometimes, when he came, he would watch her work on the house with admiration. What a woman . . . so tiny, but so determined, so indefatigable. She had the stamina of a man.

There was simply no nonsense in Beatriz's life. She knew not of passionate infatuations or long waitings for dreams to be realized by mere suppositions. She had no patience with the romanticizing of things. Things were what they were. One only had to give them order. She functioned on volition and a given routine. She was like the self-contained river-bed, dry in appearance, but with an underground network of seeming order that fed a green life.

One day he appeared with a young woman. The house had been completed the year before. To Beatriz it was a blessing. She was greatly relieved when she gave up her bed to Robles and Sofa. She considered it a lucky turn of fate and she pitied the victimized helplessness of the younger woman who in a short time became her friend. Sofa was a pretty girl. In the beginning, she was gay and lazy. She did not claim to love the pig, Robles, but she needed food and a home; now she had it. Her submission to Robles' demands in time left scars. Sofa's discontent and disgust for Robles grew. She was affectionate and wanted to please Beatriz who never seemed to stop from her labors. She would watch Beatriz plant in her garden, make candy to sell, sew canvas shoes for a local store, and work on innumerable activities that made Beatriz self-sufficient.

Beatriz was glad Sofa had come. She had been relieved of Robles and she had found a companion. When Robles was away and now that she had a friend, Beatriz's well ordered machinations of her spinster attitude and ways found a tranquility.

The order did not last. Robles was getting old and insecure about his prowess as a man, so the rampage began. Sofa had been there for a little over a year and had fallen into Beatriz's pattern of things. Now when Robles showed up in his vegetable truck, he was more drunk than usual and was becoming suspicious and jealous about Sofa's doings. All the doings were of his imagination. The filthy ways of his life were revisiting as fears. Every time now, he would come in kicking the furniture, breaking things, and beating Sofa. Beatriz had to interfere and find ways of calming him.

Sofa would huddle in a corner after being beaten unmercifully by Robles. She would remain, crumpled and whimpering, until Beatriz would dare to interfere. Beatriz knew it was impossible to stop him when the rage was high. She would keep Sofa out of the way while he broke and displaced things in the house.

"Where is that whoring bitch . . . you're hiding her from me?"

Sofa would be found by Robles and beaten. Somewhere in the blare of rage, Beatriz would place a firm hand on his arm and say in a quiet voice: "That's enough, Robles. You are tired. Here . . . here is some tea for you to rest." The pattern remained. Robles would stare at her with bleary eyes and a hanging mouth and look incredulous. He obeyed her. He was tired and beat and the rage was suddenly burned out. There was something about Beatriz's calm that brought reality to the fore.

"Here, drink your tea." Beatriz would hand him a cup filled with a steaming brew made out of Indian herbs that would tranquilize and bring sleep. She would guide his hand for him to drink. Then, she would massage his neck muscles. He would close his eyes and smile. It was good. It was rest from all things.

One day Robles beat Sofa so badly that he broke her hip. It never mended. It crippled Sofa in spirit as well as in body. The arteries of passion were severed. Sofa became a shuffling, fearful creature hoping for love. Beatriz bought her the cat one day. Sofa's eyes found a hope again. She made Mofi the receptacle of her love and stepped lightly on the passing of days.

Beatriz's technique for living did not include collapse. An order was maintained. Her skein of order was a chirping brightness that carried Sofa in its thread. After Robles' visits, Beatriz would mend the furies left behind as best she could. After the breaking, beatings, cursings, there was the herb tea. Robles would sleep the round of the clock. When Beatriz had ordered the wake of his storm and comforted the terrorized Sofa, she would gently wake the sleeping Robles.

"It's getting late. You'll be late for deliveries."

Robles would wake with a start. The brain was befuddled. He would take heed and leave in confusion. His visits were becoming more rare. But now when he came, there was an obvious sickness of the brain. He looked forward to the destruction and pain. Until the last visit . . . he had shown up with a new waif to plunder. He had found Lucretia in an abandoned farmhouse where the family had died of cholera. She was fourteen and starved.

"Clean her up. She may die of the pestilence. You two watch and see. I'll be back next week." He had not stayed this time, fearing the probability of contagion. Beatriz and Sofa nursed Lucretia back to health. Beatriz knew the beast would return to plunder. Mofi had been killed by Robles a long time before, but Beatriz had let Sofa hope and wait. . . .

Sofa stood in the kitchen doorway. She was looking out towards the distance. Her eyes were blinded by the sun. She called out, "Mofi . . . Mofi . . . Mooooo . . . fiiiii. . . . I have something good to eat . . . please come home." Beatriz watched her in silence and made up her mind to get Sofa another cat. She must also save Lucretia from Robles . . . in some way. Somewhere she must find an order to keep the girl safe. She looked at the sleeping girl who had turned around in her sleep and pillowed her face in her hands. She awoke in Beatriz a fiery protectiveness and a tenderness. So young . . . so very young. Beatriz sighed. Beatriz, in the sub-divisions of the soul, knew she could rearrange things. . . .

"Mofi doesn't answer." Sofa's plaintive voice brought her back to the daily concentration of breakfast. The cereal was ready. Beatriz set the table for Sofa and herself. Sofa limped to the stove and brought the coffee pot to the table. The bowls were filled with cereal and both women sat down to eat. They ate in silence. Lucretia stirred. Sofa's eyes filled with liquid questions. Beatriz comforted.

"Don't worry. She'll be all right."

Sofa's thoughts trailed off to her love. "I miss Mofi. Do you think he ran away?"

"He's probably lost. I'll get you another cat."

"No . . . no . . . I want Mofi. He'll come back. I know it."

Lucretia turned towards the wall again. They heard her stir and sensed an anticipatory terror. It gnawed. There was a silence again. The sun spoke . . . birds . . . crickets . . . all, in counter harmony to their concern . . . Lucretia. Again Beatriz spoke the first comfort.

"Perhaps we can help her get away."

"Where would she go? She's so young. She would be happy and safe here with us if it weren't for. . . ."

"I know. . . ."

"Look what he did to me." Sofa touched her hip to sooth the crippled heart. Beatriz frowned. It would be more than broken bones . . . that old, dirty beast would paw and take the innocence of a defenseless thing. Beatriz shivered in her tight thinness.

Sofa's face flushed darkly with the memory of her fears. Her glance fell upon the eyes of the painted Virgin on the wall. She imagined a miracle. Our Lady would intercede for the sake of womanhood. She would pray for a miracle. She closed her eyes and prayed with clenched fists.

Beatriz knew it was up to her to find and keep an order as she had always done. She must add and subtract the reality of things. There was a way out if she looked for it. The sudden clatter of bird wings outside the kitchen door reminded the women of the duties of the day. They cleared the table and set about to scrub, sweep, and keep the simple order of their lives. It was still morning when a neatness was achieved. The women had part of the morning left to their own desires. The silence of the mind and pliant bending to the sun took them outside where Sofa went to look for Mofi and Beatriz decided to trim her honeysuckle.

Outside the pale of impulse, Beatriz needed the green of wondrous tranquility that covered the one room design of her life. It was an ordinary thing, to trim the honeysuckle, but this vague ordinary thing set a peaceful rhythm, a good, clean impartiality . . . at least for a little while. With a small hatchet and the rusty spade in her hands, she observed the overgrown bottom. The traces of three days' rain were everywhere. Her strokes with the small hatchet were swift and trained. The vines could hardly breathe on the bottom. They were incrustations of life infused into a wilderness. Beatriz would give the bottom of the loveliness a form, a style without clutching, to find its way to the sun. She worked in full absorption for a long while. The church bell announced the noon hour as Beatriz came to the turn of the house where there was little sun. It was very cool here. The moisture of the rain was still quite visible on leaves and puddles. Here, too, the vines were overgrown. As she lifted them to find the main artery, the one to be salvaged from the rest that would be cut away, she saw them.

Three white, fruiting Amanitas . . . full blown, forming the usual fairy ring. The ring was completed by smaller stumps of spores that had failed fruition. But these three . . . these beautiful three were blown reproductions of a whiteness found in dreams. Beatriz stared in fascination. An excitement grew in her. In the back of her mind, there was something. She looked up at the climbing honeysuckle and felt a triumphal presence . . . the green stability was looking out for its vestal maiden. These three were a gift from the honeysuckle. Beatriz did not doubt. She touched them with a growing assurity; then, she swiftly cut them with the small hatchet and put them in the pocket of her apron. Her concentration came back to the present chore. She continued clipping the smaller vines that grew out of the main stem in brilliant timbre . . . trumpets of freedom . . . trumpets of freedom. . . .

Lucretia walked behind the stooped figure of Beatriz busy at her work. Her feet were bare and her hair was flowing. She put her hand on Beatriz's shoulder. "Can I help?" Beatriz loved the childish voice. She turned and looked at the mere girl still unbroken. Beatriz patted the hand on her shoulder and smiled her welcome. "If you want to . . . here." She handed the spade to Lucretia. Together they nursed the honeysuckle vines in a symphony of peace, a believing in something. How sweet the earth and the green blood of hope! They were lost in a finding, until Sofa called from the kitchen door, "Aren't you two hungry? I made you some soup." Her hunt for Mofi had been fruitless, so she had appeased the loneliness with a common task.

They were hungry after the vigor spent around the honeysuckle temple. They went into the house taking the heat of the sun with them. But the room was cool and in shadows now. Sofa had set the table and was spooning soup into bowls. All three sat, content with the present. They talked about the honeysuckle and the fiesta at the church the coming Sunday. The hum was light and hopeful, until Sofa remembered Mofi again.

"I looked and looked. I walked about a mile and looked everywhere. I called and called . . . Mofi did not hear." Her voice was a tension mixed with tears. The evil smell of memory . . . of Robles hitting and taking . . . was in Beatriz's mind. The wake of the last hurricane was in her mind. Sofa was longing. Lucretia was innocence. They finished their meal. Contentment seemed to have disappeared. There was a body separateness, but a synthesis of senses, of something out of nothing . . . yet everything. Beatriz and Sofa were now looking at Lucretia. A terror grew in Sofa's eyes. Sofa dared to ask: "Will Robles sell the house? He threatens everytime he comes."

Beatriz stiffened. "This is my house. I built it. I paid for every plank with great suffering. It is my house."

"It's his land. He says the law is on his side. I wish . . . I wish. . . ."

The three women were in accord with the impossible wish. Lucretia began to cry silently and looked at Beatriz with pleading eyes. The honeysuckle had given Beatriz a way . . . the inner urge, the outer deed . . . all would be obeyed. Roots were deep in the soil as they were deep in the heart . . . the house, Lucretia, Sofa . . . the calm and order of things . . . she would never give them up. Beatriz spoke lightly and without care. "Lucretia . . . I have something special for you to do today."

The girl was eager. "What?"

"I want you to plant the honeysuckle seedlings in the parish garden today."

"But you prepared the soil. Didn't you want to do it?"

"No . . . you go on . . . and after you finish, stay and help the housekeeper. She's swamped with preparations for Sunday. You can cook supper for the priest."

"That means I'll stay all afternoon."

"Why not? Just stay there and wait for us in the church. Sofa and I will meet you there for rosary services."

Beatriz got up from the table and came back with a hairbrush. She began to brush Lucretia's hair briskly. With deft movements she plaited the hair. It made a finality of the command. Lucretia looked forward to going to the church. A little while later the three women put the seedlings in a box. After that, Lucretia set out towards the tall white church as Sofa and Beatriz waved goodbye from the doorway. Sofa was full of trepidation.

"Robles is coming in a little while. He'll kill us when he finds Lucretia is not in the house. . . . I know he will. . . ."

They were still waving at Lucretia. Beatriz reassured Sofa, "I'll handle him. He won't beat you. I promise."

Beatriz felt the beginning of a whimper in the depth of Sofa . . . a deadly nausea-growth. Beatriz felt an anger. Woman . . . the victim . . . woman . . . the victim. Why? It had no order. She went into the house with Sofa following. They began to wash the lunch dishes. Sofa would not spare her.

"Beatriz . . . he'll be here in a little while."

There was a storm in Beatriz now. Why? Why?

Sofa still pried. "He'll kill us surely, this time. I'm afraid." The gall drowned Beatriz. One memory upon the other of a man who crushed the soul between his teeth. She felt the back of her mind for the thought that was a mortal gesture against the kind of death that Robles brought with him every time. She was suddenly very tired of scooping up the fragments of broken things and broken spirits. An operative evil had to be destroyed.

"Listen to me, Sofa," Beatriz went up to Sofa and held her by the arms. She looked straight into Sofa's eyes and said very deliberately, "Sofa, Robles killed Mofi." Beatriz knew it was a cruel thing to do. A twisting inside of Sofa began. "No . . . no . . . no . . . no . . . no. . . ." She sang the pain in unbelieving waves of love for the soft, furry thing that had been her warmth, a belonging. Her body shook with disbelief. Beatriz let her cry it out. Then she struck again. She had to.

"He dashed Mofi's head against the wall."

Blood waves crashed over the senses of the open wound of a woman. The pity . . . the pity . . . the pity . . . the pity . . . the hurt . . . the loss . . . the emptiness. . . . She was sobbing wildly. Beatriz knew the time was right.

"Sofa, I have a plan. Robles will never bother us again."

Sofa, wet with sorrow, looked at her questioning with her eyes.

"Instead of the herb tea, we'll offer him some lunch." Sofa did not understand. Beztriz stood before her with brilliant, excited eyes. She reached into the pocket of her apron. She put out her hand holding something. She opened up her hand and in the palm were the three white Amanitas, somewhat wilted. "Look!"

Sofa stared and saw the order Beatriz gave to freedom. She nodded

her head and cried not with sorrow, but with a sliding hope to curb the
pain so wild in her. Sofa nodded again. She was an excited part of the
plan now. She went to the stove and looked inside the pot. "There's
still enough soup for one person."

Beatriz put the Amanitas in a bowl and filled the bowl with
rainwater. She began to wash them carefully. Then she took a knife and
sliced them. Sofa watched her in fascination. Beatriz turned to Sofa.
"Add a little water to the soup before you start the fire."

There was an ecstacy close to happiness in what they did. Fear had
dwindled away. There was almost an air of festivity in their preparation
for Robles' coming. It was not long after that they heard the vegetable
truck stop in front of the house. Every thing was prepared. The women
sat down and waited. They soon recognized the steps. He was very
drunk . . . all the better. The heavy steps were uneven, accompanied by
dark muffled cursings. Robles stood in the doorway. A fungus of the
world, thought Beatriz. He was old and he was meanness, but Beatriz
felt no fear. He was a swollen poison with an evil smell.

It had been decreed long ago by man-made laws that living things
were not equal. It had been decreed that women should be possessions,
slaves, pawns in the hands of men with ways of beasts. It had been
decreed that women were to be walloped effigies to burn upon the
altars of men. It had been decreed by the superiority of brute strength
that women should be no more than durable spectacles to prove a
fearful potency that was a shudder and a blow. It had been
decreed . . . how long ago? . . . that women should approve of a
manhood that simply wasn't there . . . the subservient female loneliness. . . . It had been decreed.

Beatriz smiled at him and stood up. Robles was very drunk, but not
drunk enough to forget the young prize he had brought to them not so
long ago.

"Where's the girl?"

Sofa grimaced and closed her eyes, her lips moving in prayer, her
hands clasped tightly. Beatriz feigned gaiety.

"She's out in the back yard helping me with the honeysuckle. She's
weeding. She probably did not hear the truck."

"Go get her." His voice was unsteady. He swayed as he walked
towards a chair. Beatriz helped him to a chair and showed concern. She
peered into his face. "Do you feel all right?"

"Eh?" He shook his head as if trying to rid himself of a confusion.
He looked at Beatriz through his bleariness and repeated his command.
"Get the girl."

Beatriz did not move. She spoke softly. "Are you all right? You're
not steady on your feet. Why don't you throw some water on your face
and eat some lunch . . . that will make you feel better."

His whole body seemed to sway in a circle. "What did you say?"
Beatriz coaxed. "I bet you haven't eaten . . . have some lunch and
clear your head while I get Lucretia."

Beatriz looked into his eyes without wavering. She remained
staunchly before him. He looked at her with a puzzled look in his face,
but he could not look her in the eyes for long. He gave in to her
suggestions. Beatriz spoke soothingly "Here . . . I'll get you a wet rag
to freshen your face, then I'll get you some soup." She beckoned to
Sofa who was still a ball of fear in the background. "Sofa, get me a
washcloth." Beatriz moved behind Robles and began to rub his neck.
He sighed with pleasure. Beatriz' voice was calm and reassuring,
"There . . . doesn't that feel good?" There was no answer from Robles,
but the satisfied smile on his face was enough. Beatriz continued
smoothing the tense neck muscles in silence until Sofa came with a
damp washcloth. Beatriz's eyes said much to Sofa, but her voice was a
simple command. "Why don't you fill a nice bowl of that soup for
Robles."

Sofa did as she was told. Beatriz took the damp washcloth and gently
cleaned Robles face. "It's very good soup. There are good pieces of
chicken in it." Sofa set the bowl of hot soup on the table. Beatriz dried
his face with the edge of her apron. "There!" She guided him to the
table. "I bet I was right. You haven't eaten anything for a long time.
Mmmmm . . . doesn't it smell good?" Beatriz put the bowl before him.
"You eat all of it while we get Lucretia for you."

Beatriz took Sofa by the arm and led her towards the back door.
Robles watched them, then he picked up his spoon.

Sofa gasped and breathed in the heat of the afternoon. The fear was
still in Sofa's face. There was no fear in Beatriz' face. Sofa voiced her
bewilderment, "What are we going to do?"

Beatriz was holding her hand before her face to avoid squinting as
she surveyed the backyard in the suffocating heat.

"Well, while he eats his soup, we'll find the proper place to bury
him."

Sofa stifled a hysteria. "Bu . . . bu . . . ry him?

Beatriz in sweet cadence replied, "Yes, of course." She viewed the
honeysuckle intently. She remembered the dark place away from the
sun where she had found the mushrooms. "I know where. . . ."

Sofa followed Beatriz's eyes and stopped as Beatriz pointed,
"There . . . the ground is soft and easy . . . yes . . . under the fairy ring.
Get the shovel."

Sofa's fears tortured her face, "He'll hear us digging."

Beatriz' serenity did not waver, "It doesn't matter." Beatriz walked
around the side of the house as Sofa went to get the shovel. She stood

there estimating the depth and length. Sofa had found the shovel and now handed it to Beatriz. Beatriz planned, "I'll start the digging. When we have gone a ways we'll use the bucket to go faster. We have to hurry if we are going to go to rosary services."

They dug for a long time forgetting Robles inside the house. It was now sundown. They had talked of ordinary things as they dug, perhaps anticipating a massive charge, a violence from inside the house. But there was nothing. They continued working until they had dug a shallow hole sufficiently large. They were very tired. Without saying it, they sensed that enough time had passed for some reaction from inside the house. Still, they did nothing. They were now relaxing, letting the mind ramble. . . . Beatriz was fourteen again. "I wonder what happened to my little donkey. . . ."

"You had a donkey?"

"When I was a girl . . . when I was free. . . ."

It was a joyous idea. It gave them a new burst of spirit. Free . . . free . . . free. . . . But were they sure? It had been a long time. They looked at each other, thinking the same thing.

Sofa was the first to ask, "Do you think he's. . . ."

"No . . . it takes time."

"It's been a long time . . . hours it seems."

"They should begin now."

"Begin?"

"Yes . . . the convulsions, the coma. . . ."

Sofa was afraid again. "He'll try to kill us . . . he'll. . . ."

"Be quiet."

They sat on the sweet, fresh grass and listened. There were no sounds from the house. The sounds they heard belonged to the outside world. The steeple of the church shone with the dying sun. A thought grew in Sofa, "Do you think he left the house?"

"No . . . we would have heard the truck. . . . He's still in the house."

The stillness had a substance now. . . . Beatriz decided to go in. She got up, cleaned off her skirt and tidied her hair, the customary habit. She walked towards the house. A fresh momentum, a sturdy confidence in an end. . . . As Beatriz walked towards the house, Sofa looked around furtively and then got up and followed her. When Sofa went into the house, she saw Beatriz standing in front of the cot where Lucretia had slept. Robles was on the cot . . . dead? Beatriz turned when she heard Sofa come behind her. She smiled at Sofa as if reassuring. . . .

"He's in a coma . . . funny . . . he must have laid down to rest after eating. He must have fallen asleep . . . all that liquor in him . . . he didn't feel the pain."

Sofa looked. Robles's eyes were wide open and his mouth had a slight twitch that looked almost like a smile . . . a self-joke? Sofa stifled a scream. Beatriz quickly took her away from the cot. She sat Sofa down in a chair and stroked her hair. "Sofa, listen to me. He's better off this way. He was so unhappy . . . he had no one . . . he's never really had anyone . . . no one could ever reach him. Do you understand, Sofa?"

Sofa did not answer. She sat stiffly in the chair. Her eyes were closed. Beatriz began to pace the floor in front of Sofa as if trying to convince not only Sofa, but herself, that the nightmare had a point of justification. "I told you, Sofa . . . long ago . . . about when I worked in the fields as a very young girl. The women would bear babies and go back right away to work in the fields. The new baby was buried in the sand to keep it alive and away from the burning sun. There were many scorpions . . . so the younger ones like myself were told to kill the scorpions before they got to the babies. They were a horrible sight . . . we killed the scorpions with rocks. That's what we did all day. The scorpions kept coming. It was a good thing to do. The babies grew up healthy and happy because the poison was killed. It's the same thing now, Sofa . . . do you see? We have saved Lucretia and ourselves . . . isn't that good?"

Beatriz kneeled beside Sofa. Her voice was pleading. Sofa nodded. Things were in order now.

The death rattle cut the silence like a filament of hollowness . . . something without roots . . . something lost in the course of evolution. Then the stillness had a peace . . . the bright design that Beatriz loved.

The rest was easy. Before rosary, two women offered a human sacrifice to a Dionysian god dressed in honeysuckle vines.

RAIN OF SCORPIONS

CHAPTER I

"You don't even know what it means . . . tell me, what is the protestant ethic?" sneered Ismael.

"Screwing, that's what," Fito was bored with Ismael's argument. Ismael's face went livid at Fito's answer. "Damn Bastard! Always complaining about the system."

Fito repeated deliberately, "It means plain screwing, the American way."

"You're sour on the world, Chicano," Ismael's voice was sarcastic. Fito looked right past Ismael at Miguel who was sweeping behind the counter of Papa At's tiendita. "Hey, Mike, the bread warm?"

Ismael sniffed the air. It sure smelled good. Miguel nodded his head, "It came from the panadería about an hour ago."

Fito threw a dime on the counter, "Dame una semita de miel . . . the brown ones." Miguel nodded. He wiped his hands on his shirt and reached into the bread counter for the semita. He walked over to Fito who was sitting on a stool in the center of the store. That was a habit with Fito. Whenever he came to the store, he would pick up the stool, put it in the center of the store facing the door; then, he would sit, placing his crutches against the rungs of the stool. Miguel handed the sweetbread to Fito who stuffed it into his mouth while Ismael looked on disdainfully. Fito ignored him, "Hey, that was good . . . suave." He took out another dime and called out to Miguel, "Give me one more." He flipped the coin on the counter.

Ismael wondered about the likes of Fito. He was glad he had found the way to escape the neighborhood. He was in a college program that paid the way for smart Mexican Americans. He would never have to shovel ore at the smelter. He looked out the window to see if his bus was coming, then turned back and looked at Fito who was calmly eating. Ismael wasn't going to let the dumb flunky have the last word.

"Pigs don't cut it, man . . . hear? You're going to rot at the smelter like everybody else." Fito went on eating his semitas without bothering to answer. The bus was coming: Ismael lived on campus where he got

111

free room and board. He turned and looked at Fito one last time, "I hope you choke."

Fito followed Ismael with his eyes as he ran out of the store and got on the bus at the corner. There was amusement in his face. Ismael didn't upset him. He rather liked the guy for all his parroting. He had enough gumption to get out of the stinking hole of Smeltertown. Fito took another bite out of the semita, chewing it more slowly while he thought about things. . . . But Ismael, too, was creating another kind of stinking hole for himself . . . all those hypocritic fairy tales about American equality . . . when in the hell would people wise up? . . . words, stinking words!

He looked at Miguel who was filling brown paper bags with pinto beans from a large sack, then weighing each bag at exactly five pounds. That kid never stopped working . . . he remembered when he was that age. Yeah, all that energy, believed in something, then. . . . Hell! Miguel looked up from his work and grinned at Fito. Fito was one of his heroes, along with Papa At and El Indio Tolo. Fito sort of stood alone in the world and he wasn't afraid.

Fito could feel a creeping fear at Ismael's words, "You're going to rot. . . ." He knew the accusation too well because he had used it when he came back from the army after losing his leg in Viet Nam. He was mad at the world that had trapped him into the army, into the front line.

Miguel came up to where he was, deep in thought; "You want some more?" Fito shook his head, "What I need is some beer to wash it down."

"Papa At doesn't keep beer in the store."

"I know . . . I know . . . It was just an idea."

Fito looked at Miguel's brown sweaty face with the clear honest eyes and felt a surge of kinship with the young boy. "Oye, Miguel . . . you still sold on those stories of Papa At?"

Miguel looked at Fito straight in the eyes, "El Indio Tolo was real. He fought the gabachos the way you want to fight them."

Fito laughed and ruffled Miguel's hair. "OK, chavalo. You know something? If it's true, that Indian sure had it made . . . whenever he killed a gringo, he would go into the mountains, and who was going to catch him up there in the wilderness? Yeah, he had it made. Now, they brand you 'trouble' when you're born, then see to it that you don't make a move until they quarter you themselves."

Miguel's face was puzzled. Fito gave him a friendly push, "Never mind . . . you'll find out soon enough."

Miguel went back and opened up a Coca Cola from a tin tub filled with ice. He came back and handed it to Fito, saying casually, "It's on me."

"Hey, kid, thanks," Fito's eyes were still smiling.

Miguel went back happily to filling the bags with pinto beans.

Fito drank the syrupy liquid in long draughts. Ismael's words came back, "You're going to rot. . . ." It was a different version from what he had heard all his life. He remembered his teachers, not without a sick feeling mixed with anger. A different feeling nudged him. Sure, there had been some good ones . . . those who looked at him like a human being and not a brown tailor-made moron. The dumber the teacher, the more labels she tacked on him and all the other Mexicans. There had been a whole bunch of dumb ones in his life. He remembered the incident that had him expelled the first year of high school.

He remembered the lousy teachers' lounge. That teachers' lounge was a weird place. It was always shark time in there . . . a tearing of flesh; the smell of blood drove them wild. Here the ladies would sit and wait for dear-friends and adversaries. Fito and some other boys had chosen a shady spot where they sat against the building to eat lunch. The window from the teachers' lounge was right above them. The teachers' conversations were murder. It was a competition for "who is doing things better than who," and who can be torn to shreds for the fun of it.

"I don't know Spanish; this is my first time teaching Mexicans."

"They're really sweet . . . not too bright."

"You better lock up your purse."

Now, Fito understood, remembering the teachers, it must have been a picture of their own freaked-out selves . . . he had read that somewhere . . . poor old rucas! Fito remembered the day he asked a pal to hoist him up so he could look through the window after hearing one of their conversations. There he was with his chin over the sill. He called in "Pssss. . . ." The teachers stopped talking and looked at him in bewilderment. Fito smiled like a cherub and said sweetly, "Fuck you!"

The principal expelled him. When his parents had gone through the usual humiliations, he came back. But he never lived it down. The teachers must have seen to it that he be blamed for everything. Fito frowned. He had been to blame and he knew it. He laughed at himself. Well, he had failed every subject and had quit school at the end of the year. He couldn't find a job after that, so for three squares he joined the army.

His thoughts were interrupted when Papa At walked in with Mrs. Gómez. She was complaining about her liver trouble. Papa At nodded his head in sympathy and guided her by the elbow.

"Ya los viejos no servimos para nada," she sighed laboriously. "Give me a bottle of camphor oil and some canned milk on credit."

Mrs. Gómez had been on credit for many years. La Tienda de Los Amigos de Los Pobres was like that. Papa At seldom wrote down what was owed him; he thought numbers were too much trouble. As long as his few acres of ground down the valley gave him enough vegetables to supply the little store, Papa At was a happy man.

"Papa At, I have been a widow for thirty-two years . . . living the best way I can, but what am I going to do if I have to stay in bed? Who will take care of me?"

Papa At put the camphor oil and the canned milk in a paper sack. There was genuine concern in his eyes. He handed the sack to Mrs. Gómez, "I will stop by to see how you feel tomorrow." Fito knew he would, too.

"Ay te veo, Vato." Fito got up from the stool and reached down for his crutches. Miguel watched him and told himself, "That's one guy that's no cripple."

"See you tomorrow at your meeting!" Miguel called back with his mouth full of bubble gum. He sucked up the juice that had escaped from the sides of his mouth when he said it.

Fito looked back and grinned, "You kids going to that too?"

Miguel nodded his head vigorously, "Sure!" Fito made his way to the door and stepped carefully into the street. The damned crutches. They sure slowed down a guy. He remembered the army doctor that had cheerfully told him, "We'll give you an artificial leg in a couple of months." Fito had looked at the doctor's two whole legs, the major's insignia on his shoulder, and the fat-cat, contented look on his face. Fito had answered in a straight voice with a question, "You think that's fair exchange for the flesh and bone leg?" He had walked out very straight on his crutches not waiting for an answer.

Shit . . . He knew he had to do something about all the bile he was spilling inside his system and in the world. His crutches came down on loose gravel and crunched rhythm, "Wha . . . hope . . . wha . . . hope. . . ."

*

CHAPTER II

They went to the clinic in school buses. The lower grades sat in front, the upper grades sat in the back of the bus. Miguel with his friends in the sixth grade, Felipe, Sergio, and Diego, had joined the eighth grade boys in telling dirty jokes. Lalo was only in the fifth grade, but he hung around so much that the other boys sort of accepted him without really telling him so. They spent the ride back home making spit balls out of chewing gum wrappers and throwing them at the girls who squeaked and screamed at the boys.

The horseplay stopped when two eighth grade boys started talking about why they had gone to the clinic. They had blood tests to measure the amount of sulphur dioxide in the blood. The fumes of the smelter plants had poisoned the air for many years now. The eighth grade boys had studied about pollution and acted as if they knew everything. Pollution had been around a long time, like the dirt arroyo no one did anything about.

"You think it'll kill us . . . this sulphur . . .sulphur. . . ."

"Nah . . .my old man says if they didn't die, we won't die."

Miguel knew that Fito and some of the older boys were very angry. They had had a meeting with some ecology group to sue the smelter, and they were going to take it to court. Miguel had heard Fito talk about the uselessness of trying to be legal . . . l . . e . . g . . a . . l. That meant to have things changed by law. Fito said that never happened unless money was involved. The owners of the smelter didn't care about people dying of poisons. All they cared about was making lots of money for themselves. Miguel wondered if Fito was right. He looked out of the window and saw some yellow haired people standing and talking next to a car.

"Hey, you guys . . . anybody have something to eat?" asked Miguel to no one in particular.

Somebody threw him a Hershey bar. It went over his head and hit the bus driver on the back.

"You, kids, stop yelling and throwing things . . . or you're going to get it."

The older boys were hissing and booing when the bus stopped at the corner that led to the main street of Smeltertown.

"OK . . . you kids, clear the bus . . . cleeer the bus."

There was a stampede. The bus driver just sat there staring out of the front window. Miguel sniffed the sweaty bodies of his friends and knew what time it was in the afternoon. It was a little past noon. They didn't have to go back to school today, so he was going to go to work early at the store. Felipe and Sergio walked with him to the store.

"You want to play ball after work?" Felipe asked Miguel.

"It's payday at the smelter."

Felipe needed no other information. Every payday Miguel had a duty. He had to talk his father into going home early from Pepe's Bar. La cantina was the hangout for most of the workers at the smelter. Miguel's father would feel happy each payday and treat his friends.

Miguel's mother did not think he could afford the grand gesture, so she had trained Miguel to find his father and to gently urge him to go home because supper was waiting. Miguel liked the obligation. He liked Pepe's Bar because everybody was happy there and it was always cool and dark.

Sergio asked, "You all going to that meeting of Fito's?" Miguel and Felipe nodded. Sometimes there would be a fist fight and sometimes there would be lots of handshaking. If they went to the meeting with their parents they could stay up late although it was a school night.

Miguel observed, "Fito's going to give them hell."

A group of younger children from the lower grades ran against them and around them to go into Papa At's tiendita. Miguel remembered that Papa At had promised to tell them about El Indio Tolo. He had heard the story many times and almost knew it by heart, but he never tired of hearing it.

Felipe and Sergio went in with Miguel for a cold drink. Papa At was already passing out pilones, mostly peppermint sticks and gum to the grubby little hands eagerly reaching. Miguel looked at Felipe and shook his head. He went to the tub and took out three cokes. Sergio grabbed a piece of ice and popped it into his mouth; then, he took another piece and dropped it down Felipe's shirt.

"Hey, córtatela. Hijo, that's cold." Miguel noticed that Papa At was sitting on his favorite straw chair with the children all gathered around him. Miguel told the boys to cool it.

Felipe grinned, "The same old story he used to tell us."

Miguel defended, "It's true . . . let's listen."

Papa At was pointing toward the mountain behind the houses and the smelter. The largest smoke stack in the world stood like a sentinel beside it. "In that mountain is the Tolo Cave. The spirit of El Indio Tolo still lives there."

"Have you seen it, Papa At?"

"Many times."

Miguel knew that Papa At never lied. One small boy added, "Sometimes the spirit of El Indio comes out at night to count his gold. You can see the shine of the gold near the cave at night."

Papa At shook his head, "El Indio Tolo does not care for gold. He is a man of Nature. What you see are metal fumes . . . it is called foxfire. It's like red wind . . . free fire."

Miguel knew that fire was red wind . . . free. Papa At had told Miguel it was an illusion. Red wind . . . red wind . . . free . . . illusion. The large believing eyes of the children urged Papa At on. "Many of us are descendants of the tribe of El Indio Tolo. Indians are of the earth."

The children chorused, "Mexicans too, Mexicans, too." Red wind . . . free . . . real . . . the thought caught Miguel at the throat gently.

"Yes," Papa At agreed, "Indians and Mexicans have the strongest blood; it is the blood of the earth. It is inside all of us to understand the rhythms of the earth, the stars, the wind."

Red wind . . . red wind . . . Miguel felt a growing feeling like an echo from centuries before him. It was the long roar of a root that started with the earth and found its home in him, a Mexican. He listened intently to Papa At's description of the desert Indian and all the inheritors of this land before the white man came.

He looked at Felipe and Sergio and knew they were caught in the same excitement.

"These earthmen clustered in the valleys of the big river and where the earth was dry and parched by the sun, they followed the tall cliffs looking for water and food, and when they found it, some stayed behind and carved the mountain for their home. When the horses came . . . many rode away to follow something distant . . . but always beneath their feet was the mother they knew so well . . . earth."

Miguel saw llanos and el camino del sol. He felt la canción de cuna dentro de su ser. . . .

Papa At's voice was like a bell. "All understood their place upon the earth. Each man was part of a great, giving whole. He shared it with beasts and trees, waters and skies. The paths of seasons, light, darkness, heat and cold were his paths; Nature, earth, man . . . all one."

One child lay her head on Papa At's knees and look up at him, "Are we like that?"

"Deep, deep inside."

I don't know what it is . . . deep, deep inside, thought Miguel. He looked at the outline of the mountain and the faces of the boys and girls sitting around Papa At; there was too much outside to learn about; many beautiful things yet to be understood. He wondered if he would ever look for the things Papa At talked about inside himself.

Papa At was saying, "The order of the universe is not clean and tidy with everything in its place; it is an order that makes things equal to make them free. It is a strength with many faces, even the face of pain."

Miguel felt sad. He had seen the pain . . . and a lostness . . . was that pain?

Someone asked, "What happened to the Indians?"

Papa At shook his head, "The white man says he tamed the West; the Indian sees it another way. The white man has brought forth a new order of steel and concrete; it is called progress. Sometimes it is like the twister of the desert; this new order destroys in its path, like the killing current of a river or the hail that ruins crops. There is a word . . . caos . . . caos. . . ."

The children chorused as in a game. The word had a clean open sound that reached down, down. "¡Caos! . . . caos!"

"What does it mean?"

"When things are confused and there is pain and darkness, the twister and its moan, the killing current, the hail, the floods. . . ."

The children understood; they knew what a flood was. "It's bad, isn't it?"

Miguel, Felipe and Sergio had finished their cokes. They joined the children around Papa At. The boys sat cross-legged.

Miguel volunteered, "I learned that word in Reading. Chaos . . . is chaos . . . Ke . . . us. I think you pronounce it like that." Miguel had not known, when he learned to spell the word in class, that it had the secrets of the universe . . . mixed up with suffering. What a word! Chaos . . . caos. . . .

"Tell us about El Indio Tolo . . . how many white men did he kill?"

"Geronimo gave up; it was all he could do. They put him and his people in the Mescalero Reservation. El Indio Tolo was sixteen; he broke away from the pony soldiers on the way to the reservation and followed the pines up the Guadalupe Mountains. He was alone now . . . but he had the universe again; he was part of the whole. Many times his feet froze and he did not have food. He was very lonely and very, very sad. But the long canyons and the hidden streams had the same message he found in his own heart, so he stayed alive and learned new ways. But he was still full of hate . . . full of the caos. He sought revenge of the white men who had imprisoned his people and brought death into their eyes. He killed twenty-one men. He would ambush, and he would go into the towns at night and look for soldiers to kill. He scalped a priest on top of the bell tower. But he felt very bad when he was in his own darkness; he was not a part of the whole anymore. He found this cave after walking for many days from pines to desert, and where the cave became mountain, he went deep, deep and met the god Gotallama, the god of fire and water. He made it his home . . . unless he went with Gotallama to the green valley."

"The green valley?"

"The god, Gotallama, gave him a path to a green valley where the nature gods live. It was a deep, deep secret."

"Is he in the green valley now?"

"It is very likely."

Miguel closed his eyes and saw a greenness without shape or form.

Felipe nudged him, "You still believe the story?"

"Don't you?" Miguel looked into Felipe's eyes for an answer. Yes, Felipe believed in the green valley too.

Papa At looked out to the mountain. There was a growing inflection in him, a whisper that grew into a roar. "Gotallama knew that El Indio Tolo was not a bad man; he wanted to help El Indio find the universe again . . . the green valley was the answer to chaos."

Papa At paused again and stroked the hair of the child leaning on his knee. "I want you all to understand something very important. The end of something is always a new beginning and the conditions of the end of something live on in the new beginning. For instance, seeds are scattered by old dying plants. The dying plants become the food for the new seeds. The old plant is a chaos, but it is full of an old beauty, richer and darker than that of a new seed. But the new seed is new life. It is beautiful. The green valley has chaos. It is its food, but the green valley lives because the chaos becomes an order, a peace out of love." Papa At knew the children would only understand something about a seed, but that was enough. The rest would come to them as life.

In the green valley, the hate, the confusion became a peace; so El Indio Tolo lived with Gotallama and left the secret of the green valley in his cave."

"Have you ever seen it?"

"No one has gone that far into the crevices beyond the cave. No one has gone beyond El Hoyo."

"How do you know then?"

"It is so." The answer rang like a clear bell of truth. Everybody believed.

Felipe asked Miguel, "The secret . . . do you think it is a map?"

Miguel nodded his head, "Probably . . . maybe how to get to the green valley."

Papa At sighed deeply, then got up from his straw chair and stretched, "That is enough of El Indio Tolo for today. It is time to go home." The children made sounds of disappointment. The climate of the heart must change now . . . dizzy, dizzy is the world.

Miguel herded the children out of the door of the tiendita; they clamored and laughed. Papa At went back to his little kitchen behind the store and began to make preparations for an early supper. He would close the store early for Fito's meeting at the union hall that night. Miguel was talking to Felipe by the door.

"Tell Sergio and Diego to meet us outside the hall tonight."

"O.K."

Papa At's head popped out of the back room door, "Hey, Miguel . . . go on . . . go on."

"It's too early, Papa At . . . the five o'clock people will rush you for bread and milk."

"I can take care of it. You have to pick up your papa at Pepe's anyway . . . go on."

"You sure it's OK?"

"Sure . . . sure. . . ." Papa At waved his hands in the air and closed the matter.

"Come on," Felipe had already started out of the door. It was cooler

now. The two boys walked down the presidio street listening to the
timbre of voices, brief commotions, laughter, coming from the open
doors. Miguel noticed Mrs. Gómez' curtains fluttering in a slight breeze.

"You wanna play ball till the smelter whistle blows?" Felipe asked. .

"Nah . . . I'll wait at Pepe's for papa. It's cool in there."

Felipe ran ahead toward the schoolyard. Miguel continued on his
way toward Pepe's Bar. He thought of chaos . . . chaos . . . It was a
good word. But now, it was more than a word. It was a deep, deep
thing . . . a beautiful something . . . if . . . if a knife were plunged into
it, it would bleed . . . a bleeding, beautiful something.

Pepe's Bar . . . no society, drawing up its institutions, considered the
necessity of a corner bar. Sewage systems, jails, senate houses,
churches . . . Ah! Yes! All are part of the pattern that regulates Man's
mind and soul. But a cantina?

CHAPTER III

Spontaneous congregations create strange, wondrous things. The
local bar, like tribal councils, like fairs and carnivals, assures sunny
corners in a human life. Here is found eye to eye honesty. Even the
scale of dream-like bravado has a realness. Where else can one look for
mercy among men?

Miguel stepped into Pepe's Bar feeling the cold air from the huge
ceiling fan. Pepe was wiping the counter. He had glasses set up for
rinsing, preparation for the afternoon trade. The smelter whistle
would blow soon. Miguel looked around the room. He saw Champurrado, the neighborhood borracho. Manolo, the pots and pans salesman,
was there too with a stranger.

Pepe looked and saw Miguel come in without Sergio. Sergio was
Pepe's son.

"Where's Sergio?"

"Playing ball."

"The good-for-nothing."

There is a time to measure man. Compassion does it with a tracing
finger of illusion. Then, there is a time when Man measures himself. . . .

"If I could raise a few hundred!" Manolo was planning big deals that never happened. The stranger believed him. A good moment for them. They were drinking tequila to mix with their dream this early afternoon.

"A killing, I tell you . . . all my worries would be over." Manolo anticipated with eyes that spoke of a rawness, a compliance with the measurement of self. Manolo wanted and needed salvation. The earning of the daily bread, the begging of the daily bread, the going hungry. There was Manolo's dream, also.

Miguel offered to help Pepe with the rinsing of the glasses.

"Do two at a time." Pepe left him with that order and then went through a swinging door to the backroom. Miguel took two glasses and put them in the rinsing water. Miguel watched the glasses bob up and down in the sink. Miguel took out the glasses and placed them upside down on the draining board. He looked up and saw Champurrado drinking beer. He had a red beard, and was small and thin. He drank because his wife had run away with another man many years ago. This was his angle of repose, a point of rest . . . for a few hours, for a day, for years and years and years.

Champurrado beckoned Miguel. "Chavalo . . . otra cerveza." Miguel opened up another bottle of beer and poured it into a stein. The foam brimming, he took it to Champurrado. Champurrado looked at Miguel with soft kind eyes and smiled; then, he took the stein and drank without pausing. Finally he stopped and smiled again at Miguel. The foam had left traces of a mustache. Champurrado's eyes suddenly became pools of memories.

"I'm waiting for my body to die."

Miguel knew he said this to everyone. Champurrado didn't mean it. The statement at one time had been forged as a wallop. Now it was a comfortable habit of words. Words have reasons . . . don't they? Miguel remembered many words he had heard at Pepe's Bar. They rose like a symphony, words of confession . . . I don't know . . . I need . . . I feel bad . . . who knows . . . I try . . . maybe tomorrow . . . Words have reasons.

Miguel did not wait for Champurrado to pay. The old man did not have any money. His friends would take up a collection of nickels and dimes at the end of the day to pay for his drinks.

Champurrado confessed, "I have nothing. . . ."

There was a love, a beautiful something. Miguel shrugged, "It's OK."

Many Champurrados came and went and bared their hearts at Pepe's Bar. Champurrado smiled again. The smile was strong and good and clean. Miguel knew that Champurrado was a man who knew about life. He must know about Gotallama.

"Champurrado . . . do you believe in Gotallama?"

There was no more blurriness. The glory was there in the old man's face.

"Yes, the god of fire and water. . . ."

"Sí . . . Sí . . . el valle verde, donde viven los dioses."

Pepe came back with a plastic bag of chicharrones. He sold cracklings for ten cents. They were good with beer. Miguel looked one last time into Champurrado's eyes and saw all time. He went back to rinsing the glasses.

The universe plays its eternities. God plays all the time. . . . If there is confession, there is salvation, there is resurrection, but never without play . . . Two more glasses bobbed. Skim . . . skim . . . skim . . . There were surfaces, timeless and effortless, like water. There is mercy for what Man is.

The smelter whistle blew. Pepe told Miguel, "Finish before your papa comes."

Fito had begun to weave his plan a few weeks back, coming home on the bus from the army hospital. The plan started with a conversation he had with a man sitting beside him. Fito had been looking out of the window at the swift passage of town and desert. The man next to him had observed, "There's something special about desert country."

Fito did not turn his head. He watched the blurring, passing things a little longer, then he answered, "dreary . . . empty."

There were no more comments for a while. The man spoke again, "You live around here?"

"Yeah . . . the next stop . . . Smeltertown. You can see the beginning of our shanty town." He pointed at an old wooden building high on a hill.

The man was looking at Fito. "Going home for a visit?"

"Going home."

"Any home is as much as anything should be."

Fito was puzzled at the remark. He made no further comment, but began to feel uncomfortable at the man's frank and open scrutiny. The anger was rising again in Fito. So the man was taking stock of the local native. I'll help the old buzzard! "You noticed my skin is very brown? I'm a Mexican. We come in all sizes and shapes and the woods around here are plump full of the critters."

The man was amused, "I was also thinking about you. You're all wound up."

"Do you always go around butting into other people's business?"

The voice was thoughtful. "Yes."

Fito was interested, "You must be some special kind of nut."

"Aren't we all?"

Fito looked out the window, but his curiosity was growing. "You're not from around here?"

"Nope . . . sort of from everywhere. I move a lot. . . ."

"You getting off at Smeltertown?"

"No . . . wouldn't know what to do there."

"That describes the whole town." Somehow Fito felt bad about condemning the Mexicans in Smeltertown.

The man was thoughtful, "Smeltertown . . . eh? Another hole in the ground and slavery."

Fito was surprised. This gringo understood. He cynically added, "We also feature poisoned air."

The man nodded, "Yes . . . I remember reading about it . . . carbon disulfide, isn't it?"

Fito shrugged, "Poison."

The man looked out the window now, almost unaware of Fito. He spoke as if to himself, yet to Fito too. "Does man learn from the ant to fit into dead, unborn patterns to satisfy big business? Or is the pattern something innate, a knowledge we kept as we climbed the ladder of evolution?.But if we climbed the ladder, why are we still ants?"

Fito did not understand the route of the man's logic too well, but he understood ants. He replied, "Man should be better than ants."

The man nodded, "It's power that makes ants of men. It's power that creates shanty towns. The Indian in a wild country had it better; he made his own pattern."

Fito was bitter, "Rotten, dirty, stinking, stupid place. Damn power too."

The man reasoned, "Circumstances make Man accept power as natural. That's all he has known, being ignorant and fearful. Power is a substitute for just that, you know. It is a substitute for ignorance and fear. Human beings are OK."

"Even those with power?"

"They are only ignorant and fearful like the people who obey power. That's why they take power and use it. But we're getting out of ignorance and fear. Someday. . . ."

"You think politicians are human?"

"As much as anybody else!"

"Crud."

"We can escape the ant-hill." The man's voice was sure.

The bus had come to Fito's stop. He pulled the cord and awkwardly left his seat. He had trouble getting his crutches in place. The man did not offer to help. Fito was thankful. He looked into the man's eyes for a single second, then grinned, "Bye."

"So long."

Fito waited until the bus had taken off leaving the sharp pungent smell of burned fuel. It was a familiar smell to him. He decided to walk to Papa At's and get himself a cold drink. The unpaved, uneven street

was hard to manage on crutches. Damn it! Now that he had come back
to the news of dangerous pollution in his town, now that he felt a
wanting to fight for something, he had come back a cripple. Viet Nam
had not been his fight. All he had gotten out of it was three squares, the
rest had been shit. He had gone off to face death. Fito laughed at
himself. To face death, but somehow he never could have confronted
his draft board or the smelter bosses, or the stinking poverty of the
town. No . . . he could never confront that.

He wondered soberly, "Is it because death has a kinder face than
those other things?" Death . . . once he had seen a military cemetery.
Christ! Men's lives were cheap. That's what the thousands of white
crosses screamed out to him. There's a lot more where these came
from . . . so fight some more wars! It was a hell of a world . . . He
stopped and wiped his brow with his shirtsleeve. The anger was biting
like the sun. He remembered the man's words, "Only power, the false
pattern." Phony . . . phony . . . rules, laws, the works! When he got to
Papa At's, he saw the old man sitting on the floor bundling corn husks
for tamales. He was glad to see Fito, to find out the news from the
hospital. This showed in his face, "Well? You get your new leg
soon . . . eh?"

Fito went to the tub filled with soda pop and took a coke. He put his
crutches against the counter and leaned back on it.

"Yeah, Papa, soon, soon I will get a shiny new leg better than my
own. . . . Who are they kidding?" He opened the coke bottle with
vengeance. He drank.

Papa At had cut part of the husks into long strands. With these, he
would tie each bundle of dried, yellow husks with swift, expert fingers.
Fito sat and watched Papa At for a while. He felt good and real, just
sitting there watching Papa At. Sun, deft fingers, silence, and two men
in a room full of eating smells. Somehow it was very satisfying.

Fito remembered the man on the bus. "I met a man on the bus
something like you."

"Like me?" Papa At continued his tying without looking up.

"Well, in a way. He talked of power and used long words. He seemed
to be educated . . . sort of beyond the books . . . beyond the garbage
they throw at us."

"I never went to school." Papa At said it almost sadly.

Fito took the last part of his coke and began to roll the bottle in his
hands.

"Maybe that's good, Papa At. Maybe the best thing I ever did was
leaving that stinking school."

Papa At shook his head. "You know that is not true." He had
finished enough bundles to complete one box. So he raised himself to a
squat and began packing the bundles in a box.

Fito's eyes were far away. "He said people were ants."

"Ants?"

"Yeah . . . I remember at school una ruca reading a poem to us about an ant named Jerry. I don't remember the guy who wrote it . . . but this Jerry died in the middle of his job, the one thing he did all his life . . . he was programmed by nature like that. . . . Well, this Jerry fell down dead and the other ants were told to throw him over the side since he was no longer useful. The ants didn't care about his dying."

"People care about people dying."

"Maybe . . . maybe . . . those we grow up with . . . but there's something wrong with the whole thing. I can't work it out in my mind." He paused as if trying to figure it out, then continued, "The man put it sort of like this . . . he said all of us fit like in a slot to work for the big companies like the smelter . . . to go to war . . . then after a lifetime there is nothing . . . if we die the company doesnn't care . . . that is how we are like ants."

Papa At folded his arms in his squatting position looking forever like an Indian.

His face was perplexed. He looked up at Fito, "We stay human somehow . . . yes, we stay human."

Fito's voice was bitter, "Not much . . . not much." He put the pop bottle down with a bang on the counter. Papa At went back to making new bundles.

The anxiety in Fito's voice was felt by Papa At, "He said we could get away from the ant-hill."

Papa At stretched out his legs on the floor. He rubbed his hand on his thighs to help the circulation. His protest was mild. "We don't have to run away from the ant-hill to stay human. Everyone I know is human and beautifully brave."

Fito's voice was accusing, "You're a dreamer. You've spent your whole life in this little store . . . what do you know about life?"

"You're right, son. All I know is what I feel and the little I understand."

Fito felt ashamed. "Listen, Papa At . . . I think you're a great guy and you're smart . . . . It's just . . . It's just . . . You're too good . . . too innocent . . . you know what I mean?"

"I never went to war. I never worked for anyone else. I never wanted to leave this place. Yes . . . I agree."

Fito picked up his crutches and went over to where Papa At sat on the floor. In direct line to Papa At's eyes were the wooden crutches and one leg. Papa At felt a surge of love for this confused, hating boy so full of love and beauty. The old man wondered if he could help, but deep down, he knew the struggle was Fito's, his and his alone. He felt the boy's hand on his head. He let it lay there for a moment in silence. Their contact said so much more.

When Fito finally spoke his voice was hesitant, "I . . . I want to be free . . . I don't know how to be free. I'm pretty stupid."

Papa At got up from the floor. His body was lithe and graceful. "Well, that's enough for now." He wiped his hands on the apron he wore around the store.

Fito persisted, "Papa At . . . all the people around here that come to you hungry, El Amigo de Los Pobres, los pobres . . . shouldn't they be free from want . . . without taking charity, without losing pride?"

"Yes, there are many things that are very wrong and sad. But freedom is a very intimate thing. Some go beyond the knowing and the problems of the world. Others learn to survive with ancient feelings that are a freedom . . . struggle is a freedom."

Fito was angry again, "It doesn't make sense . . . sometimes you don't make sense!"

Papa At put an arm around Fito's shoulder, "Es hora de comer. Let's go cook us something."

Fito nodded and both men went to the kitchen behind the store.

CHAPTER IV

Lupe had read about Cleopatra. Supposedly she had been dark and fat and men had loved her. Lupe wondered about this. She was fat and dark and no man had loved her. A young queen on a barge along the Nile more than a thousand years before . . . beauty must have been a different thing. She counted patches in her life . . . ridicule that haunted . . . needs that hounded . . . unseeing eyes and mouths that persecuted . . . and the eagerness of self-punishment. Lupe ate to comfort herself. She read a lot, too, to create a world out of herself. She hushed the torments for a while.

Today her thoughts were on Fito. She loved Fito. She would live and die for Fito. He was not aware of this because he had never really been aware of her as a woman. All he saw was a fat, plain friend. There was no desire for her. To be desired mattered to Lupe. She had read about desire in books. It was the reason women existed . . . to be desired by men. She knew she would never be desired. Only pretty, slender girls were desired. She knew this without compromise. She also knew she was there, and although she was there, people could not measure that as being worth something. She always felt ignored and out of place when she was among boys and girls that searched out one another. She glanced down at her stout bare feet and wiggled her toes. She marveled at the human body. What told her toes to wiggle . . . what was the long current from mind to toe?

Sometimes she would plunge headlong into a personal conspiracy with life. It was a mind thing, all her own and very much like cotton candy . . . airy, airy candy . . . all gone and never enough after a while. Her mind was a machine that spun sugar. Fast . . . fast . . . fast . . . until a great fluff of something was formed.

Nothing solid, but a momentary sweetness that caught a special meaning. That meaning made her a heroine in life. There was always a heroine in books. She needed that personal self-made aura to go on with whatever was demanded of her in the world.

Sun from a kitchen window fell and glistened on her arm. A touch of God, she thought. Sun . . . I'm glad I'm alive! She also knew that she would never bear Fito's sons. Helping and loving him? Yes, that was already possible. It was her private privilege.

She stood up from one of the chairs around the kitchen table and went to the door. She looked out into desert mountains. Mountains keep growing, she thought. She kept her view far away, like the light of sun, far away. She did not like to look at things close. They were a desperation. Yes, she thought again, she was privileged to love and help Fito. She loved in secret. Was it a secret? Fito lived by himself in his grandfather's two room house. He fixed televisions to supplement the disabled veteran's aid he received from the government. He hated to cash the checks each month. He would cuss out the government for making him dependent, but he still cashed them. He had to eat.

Fito was helpless around the house like most men. Lupe would go to his house on weekends. She would clean and scrub and make him warm meals. She would watch Fito's contentment after a meal, when he found clean shirts and when the house was clean. What was more beautiful was when they talked together about life and about Fito.

She would spin candy with her mind again . . . whirl . . . whirl . . . spin . . . big beautiful fluff. Fito would listen and Lupe felt as if a slender, beautiful girl had escaped her gross body. She would imagine that Fito was able to see this beautiful girl of desire. No . . . no . . . he never saw. How could he? It was a sugar nothingness. Fito liked to talk to her because she talked sense and she would listen to his angers and his dreams like a sparkling fire that made his words real. He would feel very real, too, with her presence. She made him the center of the earth.

Fito admired the fact that she had read so many books and had educated herself beyond anyone he knew in the barrio. Not with schooling, although she had graduated from high school. What Fito saw in her as a form of education that was a kind of madness. The reading of too many books had grown into a madness, and that madness had grown wings. These wings took her to places she dared not go before. She visited libraries, museums, and free concerts by herself. Out of place in her poor clothes and an unsightly thing to see in her misshapen body. But there was oblivion to critical eyes then. She had the wings of a searcher and that was all that mattered. There was self-consciousness. She had no worries or thoughts about differences. She went to look, listen, and read about eternities and the wonder of human beings. Everybody thought she was strange. She knew she was strange and was glad of it. What came, what passed, what ended, her madness shoved aside. What she kept was an eternal pulse with the greatness of things.

She would never let poverty and fatness swallow her in one gulp. Fito had been popular with girls in school. He had loved a beautiful girl, slender like a reed, by the name of Belén. Belén was everything Lupe would like to be to make Fito happy. But Belén had married another boy after Fito had come back with only one leg. Fito hated women now. At least, he had no time for them. Lupe wanted to comfort him about Belén, but she couldn't. She could talk to Fito about anything in the world, but not about love between man and woman. In this sphere she did not belong.

Sometimes when she went to park concerts by herself, she would listen to the music and feel it as a kind of love. Music did not have to penetrate the eye, or the mind's concept of what beautiful people should be so they could be loved. A symphony would give bigger wings to her madness. The madness would last into the weekends with Fito. She would reach out and stroke his head in silence as Fito sat in his favorite chair. Her fingertips would tingle with a growing desire that ran through her body like flame. There was no response from him. He would be deep in thought. If the air were electric and she was electric, Fito was not a part of it.

Lupe worked in a parts factory five days of the week and supported her grandmother and herself. The grandmother spent much time in church or praying the rosary on her beads. Lupe was very much alone. Hours during the week were thin, weak and weary. But when the weekends came, they were sweet, spinning days. Lupe thought now, today is Friday . . . I shall spin sugar again.

I shall put music . . . moonlight . . . rain . . . into words and make Fito dream. But tonight she would walk to the union hall and sit in the back listening to Fito's plan. She knew about Fito's plan because he had put it together with her. Now he would tell the people. She looked at the distant mountains covered by clouds with a growing gladness. It had begun to rain softly. Mountain, cloud, rain, space . . . she thought . . . comforting. We can take them inside ourselves.

CHAPTER V

Lupe was standing in the rain outside the union hall. She held a newspaper over her head as she waited for Papa At to catch up. The hall was already full in spite of the rain. Papa At reached her side and took her by the hand leading her away from the downpour into the entrance of the building.

"Mira nomás . . . look at you, girl."

She was very wet. She would dry off soon enough. Papa At looked at her and saw something beautiful. She was like a wind carrying seed. He had always seen her as such. He sighed. If only Fito would notice. Perhaps when the knots of anger were undone.

They walked into the meeting room.

"Would you like a seat in the back?" Lupe asked. Papa At nodded. They found two empty chairs. Now, they both sat and absorbed a relishing thing: husbands . . . wives . . . children . . . friends . . . a good blending.

The best part of the meeting! The small talk between people, the smile, the handshake, the embrace . . . all good blending, a tapestry of little things . . . I saved twenty-seven dollars to buy it . . . for colic aceitito calientito . . . ¿Qué trae el loco de Fito? . . . Se casaron con el justice of the peace . . . le están saliendo los dientes . . . It's going to be a hard rain . . . a flood, you think? . . . I haven't seen you since Rosie's wedding . . . She's eighty-two, but still insists on making her breakfast . . . The boy is smart . . . así es la vida . . . Dame un cigarro . . . tapestry of little things, words that tell of life. Lupe and Papa At enjoyed in silence.

Fito came in and made his way, almost unobserved, to the front of the room. There was a clap of thunder as he stood there waiting for the people to notice him. His strong, Indian face was intense. He balanced himself well on the crutches to stand tall. He wondered . . . what am I doing up here anyway? . . . he wanted to give them a terrible sock in the jaw . . . something that would explode in their guts. Goddamit! He thought . . . I'm nobody . . . I'm a little man and little men figure little ways. Maybe my way is a little way. But they all came giving me the benefit of the doubt. It was raining very hard against the roof. Eyes were fierce; some questioned; some just looked. Fito cleared his throat. Another clap of thunder seemed to quiet the people. Most of them had seen him now, standing there waiting for their attention. His voice was something of a shout, "I think it's time we get this thing going. . . ."

They were quiet and waited for him to go on. Fito spoke hesitantly. He had prepared a beginning in his mind, "Moses . . . Moses. . . ." Why in the hell had he decided to start it that way? He floundered, "Moses led the Israelites out of Egypt . . . they were slaves to the Egyptians, remember? . . . there was a plague. . . ."

Fito felt ridiculous. Hell, he was no preacher. All these people had come to hear his plan in a rainstorm. Maybe he should thank them now. "Listen, I want to thank you for coming tonight. . . ." One of his friends among the faces encouraged, "Hey, Fito, put it together, man!"

Fito tried again, "Forget about Moses . . . take a good look at Smeltertown. Meetings! How many meetings have we had in this same room . . . can you count them? The time there was no electricity or water in the town. How long were those meetings? How many . . . eh? We even raised part of the money to bring in electricity and water, but what did they do about it for years? Ignore us! Presidio ʋwners, city officials . . . they mean nothing to me because nothing is ever done. Why argue? Problem after problem. . . . Now, pollution . . . poison we've been breathing in for years. How long have we been breathing in the stuff? How long are we going to talk about it? Takes money, doesn't it? Well, where's the money? Take a good look at the flood areas in this town. What's been done about them? Who wants to count years! The Smelter . . . they already have their lawyers and science experts to erase the problem of pollution. Oh, they will show public concern then do nothing. Nothing!"

Fito looked at the people before him. They knew futility and patience. They knew endurance. This was an old story he was telling. They had heard it too many times. Anger began to build like a red fire ball in him. Anger. "Gringo bastards! The men of the town are enslaved to their smelter. We're just things they use to make profit . . . the way they used me in Viet Nam."

"Look at me!" There was a sadness melting into the anger. Fito wiped one hand in his pants. He was perspiring and the sweat made his hand lose its hold on the crutch . . . the plan . . . the plan . . . "This time we mustn't wait for years and years. This time we cannot listen to their words and promises. They're lies!"

Someone shouted from the back, "What do we do without money? The only thing we can do . . . leave the town . . . all of us . . . every man, woman and child. Just cross the desert to somewhere." One of the old miners spoke out in anger, "You mean I came here tonight to hear that? That is not a plan. It's a whim. It's running away."

Fito had considered his plan as something even majestic. Now, to some of them, it seemed like a whim. He felt somewhat bewildered and even guilty, but he looked at their faces, "It's more than just leaving the town. There's a principle behind it."

Someone laughed.

Fito held his body straight with one arm on the crutch, held the other crutch up with the pit of his arm as he ran his thumb along the line of his jaw as if the principle weighed mightily . . . mightily. The people were still listening.

"I've been thinking about two words. The word 'work.' All of us 'work' a lifetime in one way or another. All men like work. When we work, if we do it without difficulty, without fooling around because it makes something of us . . . there's a better word for it, but I can't think of it . . . anyway, if it makes us complete, it is work. But there is work that is not work . . . that is slavery."

"I read a book in the army about how all minorities are like the slaves of a long time ago. They suffer the same way. Mexicans are a minority. We have been slaves for a long time. . . . Sometimes the dumb gringos say we don't like to work . . . what they mean is we don't like slavery. Who does?"

An angry voice protested, "We can't do anything about it. We do what we can to survive. Principle will not feed the family or put a roof over our heads. We have a life here!"

Voices rose in agreement. Fito felt helpless again, but he continued, "If we all leave . . . together . . . all of us, it will make all the papers in the country. If we make a list of the things we don't have in this town, if we make it understood we are leaving to save ourselves from the poison in the air . . . the town couldn't stand the bad publicity. It would be a stain on the American way of life to expose to the world what is going on here. . . . The city fathers would scuttle . . . like rats finding a way out."

"Who . . . them or us?"

"Both, I guess . . . but that would be better than this death-trap."

Miguel's father was angry. "This is our home. It is not a death-trap to me or to my family. There's meaning here. We're poor . . . yes, but we manage for ourselves and our children. Fito, you're crazy!"

The apostolic push and pull . . . the different points of view, all valid, all possible, would continue for some time. Papa At sat listening to the rain. It's rhythmic pattern sang a greater truth than the views of men. It seemed to sing, "there is no defeat . . . there is no defeat." It was a universal heartbeat like the smell of wet earth. Fito said the gringos brutalized and enslaved, but Papa At knew that no man is ever stamped down to nothing; no man is ever befouled by defeat. There are many ways of getting up off the ground and fighting to exist . . . so many ways, and many of those ways are not obvious to the angry eye or the confused eye or to the hating eye. But people were and they always would be. . . .

There is no defeat . . . there is no defeat. The dark, silent reality was more than sluggish fog, more than thinking and floating uncertainties. Underneath the chaos there was an even order that made all men eternal. Papa At turned to Lupe whose whole attention was on Fito's words. He could see that she was feeling all of Fito's anger and despair, all his hope and daring. Fito was a lucky boy to be loved like that. Lupe looked at Papa At with questioning eyes, "Do you think Fito can convince them?"

Papa At listened to the arguments going back and forth . . . You're a radical, Fito . . . You're satisfied with nothing . . . Chingado, we want more . . . .We do what we can . . . You want us to starve out in the desert . . . We can use our wits to survive . . . Wits! That's a funny one . . . Real funny, Fito . . . You say the company bosses lie . . . The city fathers lie . . . And what do you do, Fito? You dream . . . what is the difference between dream and lie . . . both are words . . . words . . . you don't know what you are talking about, Fito . . . back and forth.

Papa At thought . . . they are created now and from the beginning . . . nothing will change that much . . . people will see a little better. He, too, believed that work was a trial, that it was danger, that it was a struggle, and that all men loved work instinctively because it was a fulfillment, a reflection of self. Fito was right; slavery was another thing. But there was much more to this town than slavery. It was a creation of human beings who had loved and suffered and died to make it meaningful. How could a man leave that? Papa At looked at Lupe and said gently, "Everyone shall win and lose. We are all two . . . the winner and the loser . . . the lost and found. To be here together with sparks giving life, even if we hate each other for a while, that is the good of these meetings."

Lupe felt calmer. She understood. The rain was hitting the roof very hard, but the voices of the men were just as hard. It would continue for some time.

Then, the meeting would come to an end and the problem would be left a problem.

It is a good thing that problems are not really problems, for eventually they become ways.

At the end of the meeting, Miguel left with his friends. They did not go home like the rest of the people making their way in the rain to the safety and warmth of their casas. Sergio, Felipe, Diego, Lalo and Miguel had decided to smoke cigarettes behind the fire escape at the school. Tomorrow was Saturday, and they were working out a plan of their own. All of them had been excited by Fito's plan. It would be like in the movies when the wagon trains went west. Miguel and his friends visualized the whole town going through similar trials to find new homes. They liked the idea.

They found an area that was dry and small on the stairs. The rain and the dark were part of the excitement. They were not going to talk to the people about their plans. It was not a matter of talk. They were going to move, to do, to dare, to go. Huddled together while they lighted cigarettes, they talked of details. . . .

"We better start early. Before the smelter whistle. My father is bound to ask questions if he sees me." Sergio said.

The boys agreed. Most of them slept late on Saturdays, but not this Saturday.

Diego remembered, "We better take some food for along the way."

Lalo, the youngest, was still skeptical. "Can we . . . can we ever?"

All five sat there and puffed at their cigarettes and thought about El Hoyo.

"No one has gone beyond El Hoyo," warned Felipe.

Their eyes were questioning, but mixed with the question was a rapture.

"We must find the map to the green valley." Miguel's voice was firm.

"Give me another drag," Felipe asked Sergio. Sergio handed him the half-filled package of cigarettes.

Miguel continued, "If we find the map to the green valley, then all the people will be more willing to do what Fito says."

Felipe agreed, "The green valley would be much better than Smeltertown."

Sergio went back to the plans, "Listen, we'll meet by the edge of the dry wash, by the large sewer pipes in the arroyo."

"Close to where the smelter is excavating?"

"Yeah . . . all we have to do then, is climb the hill back of that. It leads right to El Indio Tolo's cave."

An effigy, a smudge of destiny, called green valley. The rain approved. Adventure seldom leaves regret. The rain anointed.

"Shall we tell anybody where we're going?"

"No. Somebody will try to stop us."

"Nobody?"

"Nobody."

It was settled. They were to go beyond El Hoyo in the cave of El Indio Tolo. They were to find the map of the green valley left somewhere in the recesses of the cliff like crevices beyond the cave. The god Gotallama had left it there for some earthman who dared to go far past. . . . The excitement in the boys was now sobered by the dark and the thoughts of the unknown.

The rain had not subsided. Somehow, they were feeling the cold a little bit too much.

"I gotta go home," Lalo said.

Yes, it was time to go home. They put out their cigarettes like dying fireflies in the dark. As each set out his separate way, he reminded the other briefly of the early start the next morning. Each found his own path home. There would be reprimands for staying out in the rain so late.

Miguel's mother was standing by the screen door waiting for him.

" ¿Dónde andabas, mi hijito? . . . Ay, ¡Andas mojado hasta los huesos! . . . Ve cámbiate." Miguel left the door of the room he shared with his little brothers ajar as he changed clothes. He could see his mother cleaning beans to soak overnight. He remembered an old habit she had. Whenever she sewed late into the night, it was a way of waiting up for her loved ones. Always too tired and worried about problems, she knew waiting best. She was a woman of the home, who provided rest and food and understanding. She would wait into the night for papa when he stayed out late. She would sit in semi-darkness, Miguel could guess . . . tears, anger, anxiety, and dreams . . . but always the waiting. She was there now, finishing the beans. She would go to bed now that Miguel had come home safely. There was a tiredness with her now after so many years of waiting and doing. With Miguel, she would be forever, deep in his own strength and his own endurance. This was her gift to him, the son. Miguel closed the door and jumped into bed with his younger brothers. Their feet were warm. He carefully pulled the finger from his little brother's mouth and covered them well. Then, he waited for sleep. He was still full of the plans for tomorrow and of the hope that was Papa At. He remembered the red wind that knows the freedom. He must learn how to be Indian again, refusing to die a little at a time.

He must help find the green valley so that the people of the town might make their own pattern, so that they might taste freedom too. The rain was still pouring down in torrents. But, they would still go tomorrow. It would be dry in the cave. The rain would not stop them now. Now, he was listening to the rain without thought . . . all was warmth, the feel of his heart-beat, the rain, the darkness, and the delicious feeling of a tired body at rest. Something in him ran, ran, ran, like a shimmering, like a wetness that was part of a whole, that was freedom and fire. . . .

Red wind . . . red wind . . . in a beginning. The god Gotallama knows well the greatest artist and architect on earth . . . red wind . . . red wind! In deserts the red wind plays, as men play, as all living things play . . . each strangely unique, for each living thing is a momentary spark of a long and complicated history of consciousness. Look! YOU ARE . . . YOU ARE NOT . . . but YOU WERE. No two samenesses, but all part of an eternal sameness. He molds, he molds . . . the red wind. One time the god Gotallama sees the red wind ride the barren flats, then rise, taking in its breast the quintessence of dust, turning, turning in growing spirals to mate with the clouds. There, the fine grain diffuses and the clouds become another being . . . red clouds . . . red clouds. Gotallama laughs and dances the freedom of the wind.

Before the momentary sparks of wondrous Man had come into existence, the red wind worked where the running water dwindled and failed in the desert to shape and mold the singing dialects of erosion. Barren gullied hill, dune and rock are symphonies of wind. But the music of the red wind has no basic element of harmony. It knows too much of universal complications and struggles. It knows that harmony is but a surface, temporary neatness . . . a stay in focus. In running play, the red wind sings a balance, works a balance, dances a balance with an artist's skill. Dissonance, like symmetry, is its excitement and its life. Catch all! Catch all! Here is creation listening to all the voices of the world. It must, like Gotallama, form life known as change. Look! YOU ARE . . . YOU'RE NOT . . . but YOU WERE. Gotallama long ago whispered in the red wind's ear, "Change is constant intermingling, different faces becoming one . . . each a beautiful consciousness giving way to another beautiful consciousness." Not harmony . . . not harmony . . . that is a kind of death. It must be embraced as belonging to all . . . but is is not elemental to creation itself.

"Listen, red wind," Gotallama said one flaming day, "Men will come upon the earth and work with harmonies because they're new. How can they see the millions of faces as one? We have to give them time. Their harmonies will be a kind of courage before they become a trap. One day, they will be like you and me, red wind. At first, the changes, violent or otherwise, they will call chaos . . . ha . . . ha . . . ha . . . ha . . . ha!"

The red wind swam in space and asked, "When will they know? When will they know?"

"That chaos is growth and hope and life?"

"Yes, when will they know?"

"Eternity stretches in the universe . . . give them time, give them time!"

The red wind shook his head and went to make a way for river waters. Then he went to make a dune. He took a free hand, and the things that were, and gave them many faces. Men later gave them names . . . lee . . . crag-and-tail . . . seifs . . . transverse . . . complex . . . longitudinal . . . heck! Those are words.

Dunes and sand and wind and stars and sun . . . life! Words to make the harmonies? Of course! The red wind humored Men. The red wind and Gotallama were given motion, up down, twist, turn, circle, run, carry, consist, assist, resist. Gotallama gave the wind its energy. In allegro, it sang as moving water vapor or shifting earth particle. The desert was the red wind's gift. Water gave life where oceans were, but in desert, it is wind that shapes another kind of life.

The balance existed before men tampered. . . .

Smeltertown was such a chaos of growth and hope and life. Man had settled here so long ago upon the sculptures of red wind and Gotallama . . . earth's murals of prairie, small caves, crevices, and mountain ranges. Men had now created other things upon this face . . . house shacks, mortared smokestacks from bulldozed caves, and gaping holes eaten away by excavations. This was the trial and error called Smeltertown. Smeltertown today stood in the middle of two propitious mountains where long ago Cabeza de Baca had ciphered the name of El Paso del Norte. After three centuries, the migration of men through these mountains had evolved a habitude. From the aspect of modern progress, Smeltertown was a failure. If men prey upon men, this town was proof of such consequences. Once, the river that abounded with deep waters from flash floods helped carve the surrounding landscapes. Now, this same river could not even receive natural drainage of flooded waters. Men had tampered.

The natural course of the river had been distorted forty years before. Men had built a dam and a flood retaining wall two feet above river bank level to keep the high waters of the perennial floods from inundating Smeltertown. The river was dry and the retaining wall sealed. Now, hasty construction to the north of Smeltertown brought floods and mud from eroding, soft mountainsides. The two received the impact of mud waters that swarmed and filled the main street and stopped the flow opposite the retaining wall of the dry river. It had rained all night and the neighborhood became a mud sponge. The men of the town built their own improvisations to save the town. They had dug ditches along a series of sand hills. It was not enough. The upper city had built its civic center, its thirty-floor concrete business building and super highways, its streets with modern drainage system, and all things to make a harmony of concrete and efficiency. Smeltertown had been forgotten. There is a law of compensation. There was nothing mechanical in the spirit of these Mexicans. They were still red wind and earth. Gotallama loved them. They had kept roots with the earth. This was their way. An eyesore? Perhaps . . . to mechanical, dead harmonies that had become a trap. To Gotallama they were salvation. But still, there were floods and Smeltertown was an arroyo flooding with heavy rain. In the desert country it did not rain too often, but the intervals of flash floods left the Mexicans in the neighborhood homeless and cold. Many times a few of the ancianos caught pneumonia and died soon after.

It had rained all night and the streets of the neighborhood were a series of charcos where swirling water was making its own private language of direction. When Miguel awoke, he could smell the oatmeal with brown sugar and cinnamon that his mother was making in the kitchen. The door of the bedroom was open. His mother must have come in to see if they were warm and covered this Saturday morning. Now she was making their favorite breakfast. There was a clap of thunder and the day was sunless, so Miguel felt like crawling deeper into the blankets with his little brothers and sleeping all morning. It was a sleepy, safe thought. No . . . no, he had to hurry and get up and meet the boys by the dry wash. He laughed to himself. It sure wasn't a dry wash any more. It must be spilling over now. He felt uneasy about the rain.

Miguel jumped out of bed and began to dress. He put on his one heavy sweater over his regular clothes. The boys had agreed to dress warmly for the cave was cold. His mother heard him moving about.

"Miguel, are you up?"

"Sí, mama."

"Come have your breakfast. Are your brothers up?"

"No . . . they're still sleeping." He looked at his little brothers asleep under the blankets. The littlest one had his finger in his mouth again.

"Let them sleep and come and have some hot cereal. It is a cold day." It was a cold day for early September. Most Septembers were hot, for summer many times lasted until winter in this part of the country. Miguel went into the kitchen where his mother had already set a place at the table for him.

"What time is it?" He didn't wait for an answer but looked at the kitchen clock himself. It was early; still too early for his papá to be up. He was glad.

His mother always rose with the dawn. It was her way. She was always there ready to serve their meals at different times, for each had a separate destiny. Only the little ones ate together. His mother looked at him out of the corner of her eye as she warmed him some wheat tortillas. He would dip them in honey and eat them with his cereal.

"Why are you up so early on Saturday, Miguel?"

"I'm meeting the gang. . . ."

"It's raining out. I think your father will probably talk to the other men about the flood. The water is very high. The men might not go to work this morning."

The smelter was about three miles up from the town and safe from the flooding; however, it would have many men absent every time there was a flood, for most men would be needed in town. The smelter bosses would grumble about schedules and time lost and deduct it from their pay. But there were times when it was necessary to evacuate, to move families to higher ground. Miguel felt somewhat uncomfortable. The last rain had been a false alarm and the adventure upon which he was about to embark was so much more important. He was doing it for the whole town. In the green valley, they would not have to live with the constant threat of floods.

"We got something important to do."

His mother shook her head, "You should wait for your father to get up." Miguel did not answer his mother. He was only twelve, but his mother treated him like a man; he in turn worked after school and gave his money to her. She never ordered him around like a child. Now he was glad of this because deep down he knew he must go. That was more important. Nevertheless, it was a matter of conscience because he could not tell her where he was going or why.

He ate his breakfast with great relish and looked out the window at the sunless day. The horizon was lost in mists. When his mother left the room, he went to the small pantry and stuffed whatever food he could find in a paper bag, then went back to finish his breakfast. He looked at the clock again. It was time to go. He called out to his mother, "I'm leaving now."

There was no answer from the back; he was somewhat relieved. He picked up his paper bag with food and slipped out the door quietly. He had taken some apples, raisins and torillas. That would have to do. He put the bag under his sweater to keep it from getting wet.

Outside, he decided to run, but periodically, he stopped under a tree or any dry spot to catch his breath. It was not raining too hard now, but it was a constant drizzle. Soon the rain would be hard again. There was a junk car on the hill above the dry wash. That was where the boys would be waiting. Diego, Sergio, Felipe and Lalo were already there. They were all half soaked and grinning.

"Hey, Mike, you're late. What's the matter with you? People are up now. What if someone sees us?"

The boys had been watching the water gush in strong streams into the wash. It was like a small river now. They looked out of the windows of the junk car to see the ditches on the other side already half full. "Come on, let's go. It's a half mile up to the cave." Miguel left the car and ran into mud that covered his shoes. It was slippery. The five boys made their way through the mud, jumping on large stones as they found the path that led to the cave. The clouds were swallowing the side of the hill. The path looked down into the side of an area where the smelter excavators had eaten into the base of the mountain that overlooked the main street of the town. The boys could see the beginning of a mud slide. The top of the excavation was becoming sliding mud, a melting mountain.

The boys stood looking at it for a moment. "Do you think it's going to get worse?" The boys looked at one another but didn't answer. Anyway, they were getting soaked to the skin.

"Let's go!"

They continued up the path until they lost sight of the excavation and found themselves where the mountain became rock covered with sagebrush and reeds.

They found a dry spot under a rock ledge where rock crushed upon rock hovered . . . a chaotic cluster unintelligible to the mind.

"Brrrrr . . . I think I'll freeze to death."

"Did anybody remember to bring matches?"

Felipe reached into his pants pocket and brought out a small round tin box. "I got some here. But there's nothing to start a fire with. Everything's wet."

Lalo began to cough. They all felt cold and miserable. "We better go on ahead to the cave. There'll be dry brush in there. There's nothing but rock here."

Beyond the ledge that covered them, the path became steep. The boys had to make their way slowly because the rocks were smoother and they had to make sure of their footing. After a while, the boys could see the opening of the cave. It looked like an opened mouth that shaped the sound of fury . . . or maybe from another view, it was a round that shaped a gentle calling.

CHAPTER VI

To the boys, it meant a place to build a fire and dry out. They ran into the cave and started to stamp themselves dry. They were too wet. They needed a fire.

"Look!" Lalo found an old wooden crate someone had left there. They wouldn't have to look for dry brush. The crate would make a fine fire. The boys broke it up with rocks and piled some of the wood in the scooped rock on the north end of the cave. Felipe brought out his tin box and opened it. The matches were dry. He struck one and the small flame looked good and inviting. The dry wood of the crate started to burn. Before long, the boys were standing around the fire. Their faces glowed with the warmth. There was still a lot of wood they had saved from the crate to keep the fire going for some time.

The scooped rock protected the flames very well. The boys felt well satisfied, but their clothes were still soaking wet.

Miguel suggested, "Let's strip and wring out our clothes!" Immediately, all five boys set upon taking off their shoes, socks and clothing until all five stood naked before the fire like druids before a sacrifice. Each boy took his clothing and wrung it out, then carefully put it before the fire to dry. The boys had taken their paper bags, and an old army satchel containing their food and placed it alongside the scooped rock. The packages looked pitiful and unappetizing. When their clothes were half dry, they decided to salvage whatever food had not been ruined by the rain. Miguel's raisins and apples were safe, but his tortillas looked like mush.

The boys laughed. All the boys' tortillas, bread and crackers were ruined. But someone had brought a long sausage. There were oranges, candy, pecans and some cans of sardines. But they could not eat now. It was to be saved for later. The boys looked at the ruined food.

Diego was hungry. He was always hungry. He hated to waste the bread.

"You know what we could do?"

"What?"

"We could take some sticks and barbecue the bread."

"Estás loco . . . gahhhhhhhhhhh!"

"You're not that hungry, hartón!"

"It was just an idea."

The fire needed building again. So Sergio and Felipe threw in some more wood. Lalo sneezed. The boys sat around the fire to wait for the clothes to dry out.

"Do you believe in the flood and Noah's ark?" Lalo asked the rest of the boys.

"Nah!"

"It's a true story." Lalo was an altar boy.

"You believe anything they tell you . . . eh?" Sergio mocked. Lalo kicked him.

"You're going to go to hell."

They all laughed. The idea stuck, for they all looked into the fire for some time.

"I know another story about floods," said Felipe solemnly. They all listened intently. Felipe read a lot of science stuff. A lot he made up.

"I read a story that the moon is the cause of the floods like the one that covered the world in Noah's time."

"How is the moon responsible?"

"Is it a legend?"

The boys sat close to the fire intent on hearing, with their naked bodies rosy and warm. Felipe continued: "The moon will end by falling on the earth."

"When? When?" The boys looked at each other truly curious.

"It is not the first time. It has happened before. The force of gravitation of the moon upon the earth gets stronger and stronger. All the waters are drawn higher and higher and whole world is flooded. It drowns everybody unless they climb to the highest mountain. Then, the cosmic rays become more powerful and those who stay alive get bigger and bigger . . . like giants."

"You're lying."

"You read it in the comics."

"No," Felipe's voice sounded serious, "It was in a book written by some German who was a friend of Hitler's."

For some reason the boys belived him. Miguel asked, "These giants are like the giants in the Bible?"

"Probably the same."

"What happens to the moon?"

"The moon will come nearer and nearer until it explodes. It will go round and round very fast; it will be a big ring of rocks and ice and water and gas. But then the earth will not have a satellite for a long time . . . until the planet Mars comes into the earth's orbit."

"You're a shit-lier."

"Shut up and listen."

"Well, then it will bump against the earth and fall into the sun because it is attracted by fire. The attraction of Mars will steal our atmosphere and what is left is to be divided into pieces in space. Then the seas will bubble with fire."

"That's some crazy story, baboso."

Miguel was thoughtful, "What will happen to the earth?"

"It will be a ball of fire that will drift into space until it becomes a ball of ice, then it will fall into the sun."

"There will be no more people?"

Felipe went on, "Yes, there will, because after this earth is gone there will be a great silence . . . then millions and millions of years later the water vapours will gather inside the sun and it will explode making another earth just like ours.

Lalo's eyes were wide with wonder, "That's a better story than the one in the Bible."

Miguel said it in a whisper, but it stunned everybody, "Gotallama is the god of fire and water. He is the god of this cave and beyond." The boys felt something grow inside of them. The fire seemed to speak a language, a knowing that they must discover.

"You . . . you think there are really giants?" Diego asked.

"You mean . . . big, big people?"

"Yes."

"I don't think so. Not now."

Miguel said softly, "There are giants inside."

"Whatcha mean?"

"People who don't see a little world, but all the world is inside them, like Papa At."

They all looked at each other and nodded. Truths were coming closer. Papa At and El Indio Tolo were part of the universe, a whole part who made their own pattern. They were giants.

"You think . . . maybe we can be giants?"

"Inside?"

"It would probably take a long time. In the world we get smaller with little worries when we grow up," Miguel commented.

"Papa At told you that."

Giants . . . fire . . . water . . . green   valley . . . own   pattern . . . the excitement grew.

Felipe suggested, "Let's get started. We've been here a long time." The fire was dying again. They threw some more wood in it. Diego had found a stick. He was holding a piece of tortilla over the fire.

"Look at him!"

The boys laughed. Diego took it away from the fire when it started to burn away.

He let it drop and then picked up the burned tortilla that was half carbon and began to eat it. "Hey, you guys, it's not bad . . . not bad at all."

Breakfast was far in their memory and they did not want to eat the other food because they needed it for the journey. So the boys took up pieces of bread and held them over the fire. The bread did taste good. The whole world tasted good. When they had finished eating what they could, they began to put on their clothes. The clothes were still damp, but it was much better than soaking wet.

Diego observed, "All the paper bags are wet. Let's put all the food in my army satchel." The canvas was stinking and dirty with mud, but all the food fitted. Diego smiled and put the satchel over his shoulder. Felipe walked back to the mouth of the cave to see if it was still raining. All the boys followed him. All of a sudden, there was a clap of thunder accompanied by a flash of lightning that lighted up the mouth of the cave. The boys fell backward.

"Whew! That was close."

The rain was still pouring. Sergio pointed towards the excavation that seemed far, far away from the height they were in. "Miren . . . the mud is snaking down into the town, like chocolate."

The boys drew near to look. The hill over the excavation seemed about to collapse.

The boys looked at each other.

Felipe looked at Miguel and asked, "You think we should go back?"

"No . . . we need the map. The whole town needs the map."

Lalo suggested pessimistically, "What if there isn't any map?"

Miguel's voice was sure, "There is a map." No one doubted him. They had to go on. They walked away from the mouth of the cave and far beyond where they had built a fire. The storm disappeared in the darkness of high granite. The cave was narrow, and Miguel led the way through the narrow passageway. The ground had been smooth under their feet, but now in this area, they felt soft gravel. Some of it seemed to break like sugar cubes under the pressure of their weight. They had all put on their shoes except Lalo who was carrying them. Suddenly, he yelled, "Awwwwwwwww!"

"What's the matter?" The boys stopped and turned to look at Lalo who was the last one in the group. He was holding his foot in his hands, "I think I cut it."

Lalo was standing there looking like a crane on one leg.

Miguel looked at the cut and then looked at Lalo. "Maybe we better go back."

"No!" Lalo's voice was loud and created a small echo in the cave. "I can wear my shoe. Awwwwwwwwwwwwwwww, vatos, it's nothing." He sat down on a rock and deliberately put on his shoes. There was no expression on Lalo's face, but the boys knew that it hurt when he put the shoe on.

Beyond the belly of the chamber where they sat, they all knew there was a long winding passage . . . almost a mile of walking before they came to the chasm.

No one had dared go beyond the chasm except El Indio Tolo, no one in the neighborhood, that is. The silence gave the feel of a deep, deep mystery . . . something bigger than all of them.

Miguel remembered Papa At's explanation of the parts of the whole. The whole was beyond anyone's understanding. And like the seasons and the wind, the whole was ageless.

Felipe warned, "We have to be very careful when we cross El Hoyo." The chasm was a bottomless pit. Miguel swallowed his fear silently; he knew the others felt as he did, but they must go on . . . they must find the map to the green valley. If the smelter fumes were poisonous, the green valley would be the ideal place; it would be the promised land for the people of Smeltertown. That is the reason why they were all here and why they could not be afraid.

Diego stuttered, "Di . . . di . . . did el Go . . . gota . . . lla . . . llama put it there to stop people from going any farther?"

There was silence; then, Miguel assuming the bell-like voice of Papa At, explained it as Papa At had explained it to him. "Gotallama is a river god and a cave god. It is water and fire that makes caves and all things go on and on and on like Gotallama. . . ."

Lalo asked, "Is that why he is a god because he goes on and on and on?"

"Yes."

"He goes on doing what?"

"Living."

"Is that all?"

Miguel's voice was deliberate, "Papa At says that *is all.*" The words stayed with the boys, "Living is all . . . living is all. . . ." Erosion spoke for the mountain that held the cave. Here the solvent action of steam, gases, waves, and water ran silently through rock creating a history, a being in granite, a making of eternity. The stone was mute and voiceless, yet was all voice calling out creation in a silent, moving thunder.

"Gotallama," Miguel continued, "doesn't love or hate. He just is and he just changes and becomes. If he made the chasm, he made it because it was part of change."

"That's crazy . . ." Felipe scowled in though, "All the stories about Indian gods . . . gods are always angry or punishing men or each other. Are you sure he is an Indian god?"

Miguel was sure. "He is an earth god."

Diego reasoned, "We're earth . . . the Bible says so. Are we all gods?"

Lalo warned, "Don't say that or you'll go to hell. It's a mortal sin." He crossed himself.

"Watcha el altar boy," Diego pushed Lalo playfully. Sergio looked from one boy to the next and then his eyes became glued to the opening that led further into the cave. "Are we going to go on?"

When the question was asked, the boys resumed their journey. Miguel offered, "I'll go first."

They were now coming to the end of the cave. However, the high crevices came almost one upon the other high in the sky. It seemed that the crevices were an elongation of the cave now broken in two with a history of growing, slanting, curving rock.

There was no rain here for some reason. The sky could not be seen through the overlapping rocks. They were now in an area that was high and spacious, near the tunnel that crossed to El Hoyo. There was still light that sifted through high shafts in the rocks. But once they began their journey into the coming tunnel, it would become dark and the passageway became very small until they reached the entrance to the chasm. Again, one would follow the other, for only one person could go through the tunnel at a time. Miguel led the way. They felt their way, for the snaking passage way was dark and narrow. Miguel held out his hands to touch the sides of the narrow funnel and small particles of dirt and rock rained against his chest.

He remembered a warning of Papa At's, "The snake and scorpion don't like it. . . ." He assured himself there was nothing to fear. Diego followed Miguel. Miguel could hear Diego breathing. After Diego came Sergio, then Felipe and last of all, Lalo putting his weight on one good foot. They followed the passageway in silence for a while. Only the sound of debris falling and feet finding their way among rocks was audible. It was a long dark finding . . . a dark finding . . . were they doing wrong? Miguel thought of Gotallama's green valley, a map carved on a flat stone by El Indio Tolo as Gotallama had instructed him in a dream. No more desert or want, no more pain and defeat in people's eyes.

El Indio Tolo had placed that stone tablet in a niche carved into a glowing stone somewhere deep in the cave . . . no one had gone beyond the chasm to look for it. But they were going . . . because it was time that they do something as men. Each boy carried the burden and the dream as he stumbled, fell, and got up to go in his dark finding. From far behind, Lalo began to whistle. One by one the boys joined it. It was a hope in the dark stillness.

It seemed, after a while, as if the passage had no end. The funnel with its sharp angles and zigzags gave a feeling of helplessness, of utter lostness. Now the passageway branched off into three directions. Miguel shouted, "Stay to the right!"

"Stay to the right!" echoed the resounding shaft.

Miguel felt very tired. He called back to the boys, "Rest . . . just lie there and rest!"

Miguel knew he must crawl all the way in the funnel of the catacomb that led to El Hoyo until the roof rose again into a large chamber. In this chamber they would find a stone guard, granite, stern and solitary. Papa At had told them about the stone guard that stood before El Hoyo. It had been carved by the power of Gotallama, by his water and fire, through the centuries.

Now these children of the sun, these collectors of light . . . breathless, tired . . . lay on the smooth ground of the hollow way and rested. Their minds did not rest. How long had they been in the cave? Would they cross El Hoyo after they faced it? Would they find the crystal chamber of El Indio Tolo after that? The map? Would they find the stone stairway leading out into the world? Would it be their world? Or would it be a world of green gods that kept all things in motion . . . growing? Would they die? Miguel's body felt very tired. Now he floated in a lightness with the darkness and the silence. He wondered if his friends were feeling what he was feeling. After a while, Sergio's voice broke the stillness. "Hey, muevanse!" Miguel felt his mouth full of dirt; he could hardly breathe and his eyes were smarting. He must turn over on his back and drag himself up for the rest of the way. He turned himself; then began dragging himself forward by drawing up his legs and then pushing up. After another long while, he saw the light at a distance.

They had made it! The narrow passage was now becoming wider and wider, like a caracol, until it became the entrance to a lighted chamber. Light was sifted into the chamber through jagged gigantic boulders that formed a steeple, high over Miguel's head.

Miguel stood up, dirty and tired, and stretched after the long cramped journey. One by one, the other boys appeared at the entrance.

As Lalo came through the opening, the rest of the boys were exploring the chamber.

There was light. The sky was now visible. There were puddles on the ground and the rocks glistened wet. The patch of sky that was visible showed a trace of blue among the clouds.

Before them was the stone guard. It was composed of three huge rocks. It had no outline of feet. But from the second rock, there curiously projected two arm stumps, one of them raised upward. The top stone was rounded off with a canopy that resembled a floating helmet. This was the stone guard Papa At had described to them. They inspected the mute sentinel that knew the centuries better than they did. Miguel pointed ahead. About four hundred yards away they saw a curved mount resembling a narrow bridge. It was a natural ledge over El Hoyo. They had to be very careful now. They walked cautiously the rest of the way until they came to the edge of El Hoyo. They looked down the abyss holding their bodies well back. Miguel could hear his heart pounding. The boys looked at each other asking the unavoidable with their eyes. "Who will go first?" The fathomless darkness spoke of terrible unknowns.

The ledge arched across El Hoyo and through its axis, there was a long diminishing view of jagged rocks whose symmetry was broken by ripples of small crevices. The narrow natural bridge traversed the yawning mouth of darkness. They must be sure-footed and brave. The thoughts of misadventure were heavy . . . five pounding hearts and full throats of boys who knew there was only one thing to do . . . to go across to the other side. Fear, like darkness, hovered.

Miguel whispered, "I'll go first."

He knew he must not look down into the inky gulf. His feet, his hands, his feel would find direction more than his eyes. It was a risky thing. He walked to the edge of the ledge and put his right foot firmly down as he used his right hand to grab ahold of a protruding rock. He slowly balanced his body with the hold and made his way slowly and steadfastly across. Each time he would put out his right foot for sure ground. Then he would lean his body slightly to make his right hand reach out for some secure support. Once this was done, he would bring his left foot next to the right foot and his left hand would also find a security. If darkness revelled in its power to frighten, so did brightness encourage the will to do among five boys.

The pre-emptive role had been assumed by Miguel, now one by one, the other boys, first Diego, then Sergio, then Felipe followed Miguel along the ledge. Lalo was the last, and once the other boys had made it across the ledge, they watched Lalo's crossing with a prayer, for his foot was injured and it was more difficult for him. He made it safely across and everybody breathed more easily. All five boys could not resist looking back at their feat; they had conquered El Hoyo. They walked to the edge of the open throat of death and felt a bigness in themselves and a secret thankfulness.

"It's a good thing there was light," commented Miguel. He suddenly looked up at the other boys and grinned. They grinned back. In a corner of the area where they now stood was a wide stone platform, yellowish grey in color with spotted red tuff and black basalt.

Felipe suggested, "That's a good place to eat. I'm starved." They all agreed. They scampered up the platform and Diego opened up the satchel. He spread out the food. Apples, sausage, sardines, oranges, raisins, pecans, Ah! They ate and ate and ate. Food had never tasted that good.

"We better find our way out of here before we starve again," said Diego with his mouth full. The boys were too content now to think about that. Miguel looked up. The sky was no longer blue. It was dark now. He looked at the other guys and noticed that he could hardly make out their faces now.

"It must be night."

Sergio was already lying down on the platform. "I'm so tired. Why don't we sleep here?"

It was a good idea. They all lay down and were quiet. Sergio suddenly asked, "Do you hear what I hear?" They listened.

"Sounds like water hitting rock."

"It's still raining."

"No . . . if it were, we would be getting wet, dummy!"

"Then what is it?"

"I don't know. It sounds more like a running stream."

They listened again. The sound reminded them of the river stream on the edge of town.

"It could be Gotallama warning us," suggested Sergio.

"Warning us about what?"

"He will do something terrible if we go on."

"Don't be silly," admonished Miguel. "Nature gods are all good; only men are bad to one another."

They all felt better. Lalo asked Felipe, "Is it true . . . your story about the earth and the sun and giants?"

"Of course."

"I don't believe it. Do you believe it, Miguel?"

"I don't know. Papa At says that all truths are false and all falsehood is truth."

"That doesn't make sense."

The word came like a bell from Miguel's throat, "Chaos."

The exhausted boys were soon asleep.

CHAPTER VII

It was Saturday morning and Lupe was getting ready to go to Fito's house, when she heard a hard thud that crashed against the outside wall; then, she heard her grandmother scream. She ran from the kitchen to the front room where she saw her grandmother standing, pointing at the front window. The window was covered with mud. It oozed down the window. In its midst clung the sprawled figure of a scorpion, the biggest scorpion Lupe had ever seen.

"¡Jesucristo! ¿Qué pasa?" She ran to the window and looked out beyond the horror of the sprawled scorpion. The whole main street was flooded with mud. In the mud, she saw hundreds of dead scorpions floating, carried along with the impact of the mud. She was frightened, but she tried to look calm as she turned towards the anciana.

"Every thing is all right, grandmother. No se apure."

The old lady was praying against her fingers with her eyes closed, "Ave María, Madre de Dios. . . ."

Lupe went up to her and put her arm around her, "Ya, ya mamacita, no se asuste."

But she was very frightened herself. What on earth had happened? She held the trembling body of the old woman and kissed her cheek, then she helped her over to a chair. The grandmother sat down and began to cry. "Let me get you a glass of water," Lupe ran back to the kitchen for the water, but more important to confirm her suspicion. She looked outside the kitchen window. Yes . . . the sea of mud and scorpions was all around. She couldn't tell how high, but it was high. The rain, falling furiously on the mud, made swirls. The floating scorpions would turn with the swirls in a rain dance. A frightening idea gathered in Lupe. If the mud kept coming, they might drown in it. It could well cover the whole building. Lupe could now hear scream after scream outside the house.

She pieced the situation together in her mind. The main street was a gully; the mountain over the excavation had fallen right into the main street of the town. She remembered that morning, seeing the men of the neighborhood rush over to the school that was on higher ground. The ditches were overflowing and water was rising to sidewalk level. They were gathering to make plans for possible evacuation if the rain did not stop. But this, the whole side of a mountain turned into mud . . . this . . . who expected this?

Lupe had already considered taking her grandmother with her to Fito's house if the rain did not let up. His house was behind the school and relatively safe. But the presidio where she lived was on low ground.

Prodigious quantities of water had seeped down into the main street all morning. It was the main artery and the water rose and rose. The ditches were overflowing and could very well give way. Water had begun edging into the houses since early morning. Lupe looked at the doors. Now it was no longer water that was seeping through. There were signs of thick mud pressing against the doors and curling in slowly at the bottom.

She went to the front room that served as a bedroom and gave her grandmother a few sips of water. The old woman was praying her rosary. She seemed not to want to know what had happened. Lupe did not want to alarm her any more than she had to. She suggested gently, "It's the storm, grandmother. Lie down while I figure out how to get us to Fito's house. His house is high."

The grandmother kept praying. She looked up at Lupe and gave her her old withered hand. Lupe helped her up and took her grandmother to bed.

"Just lie down for a little while."

The old grandmother lay down and closed her eyes serenely. Lupe went back to the front window to see if the mud was rising. The litany of rain had taken tragic proportions. An avalanche had occurred, and all the people on Main Street were the victims. The slope over the excavation must have yielded to the pressures of the water. She peered out of the window where the dead scorpion still tenaciously held on, dead as it was. Of course, it's not holding on, thought Lupe. It's stuck to the mud! She wanted to laugh. Then, she saw men wading through the mud coming from the direction of the school. They were coming to help the people on Main Street. God bless them! Now she could see people coming out of the presidio and other houses in the area. The mud was well over their knees. Women held children on their shoulders. There was no thought of saving personal belongings. Lupe knew that she had to save herself and her grandmother. Men coming towards the presidio would have their hands full saving the children that lived along Main Street.

She looked at the helpless anciana lying on the bed. How was she to do it? She knew that as soon as she opened the door, the sea of mud and scorpions would invade the little room. She knew she must stay away from the door as soon as she opened it, for the ills of the mountain would take her and her grandmother along with them. She had to decide right away. She went up to her grandmother and sat besides her on the bed. "Abuelita . . . abuelita. . . ."

" ¿ Qué, hijita?"

"You must do as I say, abuelita."

"¿ Qué?"

"I want you to climb on my back. The whole street is filled with mud, and we have to get out. I don't want you to get wet. We must leave right away. Do you understand? You must ride on my back."

La anciana shook her head, "No . . . no . . . estoy muy pesada. It is too much for you, Ave María Purísima!"

"You have to do as I say, do you hear, grandmother?" She helped her grandmother get out of bed. Then she found a coat. She put it on her grandmother. Next, she went to the kitchen table and took off the oilcloth with pink flowers. She put it over her grandmother's shoulders and told her to hold it at the throat like a hood.

"When you get on my back, grandmother, use only one hand to hold the oilcloth; then, put the other hand tight around my neck. Do as I say." La anciana nodded.

Lupe led her grandmother to the kitchen table. "Get up on the table. This kitchen door is better than the front door. When I open it, the impact of the mud will not be as great. Now, no matter what happens, stay on top of the table. The mud is going to come in, but we must let it come in until there is a clearing at the door. Then, I will come to you and let you get on my back.

"Hijita, déjame morir. Save yourself."

Lupe helped her grandmother get up on the kitchen table. The old woman stood there holding the oilcloth with the flowers tightly over her head. When Lupe made sure her grandmother was safe, she went to the door. She must move away from the door as soon as she opened it. She turned the knob and the door swung open. Quickly, she stepped away. She could hear her grandmother screaming and the swish of the mud behind her. She went over to the anciana and quieted her, "Don't be afraid. Just get on my back when I tell you and close your eyes and pray."

The grandmother closed her eyes and began to pray. Mud and scorpions were spilling into the kitchen like gasps of vomit. Lupe watched in horror. After a while, the kitchen floor was evenly covered with mud; the flow was coming in low. She told her grandmother, "Get on my back."

The old woman got on Lupe's back. This was one time Lupe was thankful for her big body. The little grandmother did not seem to be so heavy at first. "Put your legs around my waist, grandmother." The grandmother did as she was told. One hand was holding tight to Lupe's neck. It made it difficult for Lupe to breathe. Lupe started towards the door. She walked carefully. The first fifty yards outside the house were hopeful, but after she passed the huge elm on the side of the street, she began to feel the full weight of the effort. She had come to the edge of the sidewalk with great trepidation. She put one foot ahead to feel her way. Luckily, she hit the edge of the sidewalk. The next step must be down. The weight on her shoulders would feel the impact of the stepping down. She held her body taut, as she stepped down. She made it without falling. Thank God!

She went on a few more yards out of pure courage, but now, scorpions, like rage, fell and clung to her clothing and hair. One hit Lupe's mouth as she gasped for breath. She felt its cold, hard, lifeless tentacles. A scream formed and gagged. But she did not scream. She clenched her teeth and twisted her head violently to throw off the scorpion. The rain washed her face free. Her spirit was quailing and crying. She pressed on forward. Her grandmother's hands were clawing in desperation. Lupe felt as if her back were breaking with the weight of her grandmother. Her feet now felt heavy as she trudged the mud toward the faces of two men coming towards her.

Scorpions clung; rain washed them away. This image would be hoarded in her mind forever. Suddenly she felt a dizziness. Little by little she was giving way. She fell on one shaky knee and the taste of mud was harsh in her mouth. She could not tread the mud any more. She fell headlong into the sea of scorpions. The last thing she remembered was her grandmother whimpering. . . .

Miguel opened his eyes. It was still the same darkness with ribbon films of distant light from an unknown beginning. He kept still and looked around at the shadows created by the light, low-flung into a shimmering. An arklike boulder sprawled on the right, and to the left were outlines of dark, opaque masses of rock formations that fed the imagination. There was a panther tearing a victim to pieces with its claws; there was the outline of a thin long rock caught in strangulation by smaller, jagged adversaries. Miguel turned to the right again and the embryonic substance of a vision grew and grew . . . a moving, growing transformation . . . what is it? Miguel held his breath. The vision took form. It was a man, the shape of El Indio Tolo beckoning . . . it is just my imagination! It is only the shadow of the boulder, no more.

"Sergio!" Miguel nudged the sleeping body beside him.

"Yeah?"

"You awake?"

"Yeah. . . ."

"I think it's morning."

"Maybe it's still night. . . ."

"We slept a long time."

Felipe's voice joined in. "You think we'll find our way out?"

Miguel assured him. "As soon as we reach the crystal room."

Felipe was skeptical. "What if it isn't there?"

Miguel's voice was certain, "It'll be there. Papa At said so."

"Papa At has never come this far. How does he know?"

"El Indio Tolo found it."

"Maybe it's just a story. . . ."

Lalo's voice was a whisper, "You think we're going to die?"

"I'm hungry." Diego's matter-of-fact voice made things possible.

Miguel listened, "Sh . . . sh!"

The intonation of flowing water was clear in the silence, far, far away it seemed.

The sound went deep into the senses. The powerful harmony in the essence of rock was felt too, but there was a dismal and pitiless deadness also. Miguel tried to find courage.

"There's some light coming from somewhere . . . and the water . . . there's a way out."

Felipe shared the optimism, "And we'll find the crystal room and El Indio Tolo's map to the green valley."

"Sure!" Sergio's voice was excited, "And when we do, we'll all go there to live, all the people in the neighborhood. We'll tell Fito there is a place where there are no poisons for the lungs.

Lalo asked, "Is it like the Garden of Eden?"

Diego scoffed, "That's a fairy-tale."

Lalo kicked him with his good foot, "The Bible's not a fairy-tale."

Felipe remembered what Papa At had said, "It's a green valley with wheat fields and sunflowers and a waterfall."

Sergio, suddenly filled with apprehension, "Maybe somebody already found it. Maybe now it is a city with tall buildings and cars and a smeltertown like ours. . . ."

Miguel's voice was angry, "No . . . it is a valley that was meant for people of the earth. The gods of the valley predicted it to El Indio Tolo. It is not to be found by people who . . . who. . . ."

"Who what?"

"I don't know, but los gabachos . . . they're like machines, like their cars and their buildings and their smelter. The valley is not for them."

Miguel felt something in himself. The Indian in him was in harmony with earth things. He looked up at the pilings of centuries. And felt the perfect composure of time, but he knew they must not sit around and talk too long. They didn't know how far they had to go. He reminded the boys, "We better look for the passage out of here." The boys felt the platform where they had slept and began to feel their way among the huge boulders. Miguel remembered the vision conjured by his mind. He walked toward the arklike boulder and investigated one side and then the other. On the right side of the boulder was a narrow cleft, not even big enough for one person to squeeze through. Miguel decided it was not the way. He joined the other boys whose search had also been fruitless.

Sergio suggested, "Maybe the only way out is the way we came and this is the end of the cave. Maybe El Indio Tolo is a fairy-tale like the Garden of Eden."

The rest of the boys were silent. Felipe spoke after a while, "Let's take another look. . . ."

The boys got up disheartedly and began another search around the cave, carefully feeling the curvatures of the rock formations on all sides. Miguel remembered the small cleft behind the arklike boulder and decided to see if he could squeeze through. He held himself tall and straight and squeezed his body sideways through the cleft. His face was pressed against hard rock. The rock was not loose and grainy, but smooth and slippery. He could feel small protruding edges dig into his body. But it did not hurt. His body fit through, although he had to hold his face up and it was hard to breathe. The higher the cleft, the wider it became. He knew he had found the passageway. He remembered the vision and felt an excitement in him. He stopped and decided to go back and tell the boys.

He edged his way out and called out to the rest, "Over here . . . I think I've found it."

When the boys looked at the narrow cleft they did not believe it was the way. Miguel told them that the higher it was, the larger the passageway became. Sergio was the tall one in the group. He was one head taller than the rest. He decided to find the way through. The boys watched him as he made his way sideways through the cleft. They watched until they could no longer see him.

Miguel called out, "Are you all right?"

Sergio's voice came back loud and clear, "I'm all right. . . . It's getting bigger now. . . . Hey! There's a light up ahead!"

They waited in expectation for about fifteen minutes. It seemed an eternity, but Sergio was whistling to let them know he was all right. The whistling became a faint swirling noise as the sound was carried through the narrow cleft, but it was reassuring. Then, Sergio's voice called out, "I've found it . . . I've found it . . . oh, my God . . . wait until you see it!"

Miguel waited no longer. He started to make his way through the cleft. One by one the other boys followed at a distance so as not to crowd each other. Miguel felt the space grow as he made his way through. He was hardly conscious of the closeness any more. His mind kept singing, "The crystal room . . . the crystal room. . . ." He moved his body with faster thrusts leading with his left shoulder . . . and feet that easily tangled up under him . . . but he had to be careful. He swallowed hard and felt his way carefully. Again he wondered, "Did Sergio mean the crystal room when he had called out? . . . or was it the passage he was talking about?"

He listened to catch any thing Sergio might call out, but nothing was heard. Only the scraping of bodies against the narrow cleft resounded in his ears. Before long his body was no longer pressed against the sides of the cleft. He could turn himself, yes. He could turn himself full body. The area was now completely lighted, and the shades of rock became flesh-colored and clear. Miguel's feet were wet. He could look down now and see scattered small remnants of water making puddles in the small recesses along the edge of the passageway. Here the tunnel became high and the beginning of limestone formations began. He was now in the crystal room. Floods of sunlight glowed on the rocks ... perpendicular joints rising, red and white, one fitted on the other, convex, concave ... Gotallama had seen to it that the toll of solvent action left its magic, steam and gases and waves and water from an old ocean running silently through rock. The majesty of erosion had hewn mysteries of an eternity. There were prisms of crystal, feldspar and black tourmaline forming geometric adventures of light. The feldspar was brilliant flesh-red and blue color as if highly polished by the sunlight streaming from a heaven very clear to the eyes. Miguel looked up and felt a holiness. The light streamed down into a million colors upon stalagmites petrified between the claws of granite jutting from the ground. And in the stream of rainbow light was a pool, limpid and silent as the reflection of all time.

Miguel could do no more than look in utter wonder. Now he understood why Sergio had remained silent once he had come upon the crystal room. It demanded the silence of a cathedral ... it demanded the awe for godly things. Lalo clutched at Miguel's arm and pointed. A stream of crystal water fell over pastel rocks. It hurried over a bed of rock ledges and widened into a pool. They both hurried over to the pool, clear and quiet, and looked down. The bottom of the pool was covered by pink and creamy gravel. It was so beautiful, Miguel grinned at Lalo in disbelief but with a knowing joy of goodness in the world.

Miguel's heart was pounding hard. They had found the crystal room! El Indio Tolo had been right! Bless Papa At and his dreams! The green valley ... somewhere in this cave room was a map of another dream, a dream that belonged to earth-people.

All the boys were now in this room of light. Silently they walked around with amazement in their eyes. Then Miguel gave a whoop, "Aieeee ... eeee ... eeeeee!"

All the boys gave way and they began to shout and horse around with the freedom of earth-Indians. After a while, they all fell upon the clear water of the pool and drank and drank, then lay down upon the ground and caught the streaming light from the sun with closed eyes that felt a world they missed while in the belly of the earth. Their happiness was as brilliant as the prisms of the cave, and the many shades of doubt and fear were lost to light, and a faith and hope regained.

The boys were between reality and dream; they were in a silent world of color. Color is free and is given life by light, a wild life that catches fancy. Miguel's mind clicked, "This is God." Here was a clarity so wide, so wide. None of them could imagine such distances.

"Would you like to stay here forever?" Felipe asked through half-closed lids that caught the magic of the light.

"What about food?" Diego asked. The rest of the boys were thinking about living in the cave . . . wild thoughts, free thoughts, thoughts of earthmen who know there is a wild god in the world, for the order of things lies in changing chaos, leaving only the most intricate patterns. Chaos of Man or chaos of Nature, it is part of a deep wildness from a time when earth was taking form and creating changing life, all an orderly chaos. Man creates the same way, then he is angered or he despairs at the ordered chaos. Sometimes he lets it all be and laughs and finds a balance in himself to love the chaos of his world . . . the wild God. The boys felt him now. The long way to the crystal room had been an impenetrable darkness, for that reason they now knew light. It was the geometer of light within the heart of five boys lying on the ground, feeling beyond themselves. Miguel's mind clicked again, "This is God." This was a procession of the heart not too easily disturbed.

"If we could stay here, we would never see the people. . . ." Felipe said, picking up a piece of pink gravel and putting it against his eye to see through it.

"Maybe, they would all come. . . ." Diego suggested.

"That's a dream, nothing else," Miguel retorted remembering another way.

"The valley of the gods . . . the map . . . it is more beautiful than this cave; there are living things in it."

They all looked up at the opening letting in the light. It was so far away; it seemed miles up. The light was soft as early afternoon. They looked again and could not tell where the mountain ended and the sky began. . . .

Miguel squinted until shapes were lost to his vision and all he saw was a round glow . . . perhaps the god Gotallama? He opened his eyes again and told himself the truth. It was the sky and the opening in the mountain letting in the light . . . but it was still a part of God. He sat up and looked around at the boys who, on seeing him get up, did the same. They went to the edge of the pool and squatted like Indians looking across at what seemed to be a stone altar in the middle of the pool. The streaming water behind it gave it a living shape.

"What do you think it is?"

"Some stone that grew in the middle."

"Stones don't grow, dummy. . . ."

"Sure . . . very slow . . . not like plants."

"That's silly. . . ."

"No . . . it's true."

Miguel knew what it was. He looked at it and felt a lump in his throat.

"The map is there," he said.

"How do you know?"

"I know." He knew he sounded foolish, but he knew that he knew.

The boys were impressed by the certainty in his voice. Miguel was like that. He felt things others did not. They believed him.

"How do we get to it?"

"Swim . . . it's too deep to wade to it."

"It looks too high . . . do you think we can reach it?"

They looked at the huge red stone shaped in tiers of small columns holding smaller skeletal arms of stones like a web . . . chaos finding order in stone. It was a curious thing to see. A niche, an altar, a hiding place, a dream . . . it did not matter; it was there, solitary and strange waiting . . . waiting. . . .

Felipe was excited, "Let's all swim across . . . then one of us can pull himself to the tangled part."

Miguel nodded, then one by one they plunged into the pool. The water was warmed by the brilliance of the sun. All the boys swam quietly. It seemed to be a most serious thing. Wide eyes in dripping faces now looked at an insoluble state, a creation of Gotallama.

"Hey, look!" Lalo had pulled himself up by bracing himself on one of the columns. He was now sitting in the maze of stone, "There's something in the middle. . . ."

"Miguel was right!"

The boys hoisted themselves up and found a place to sit in the stone maze. They looked and saw three ceramic jars of a pure orange shade. Someone had put them there. They were man-made. Alongside the three jars, was a beautiful carved stone of prism colors. It was a slab the size of a writing tablet. Miguel knew what he had to do. He raised himself and made his way gingerly to the middle of the maze where the objects were. He took one jar and handed it to Felipe; then he took the other two jars and gave them to Diego and Sergio. He then picked up the slab and handed it to Lalo who took it with great care. Then, Miguel walked back to where the other boys sat holding the objects with one hand.

Sergio suggested, "We can drop them in the water; they won't break." He dropped his jar and it fell and floated on the surface of the pool. The other boys followed suit, except Lalo who turned and looked at Miguel waiting for him to say something.

"Not the slab," Miguel said, "It's flat and it may break. Here . . . Lalo, I'll jump into the water, then you can hand it to me." He dived into the water creating ripples, making the orange jars bob around him.

He looked up and reached out for the slab. Lalo leaned out into the water and handed it to Miguel. The boys then slid off their columns and fell into the water. They did not dive in as Miguel had done.

He had come too close to the floating jars. When Miguel reached the edge of the pool, he waited until Lalo had gone over the narrow stone edge leading out of the pool, then he handed him the slab. Felipe, Sergio and Diego pulled themselves out of the pool then leaned over to catch the floating jars. When the boys had secured them, all five sat down, dripping wet, and felt the glow of discovery.

They looked at one another, then all eyes were on Miguel who held the slab in his hands. He was looking at it intently, tracing it with his fingers. As if by impulse, he turned it around the scrutinized the back of it carefully.

Felipe's voice was now impatient: "Well, ¿es o no es?"

Miguel looked up with a puzzled look. He handed the slab to Felipe. Felipe looked at it eagerly, then his heart sank; the slab was absolutely smooth on one side. The other side had one circle with an Indian word in the middle. Felipe made out the letters, "K . . . e . . . a . . . r . . . ." He looked at Miguel and asked, "What does it mean?"

Miguel shook his head, but his voice was not disappointed, "I don't know."

Felipe looked at it, but there was nothing more. "Well, this sure isn't the map to the green valley." He handed it to the other boys. They too seemed disappointed. Lalo suggested, "Let's look around some more . . . maybe it's somewhere else." He jumped up and began exploring. Sergio and Diego eventually did the same. Felipe turned to Miguel as if waiting for his decision.

Miguel's voice was sure, "This is the map."

Felipe scowled, "Estás loco . . . one circle and an Indian word? You don't even know what the word means."

Miguel's voice was certain, "It's the map. I feel it, I can't . . . can't explain . . . but I feel it is the map."

"You call it a map?" Felipe's voice was a jeer. The other boys gathered around Miguel, "You think it's the map, Miguel? How you know . . . eh?"

"I don't know . . . that is my mind doesn't know . . . but I feel it is the map."

Felipe was still incredulous. "Well, we're not taking your word for it. We're just going to look around some more. We didn't come all the way just for that." Miguel did not answer. They all looked at him accusingly for a moment before setting out on another search around the crystal room. It became a frolic. Everywhere the boys looked they did not find the map, but they did find strange, fragile formations of light and rock. They filled their trousers' pockets with the clear rocks as if they were gold. Miguel sat still holding the slab on his lap. Once in a while he would look up toward the opening, as if he wanted an answer from Gotallama himself.

Miguel felt outside himself; his senses were crystallized. He looked at the slab again and intuitively knew it was the map. There was no need to look any farther. He was at peace in this sanctuary of light, and the unerring images cast by the reflections of crystals and sun seemed to sing, "Map of hope, map of love, map of peace." He watched the boys, silently, busy in their search. But they must find out for themselves. He felt the room; millions and millions of years of Nature making . . . Nature making. Miguel was now a remoteness, a part of light. He looked at the slab again and circles whirled and expanded, contracted and sprang forward, spoke of a surety of being part of Nature making. It was too much to bear, this communication with stone, so Miguel put it aside and picked up some smooth, round pebbles the color of cream and tossed them into the pool. The pebbles struck the water and the ripples melted the colored reflections of the sun. Miguel felt a whisper inside himself, "That's me . . . the stone, the light, the slab. . . ." He suddenly frowned. He didn't know why he had said that to himself, but he knew it was true.

"K . . . E . . . A . . . R," Miguel said the letters slowly and carefully. He did not know what they meant, but they thrilled him somehow. Sergio came up to him shaking himself: "Mira . . . I'm dry . . . look what I found." Sergio handed him an ebony stone veined in gold. "You think it's valuable?"

"I don't know . . . but it's beautiful."

Both boys looked at it admiringly. Lalo sat down on the ground next to them and voiced something that was in everybody's mind, "Let's go home."

Miguel assured them without hesitation, "We have the map." The boys did not question any more. Somehow, they could do no more than believe Miguel. There was something inexplicably authentic about his certainty. They had the map.

Sergio remembered Papa At's words, "In the crystal room, El Indio Tolo found a stairway leading out. . . ."

Felipe asked, "Into the green valley?"

"He didn't say . . . but it was the way out of the cave . . . the only other way is going back to El Hoyo."

The courage would not be found to cross El Hoyo again . . . the magic of anticipation had curved valor and daring. They were tired and very hungry; and, perhaps without admitting it, a little afraid.

Diego stood up. "Let's start looking."

Felipe was doubtful, "Listen, we covered every inch of the room looking for the map . . . I didn't see any opening. There's no way out of this place except through the way we came, unless . . . unless there is a secret passage way or something like that."

Miguel again was certain. He did not doubt the story of El Indio Tolo in the least. "There is," he said.

Now the search was in unlikely places for movable rocks or narrow crevices or openings between rocks. They were excited again. Hunger and fatigue were forgotten. They all wanted to find the way. It was Lalo who found it. It was a rectangular boulder covering what seemed like a very low funnel close to the lighted side of the room, close to the open sky so high above. Together the boys rolled away the boulder and saw what looked like a wallcrypt. It did not look any larger, except that it led up toward an opening. Through the opening could be seen tendrils of light. If there was light, there was a way out; the boys knew this. Now the thing to do was for one of them to lie down on the crypt-like opening and push himself through to investigate where the light was coming from. Lalo, being the smallest and the one who found the way, volunteered. Once he had pushed himself up into the crypt, he called out excitedly, "It's leading up . . . I can see pieces of the sky." What Lalo saw was a continuous serpentine system fashioned by nature into a natural stairway. The center was one right-angle circle with the same tendrils of falling light. This was the way out. Lalo pushed his body up until it was at a standing position. The opening was wider than the crypt and he had enough room to extend his arms out to the side as he followed the circular dimensions of the hard basalt with holes deep enough to secure a footing. The right angle turns continued up. After a while, Lalo realized it was night in the outside world.

The tendrils of light had disappeared, gently leaving behind streaming greys of dusk. It was hard to find secure footing, so he worked himself up more slowly. The rest of the boys followed not far behind him, so he called out, "How you doing?" The voices came up to Lalo somewhat hollowed in an echo of full chorus. He was reassured. He put more effort in his climb, and it was not long before he saw a new kind of beam streaming down in narrow ribbons upon the rocks. It was the moon. There was a full moon. He sighed deeply as if anticipating the outer world. He looked up. He saw an opening in what seemed to him a great distance up. There was still some way to go. He thought about the green valley, but his mind could not stay on it. The thought of the outside world made him think of his nice, clean bed and his mother stroking his head while he slept. He gulped back tears and felt ashamed that he wanted to cry. His arms ached beyond pain, but he stubbornly held tight to the sides as he made his way up slowly and carefully, knowing he would reach the top.

Suddenly he noticed what seemed like rat holes clustered on the sides of the rock wall. In some places small scraps of green growth could be seen now. He was coming to a surface. Lalo looked up and realized that he could almost touch the opening. It was covered with stones that left small openings for the tendrils of light that had guided him to the top. When he reached the top, he waited for the other boys.

There was a circular ledge close to the opening with enough room for all of them to stand safely. He now stood on the ledge and waited for the other to reach the top. One by one each boy, panting and tired, reached the ledge. First there was Miguel with the bulging slab inside his shirt. Lalo thought how hard it must have been for Miguel to make his way with the extra weight. Behind him came Felipe, almost at Miguel's heels. When Miguel and Felipe reached the ledge, they said nothing. But there was a thankfulness. Here, the filtered light had found its way to the depths. But here was its beginning. This was not the light of the sun. It had a coldness of the moon. Miguel and Felipe watched the other boys climb up to where they stood on the top ledge. At instances the threads of light would fall upon the moving bodies giving a fluency and strangeness to the climbing figures. When Diego and Sergio also reached the ledge, there was a feeling of relief. Now they all stood silently looking up at the stones covering the opening to the outside world. They felt a soft breeze smelling of night finding its way in the cradle of light. It was a joining that felt familiar deep in the instinct still dormant in the breathing bodies of the boys. It said too much. Diego observed, 'We'll have to roll back one of the rocks."

The boys pooled their weight against the smaller stone close to the bottom of the opening. It took a lot of effort for what seemed an interminable time. Finally, the stone separated from its granite mates. The second stone rolled back with greater ease. Now the light was a flood of serene undulations. The opening was large enough for one person to make his way out of the cave. Lalo again pushed himself up and out of the cave. His foot was now in great pain. But the excitement of the project dulled the pain somewhat. He tried to forget the pulsating hurt. The opening was just big enough for him. It was necessary that he push away another stone before the other boys could push themselves out of the cave. Once Lalo was out, the rest of the boys waited for him to do just this.

"He's sure taking his time," Felipe complained as they waited impatiently for some time. There was no move from Lalo, but after a time his voice called out, "It's the middle of the desert." It was then that he pushed away another stone from the outside. Now the opening was big enough for two boys abreast. The moon was visible. Lalo reached down to help Diego out. Then both lent a hand to the other boys. Now, all five were outside in the middle of the desert. A ridge of mountains loomed in shadows at a distance. . . .

There was always warmths in distant and shadowy beginings. Gotallama is always there.

The red wind breathes through the pulse of Gotallama. Things move . . . Gotallama is always there.

One sun, two suns, three suns. . . .

All suns are Gotallama plunging into seas for love. . . .

Warmth, new life, continuing life . . . water and fire are today . . . Incalculable. . . . .

Hordes creeping . . . hordes still creeping . . . hordes to creep. . . .

Soft and bright, green and white . . . Gotallama is always there.

When men came and calculated ciphers, clues, codes, charts to make systems . . . HARMONIES . . . temporary foci. . . .

Gotallama clapped his hands. Bravo!

Man always learning what the crust of the earth had done from its beginning. Look! There! Creation inscribed in its womb!

Men are clever. Have they not explained proliferation?

They are piecing the puzzle . . . Hurrah! Hurrah! Formations of species . . . of stars . . . of planets. Men restructure. They must be looking for God.

Harmonies dissolve in finding. . . .

YOU! YES YOU! YOU ARE . . . YOU'RE NOT . . . BUT YOU WERE. HO . . . HUM!

Gotallama sings as it drifts with the red wind. The mind can only do so much. . . .

The red wind whispers, "It could take them forever, you know."

Gotallama answered gravely, "Endless form . . . formless ends. . . ."

Then they went to play.

CHAPTER VIII

Papa At captured thoughts in la tiendieta. El amigo de los pobres had been spared. The whole presidio along that street had been spared; Mrs. Gómez's pretty curtains had been spared. The block was an incline set at a higher level from the rest of the basin that was main street. There had been mud and scorpions, but not with full impact. This presidio was close to the highway. It was almost as high as the location of the school and the church on the opposite side of main street, but not as high as the black, charcoal face of the smelter itself. Now Papa At was sifting light from dark. Strange . . . when there is nothing left in oneself . . . there is a fusion with all things. It was dawn of a very unusual Sunday. He was salvaging what supplies had been hit by the mud. After the mud slide on Saturday, the whole town had been

invaded by television cameras and charitable groups who had come
forth to help. Newsmen and blinking cameras were not favorites with
Papa At. Tragic circumstances should not be "news," he thought.

Counteractions of interest and sympathy after long years of
indifference and disdain . . . what comes of it? It was time for grief.
Five boys had been buried alive by an avalanche. They could not be
found. The search had begun on radio and television after the mud
slide. It was now Sunday and no one had heard anything about the
boys. Grief, a grand opus, has no words. The mind worked out a silent
speculation of hope. The neighborhood had decided the boys were
dead. One woman had seen the boys climbing the hill behind the
excavation that had given way early Saturday morning. Papa At had
searched all night with the rest of the men from the town.
Nothing . . . It was assumed that the boys were buried deep, under the
falling of half a hill.

Papa At carried a large bag of dried red chile over his shoulder into
the storeroom. He set down the bag of chiles on a low wooden table.
He straightened his tired body and decided to put some coffee on the
stove. The back window of his little kitchen was streaked with mud.
Papa At sniffed the air.

The rotten timbers of the old building gave off a pungent smell.
Wetness . . . an aftermath of a trial was giving off the consequences of
new experience. He sniffed again. No good . . . not bad . . . just strange
and somewhat exciting because of its newness. Papa At rubbed the
knuckles of his hands. He was feeling a little rheumatism. Broken
things . . . broken   things . . . scorpions . . . people . . . ways . . . five
boys? The men had contemplated digging into the tons of mud that had
collapsed on the spot where the men thought the boys had been buried
at the bottom of the hill leading to the main street. They had given up
the thought, for the feat was impossible. They could not possibly dig all
that mud to look for the five bodies. The city was bringing pumps later
in the day to suck the main street free of mud. Then there would be the
iron caterpillars. Maybe then. Better leave well enough alone until then.
He felt forlorn. Tears welled up. He went to the stove and poured
himself a cup of coffee. Maybe the boys are still alive . . . he felt they
were still alive. Still, he was overwhelmed and pinned to a sorrow. He
had even thought about El Indio Tolo's cave . . . perhaps? When it was
raining so hard? Maybe not . . . but then, one never knows. He would
talk about it later to the men today . . . or after the pumps sucked the
mud from the street. If they were in the cave, Papa At hoped, they
would be safe. They were with Gotallama. Heaviness . . . lightness. . . .
He sipped his coffee, wondering. Sunday evening there was to be a
special mass to pray thankfulness for the living and hope for the five
boys being alive. He did not go to church, but he was going this time. It
was a time to gather and share in faith.

Rain, like wind, has kissed the whole face of the earth for skies are opened arms. But rain is capricious. It does not know of harmony. Desert rain often comes down in torrential downpour. The hot baked surfaces of earth are first indifferent to the touch of rain. But then, rain will not be ignored. It persists until it runs off in sheets across flats, or it winds down deep canyons in heights of great passion, a savage passion that is furious in its charge. Go . . . gash . . . tear . . . destroy . . . erode . . . then, then, find a bosom for a home, a warmth. Rest and go deep into the pores to find a love.

Rain and earth . . . rain and earth . . . storm and mud . . . red wind circling . . . Gotallama knowing that the sun will come again. The desert earth will once more have a cracking face with new contours, tributaries, rivulets . . . and waiting ocotillo blossoms in desire. The desert having tasted passion for a little while remembers purple-cacti bodies, forms only seen in dreams that create contortions of strange balances. Purple cacti lost in rain. The rain has a purple tongue, moist, cool and warm . . . the earth feels it. How violent is love . . . how beautiful.

Purple cacti and purple tongues are real in swift, short moments that come to be, to search and find much more than desert, much more than sun. And if it pours a life into a death? Or is it a death into a life?

Is it forgiven? Is it remembered in desert times? It is the play that keeps things whole, says Gotallama.

Lupe was lying on Fito's bed. Fito insisted that they take her to his house when the men brought her unconscious, half-drowned, to the school where all the victims of main street were gathered. Everybody was looking after them. All of them had help from friends and relatives. The grandmother was safe. She had wanted to remain with the other ancianos. They had things to share as old people will share. The tragedy had given a freshness to their comradeship.

Lupe could hear Fito in the kitchen making her a cup of tea. She stretched out leisurely under the covers. She felt happy and warm and for the moment she erased the thoughts of the last hours. This was a different time and a different place. Fito was making *her* some tea! She had never been waited on before. There had been many times she cringed and suffered. There had been hurt and loneliness. There would be many times like that again. But now she felt warm and shy and happy. There was a newness to her hope, strangely like in storybooks. Fito came into the room with a cup of tea. Lupe watched him admiringly as he made his way expertly on crutches carrying the cup of tea. She sat up and smiled at him. Her dark hair was loose over her shoulders and her dark eyes were bright. She reached for the cup, "You shouldn't be doing this for me. I'm all right. I should be up."

Fito protested, "You stay where you are, woman. It's my turn. Everybody should have a turn."

Joy opened like a flower in her. Without guilt, without shame, her heart and mind shaped the words, "I love you." She couldn't say the words out loud. They were too precious. She felt herself beautiful. Fito sat on the bed next to her as he put the cup in her hands. He sat there looking, and Lupe knew that he saw. A single eye was splitting sun and all impulses in creation. She was Cleopatra. She sipped her tea in utter happiness. He just sat there watching. A part of her mind, nevertheless, was still with the past hours. She put down her cup and looked at Fito with serious eyes. "The scorpions?   Those things are a nightmare."

She bit her lip and nodded. He explained, "The mud slide must have hit a large cache of them. With the excavation, they came to the surface. Then, the long rain. Their world sort of came apart."

Lupe was somewhat puzzled. "Their world?"

Fito laughed. "Sure, why not? They live, don't they?"

Lupe closed her eyes and remembered, "I never saw so many. They looked alive on top of the mud. I thought it was raining scorpions."

"Many people did. The papers are playing that up. Some people thought it was the end of the world. Funny, isn't it, what people imagine?"

Oh, yes, thought Lupe, it's funny, it's funny . . . the mind. She remembered his little brother, Lalo. She could sense a quiet anguish in him.

"Is there hope for the boys?"

There was a hesitation. Fito was salvaging. "Half the hill fell . . . enough to bury dozens of men; but I keep thinking there are other possibilities. I keep hoping. No one is really sure of anything."

"Maybe they ran away."

"No . . . they would have heard about the search and would have come back or let us know."

"But you thing there's hope?"

"It's a feeling, that's all."

They both felt it was enough. Among earth-people intuition is a greater reality than speculation or theory.

Outside the bedroom window, Lupe could see a pearl sky. The rain had stopped. The sun had come back. The side of the mind, heavy with past hours, was giving way to another part, an impenitent surge of desire for new ways, new feelings, clean and young, that no thought of worthlessness or ugliness could imprison. Funny how feelings work. But this was much more of a mindlessness. She wanted to be just pearl sky, sun and warm blankets. She enjoyed this new circumstance where the mind did not trap. She searched Fito's face and found the beginning of peace.

"And your plan, Fito . . . about leaving?" She asked it half-afraid.

"Before storm?" He laughed, then added somewhat sadly, "Many storms are past."

"You want to stay here in Smeltertown?"

Fito shrugged, looking thoughtfully out of the window, "I can't say . . . but, lots of people here . . . they have something. I . . . I want to find something myself . . . something without anger."

"A world."

"What?"

You said earlier that even scorpions had a world. What's a world? A purpose that is ourself . . . isn't that it?"

Fito remembered his plan. An expression of pain crossed his face, "A world can't be busted . . . no, you can't do that to people. I didn't know better."

Lupe wanted to put her arms around him, to comfort and reassure. She whispered, "I still think you're a Moses."

"I'm just Fito."

"That's even better." She put the back of her hand on his cheek.

His face was stubby and his eyes were sad. She reached out and took his head and lay it on her bosom. She was a mother of the earth. There was no spinning candy. She felt his need for her faith. She stroked his head and knew that theirs would never be a great love story. It didn't have to be a great love story. Little "nows" were enough. Between the struggle, the disappointment, the confusions, these small stillnesses would be the architects of purpose. It was all a making of ordinary things that had nothing to do with books and mind, with words of heroines. She felt very alive. She didn't want to be Cleopatra anymore. She wanted to be Lupe loving Fito the way she knew how. After a while Fito looked up and asked, "You'll stay, won't you?"

"Yes, I'll stay."

CHAPTER IX

Diego's stomach growled; he said with a lilt in his voice, "When I get home, I'm going to eat everything in sight . . . oh, man, some of my mother's caldillo, a whole quart of milk, a lot of sugar doughnuts. . . ."

"Shut up!"

No one wanted to think of food. The thought of food made them feel weak. They were also thirsty. When they left the crystal room and journeyed up and out of the cave, Sergio, Felipe and Diego, who were carrying the orange jars, had filled them with water and had stuffed the neck of the jars with stone wrapped with a piece of Sergio's undershirt chosen for the occasion. However, on the way up, the water had seeped out and spilled. Diego's jar had slipped under his shirt, and had broken to pieces. Felipe and Sergio still carried the orange jars, but they were empty. Miguel hugged the slab with the map under his shirts.

"All I want to find is the highway," Miguel countered.

Felipe had suggested that they keep traveling because it was night. When the sun rose, no one traveled in the desert. They had been walking for some time. Miguel had looked up at the sky to find the North Star. They had estimated that the path of the cave had been toward the north. If they were setting out for home, they had to travel the opposite way against the North Star. The North Star was clear among the smaller stars, solar stones of light. They stayed away from the density of mountain. The black mesas soared out of the east in the moonlit night. The sagebrush smelled green after the long rain. They were on the lookout for a road, a highway, or the long steel arm of progress, the freeway, more discernible from a distance. But all they saw before them were stretches and stretches of endless horizon.

Lalo had fallen behind. Miguel turned and saw him nursing his hurt foot.

He walked back to where Lalo sat in the dark and asked, "What's the matter . . . your foot hurt?"

"I think it's infected." Miguel looked at the foot and saw the swollen area. It was very much infected.

"Here," said Miguel, helping Lalo to his feet, "lean on me. You better not use that foot."

"No . . . I'll be all right." He was determined to walk by himself, but when he put the weight on his infected foot, he grimaced and looked at Miguel apologetically.

"Hold on to me." Miguel was matter-of-fact about his order. Lalo did as he was told.

Sergio called out from the darkness in front of them, "Hey, where are you?"

"Right behind you," called out Miguel. "Let's slow down a bit. Lalo's foot is infected . . . that hurts like hell. . . ." The rest of the boys waited until Miguel and Lalo caught up with them.

When dawn came, it seemed as if they had walked forever. The coming of dawn gave them a new kind of hope. They looked in all directions, but still saw nothing. They decided to rest for a short while against tall scrub on the side of the hill.

When the sun came up, Miguel observed, "We better make time until noon. After that we better find shelter against the heat." He pointed to the southwest. There was a long strip of light smooth ground. 'That looks like the old cattle road leading to the border. If it is, the highway will show after a while." They all felt relieved and kept up their walking until they were utterly exhausted. The heat broke their parched lips and their bodies ached. Felipe spied some tall mesquite clustered in a wide area. It offered the best shade around. They found a clearing that was somewhat cool. Then all of them sat in the patch of shade and waited for the unmerciful sun to give way. They fell asleep.

Miguel awoke when he felt something run up his legs. It was a lizard sitting placidly on the slab Miguel had under his shirt. Carefully he cupped his right hand and swooped down on the lizard. He caught it. The rest of the boys were awakened by Miguel's movement.

"Hey, you guys, look what I caught."

Felipe rubbed his eyes, "We sleep long?"

Miguel observed, "Not long. The sun is still hot . . . look!" There was another lizard behind a clump of mesquite. "Catch it! They have water. It doesn't taste very good, but it is wet." Miguel bit into his lizard bravely. It tasted somewhat bitter and smelled acrid like ants, but it was wet. The other boys set about catching lizards. Diego caught one. He bit into it and gulped it down complaining, "It sure don't taste like sugar doughnuts."

"Shut up!"

The rest of the boys looked behind mesquite bushes, around spiny chollas, and giant sahuaros with their hidden water. The boys did not know. They found the shade of joyoba bush where the heat was not too intense. They sat down somewhat despondent over a fruitless search for lizards.

"Should we wait until a lizard comes around?" Sergio asked. He wanted a lizard; his mouth was dry.

"No," Miguel stood and peered up at the sun. "We better move on now."

"It's still too hot."

"If we walk slow, we'll run into the highway before long."

The rest of the boys were undecided. The heat had taken too much out of them.

Miguel insisted, "We can't just sit around under this mesquite." The other boys agreed. They scrambled to their feet. Felipe helped Lalo to his feet. The foot was very swollen. They were all worried about Lalo's foot, but they didn't say anything. One by one, the boys took turns helping him walk. They walked for about an hour, but still no highway. Felipe was disgusted. "We better find another spot with shade. I feel terrible." Sergio doubled over and fell to the ground. They looked down at him. Miguel asked anxiously, "Are you all right?"

Sergio nodded, but he seemed to just want to lie there, lifeless in the sun. Miguel told him, "Get up, Sergio, we have to go on, get up!" Sergio just lay there. Felipe hurried on ahead. He wanted to see if the highway was anywhere near or whether he would see some kind of protection from the sun. Diego, Lalo and Miguel sat around Sergio and watched his curled up body. Miguel asked again, "Are you all right?" Sergio nodded, but didn't say anything. They saw Felipe coming back almost in a run.

"The highway's over there! I saw a car. It's over that way!" He pointed south. Miguel was already helping Lalo to his feet. Diego touched Sergio's shoulder, "Hey, Sergio, Felipe found the highway. Get up, man! Come on."

Sergio slowly got on his feet staggering. Diego asked, "You wanna hold on to me?"

Sergio shook his head, "No . . . I'm fine now. I'll make it."

They all walked together towards the direction where Felipe had seen the highway. Before long all of them were able to see the long scar of highway at a distance. Relief was like fresh air. They walked a little faster. Once they came to the highway, they all sat down about three hundred yards away to wait for a passing car. The sun was still very hot. Felipe stood up and looked towards the north to see if any cars were approaching. There was nothing.

"This is the old highway. It's hardly ever used. All the cars use the freeway now." Diego was skeptical. Sergio had his head between his legs. He didn't seem to be aware of any thing. They felt as if they were burning alive. The dryness hurt. They waited for what seemed an interminable time. It was getting cooler now. No one said any thing. Suddenly, Felipe saw a truck coming from the north.

"A truck . . . look, fellows, a truck!" He forgot his exhaustion. He was jumping up and down. Miguel ran to where Felipe stood and helped him wave to make the driver stop. When the truck stopped, they saw it was a vegetable truck. Diego was the first one to reach the driver.

"Can we have some of your vegetables . . . please, we haven't eaten."

The driver of the truck stared at them in disbelief . . . five bedraggled boys in the middle of the desert. "¿Qué pasa? Where did you kids come from?"

Diego persisted, "Can we have some of your vegetables?" He didn't wait for an answer this time. He went to the back of the truck and climbed it. The vegetable baskets were covered over with burlap. He opened one of the baskets and saw that it was full of potatoes. He grabbed one and bit into it. The rest of the boys climbed the back of the truck as Miguel talked to the driver.

"We were exploring a cave. The cave of El Indio Tolo. It starts at Smeltertown."

He looked towards the back of the truck where the rest of the boys were eating potatoes. Someone had found a basket of turnips. "Listen, my friends are helping themselves to your potatoes. We haven't eaten for a long time."

The driver looked at the boys and laughed, "That's all right. I guess they taste just fine when you haven't eaten." He looked at Miguel and suggested, "Climb on and have a potato yourself."

Miguel climbed the back of the truck and Felipe handed him a potato. It was good. The driver watched them eat for a while, then, still incredulous, asked, "You mean the Smeltertown across the stateline?" The boys looked at each other. Felipe asked, "You mean we're not in Texas any more?"

Diego asked the driver, "Have you any water around?"

The driver shook his head before answering Felipe. "The state line is about twelve miles south. You boys are in New Mexico."

"Hijo'e. . . ."

"Can you beat that?"

The truckdriver suddenly remembered what he had heard on the car radio several times that morning. "You kids from Smeltertown . . . eh?"

"Yeah."

"There was a flood there, a mud slide and they're looking for five boys."

"A hill fell?"

"Yeah . . . full of scorpions. I bet the devil you're. . . ."

Miguel was concerned, "Was anybody hurt?"

"You five are supposed to have been killed. You got everybody worried."

Miguel asked anxiously, "You'll drive us there, won't you?"

"Sure, sure."

The driver went back to the front seat of the car and called out, "Anybody want to sit here in front?"

"No . . . thanks . . . we're O.K. here."

The driver started the truck and they were on their way.

The boys were silent in the back. They were getting full and they felt guilty about what they had heard. The town thought they were dead. They had been revived with potatoes and were now full of worry. Sergio was well enough to warn ominously, "We're going to get it." Felipe and Miguel looked at each other.

Miguel said, "It was my idea in the first place, so I'll take the blame." All the boys protested at once, then Miguel commented, touching the slab under his shirt, "We got the map."

The rest of the boys looked at each other in silence and remembered the crystal room and the pool. They remembered the fire in the cave and the miracles of Nature inside mountains. Felipe spoke what they all felt, "I'd do it all over again. It was great. We all did something . . . something special."

The truck rattled on southward with five boys sitting on baskets full of potatoes and turnips.

. . . .

"Do you remember your Padre Nuestro?" Fito asked Papa At. Papa At smiled. Inside his head were images more than just a prayer . . . Santificado sea tu nombre . . . the face of the earth . . . Danos el pan de cada día . . . the face of man . . . Papa At looked at Fito and asked, "How's Lupe?"

"Staying at my house."

"You're a happy man . . . eh?"

"I have to straighten myself out a lot. She understands."

They walked in silence for a little way. They were circling the main street at a higher level on their way to the church for the special mass. The pumps and the caterpillars operated by city engineers had worked all day Sunday cleaning out Main Street. The engineers had torn into the old wall to use an old excavation for the sea of mud and scorpions. It was a beginning, the tearing of the wall. The two men walked slowly enjoying the greenness left by the rain. They looked down into the town and saw the cluster of old brown buildings and muddy streets isolated now that the engineers had left. The pumps were still there; so were the caterpillars. It would be the work of more than one day. When they had finished the main area, they were to dig directly underneath the hill to look for the bodies of the boys. The living had to be taken care of first. Papa At caught sight of the hill just above the path where they were walking. There was a conspicuous show of life. Plants of thorns, and brittle bushes, bearing live roots, flourished.

Papa At suggested, "Let's wander a little. Come on."

Fito hesitated, "Is there time?"

Papa At was already walking up a small clearing. Fito followed with some effort. Climbing was difficult with crutches. Papa At was pointing to a single creamy blossom on a sahuaro, "Look!" He began to climb higher, searching among the cacti and the green sagebrush.

"What are you looking for?"

"Mariposa lilies."

"I think you're crazy, old man."

"You're right. I'm a crazy old man." The little red lilies usually died during long droughts, but the roots stayed alive, and when the rains came, the little red flower would live again for a brief, lovely period like all the ephemeral plants of the desert. They both searched for a while, then they sat down.

Fito observed, "It's getting hot again. The flowers won't last."

"Swift life . . . swift death. . . ."

The desert was rejoicing. The desert was rejoicing.

"What are you thinking, Papa At?"

"Nothing really. I'm just enjoying."

Fito decided to do the same. After a while they heard the church bell. It was time to go. They had a ways to go. They did not want to be late. They made their way back to the path that led to the church. As they came down, they looked at Main Street again. The sight created questions in their minds after the brief period with the flowers. Neither man wanted to think just now. They walked in silence to the church . . . The Church of El Sagrado Corazón de Jesús had become a house divided between old ways and new ways. The old ways persisted because the old people were attached to the church. It was hard to convince the very young of its importance. There were changes in the world that were beyond the old patterns.

To the old people, who were part of El Sagrado Corazón, faith had to have an undisputed foundation. These old people still accepted the kind authority of Father Santiago. Heaven and Hell were black and white concepts. God was a personal God with anger and love. It was an old love affair that could not be destroyed by the young who wanted more of a realness. The ancient ways said . . . bondage would lead them out of bondage . . . the way of the poor. The church bell rang again.

When Papa At and Fito arrived at the church, they saw it was already full. Papa At and Fito found a back row. Papa At began to familiarize himself with what he had long forgotten. The paraphernalia of conventionality made him uncomfortable. But it was also a force and a fascination. It was a proud face of an old world. Upward inspiration towards Heaven . . . upward . . . upward. The imaginative mind of man surrounded the church . . . plaster saints standing or moving humanly in pose, plaster faces with human expressions of rapture, grief, wonder, worship. Chubby infant heads without bodies wearing wings, little pages in the royal court of God. The royal court of God? The ancianos were like those hovering, adoring little faces attending the glory of God. How fortunate are believers!

"Candles burn and flowers adorn the altar which holds the mystery of flesh and blood," thought Papa At. They bring God into the church. Liquor on the breath, stomach ache, lovers holding hands, children fidgeting, women believing, men withstanding . . . they were the flesh and blood, and a mystery to remain undefined. The pagan in Papa At had been touched. God has guts, he thought. He is the natural experience.

Old women praying beads were warriors of the ancient religion. Here they fought off ancient instincts with the Cross. Why, Ladies, why? The oxygen of the air had a God more real than an agonized Christ on a Cross. That was an idea . . . only . . . an idea? Error and pain and forgiveness are what men know of God and that should be enough. The mothers of the lost boys were sitting together as if to gather comfort from one another. They wore black, in mourning . . . mourning . . . mourning women. The mass was about to start.

The holy sacrifice of the Mass. Christ was Father Santiago as priest.

Christ was victim now. Man, too, is priest and victim. Why must we be constantly reminded of Christ's death? Jesus's life . . . ah! That's something else. Who remembers his silent journey away from temple and priest to find and share with simple people? But now Father Santiago is offering us the life of Christ in payment for the sins of Men, Papa At felt a protest . . . no . . . no . . . Stop! Jesus never defined sin. He spoke very little and he loved all men and loved all life. Could it be he didn't want to die?

The series of prayer and movements continued . . . kneel . . . stand . . . sit . . . kneel . . . stand . . . follow the leader . . . Amen!

Father Santiago had turned to the altar where he was calling upon the heart and the hand and the brain and all human effort every which way . . . What is unworthy? Papa At didn't know. He wondered if the congregation knew. Now he bowed his head with the rest of them in contrition. Papa At struggled hard for a pure mind. Maybe if he called upon the merit of the saints like Father Santiago was doing. Somewhere he had heard that saints and madmen were one. If so, he could trust the saints. Kyrie Eleison . . . Yes, God does have mercy! Gloria! All the people praised. Father Santiago turned to give grace to all who gathered here in his church . . . share the bounty of grace. What the seasons give? And light? and dark? And the honest gestures of men?

After a while he read an epistle and a Gospel that told old stories made new. Then everybody recited the creed, some mouthing words, others said them loudly, sure and with authority. Papa At remained silent. He simply didn't remember it. All of that had been in a child's world. Soon Father Santiago would offer the divine gift of body and blood. It was said that Isaías saw the vision of God and the angels crying out to one another, "HOLY, HOLY, HOLY!"

Papa At noticed that the transformation took a little time, from Sanctus to Pater Noster. But the consecration was so swift and ephemeral, just like the life of the Mariposa lilies. Christ, the victim, had given all of them the gift of blood and body.

> Through Him
> And with Him
> And in Him

Papa At looked up and saw that Gotallama was streaming down from the glass stained windows pouring warmth. The people were warm and alive; the earth was warm and alive.

> Through him
> And with him
> And in him.

Things as they are . . . that is the mystery and the wonder of a life or a death. Take the scorpions, for instance. They are a certain combination in a long evolutionary process. These ugly, awkward creatures, vile to the touch, looking ominously fatal, are a moment of accident. It is a chemical turbulence, an organic compound, the touch of sun, the sense of water that gives them life. Like all living things, scorpions serve beauty too. Deep, deep they dig to turn the soil, to give it breath, perhaps offering a chance to something like the Mariposa lily. They were a part of a whole.

In Smeltertown a sea of dead scorpions were something else now. Withered bits of black, dismembered and lost in drying mud. But there is still a sun and a chemical turbulence and an organic change that will give them their own kind of place. . . .

"Scorpions?" Miguel's voice was incredulous. The truck driver was telling the five boys about the flood. All six were walking through the same path Papa At and Fito had walked overlooking the main street of the town. They had parked the vegetable truck just on the edge of the entrance to Main Street. The street had been closed. There were warning signs already posted by the city department. The bleak, muddy appearance in the middle of the street, created anxiety among the boys. Sergio was crying unashamedly. Of the five boys, he was the one who was most concerned because his father's bar was right on Main Street. All the other boys lived on higher areas, so they were not as distressed.

"Is my papa all right?" asked Sergio, forgetting that no one could give him an answer.

The truck driver comforted, "I heard on the radio that no one was hurt . . . just you boys. You're supposed to be buried under the mud just where the hill fell."

All eyes turned towards the fallen hill. The boys were silent thinking of the morning they had seen the beginning of the mud slide. Now, a fallen hill had been ordained as a gentle, flood-plain with a series of ridges, a tale of force and rain. All was still now. Not a single cloud in the sky to verify the recent storm. The air was lucent, like glass, casting a blaze of orange against a blue sky, a new impulse of color. The only evidence was the wash channel full of damp mud. Soon the sun would leave dry, cracking creases. Then the wind would later ride the plain, making red clouds against the sky.

"We're supposed to be buried under that?" asked Felipe, then gave a long, low whistle. The church bell could be heard in the distance. The truck driver pointed toward the church and remembered, "I think they're having some sort of services for you boys."

Miguel gasped, "Funeral services?"

The man shrugged, "I don't know."

The boys looked at each other uncomfortably. They had better hurry to the church. Miguel observed, hugging the slab under his shirt,

"We better get there in a hurry." They hastened their steps; the truck driver following. This was one church service he had to attend.

Felipe reasoned hopefully, "I don't think it's a funeral mass. They would have to dig us up before they had a funeral service."

Lalo, who had been leaning on Diego, suddenly said. "Listen, vatos, my foot is in pain." He sat down on the incline of the hill where the path came to an end. The church was now in view.

Miguel was skeptical. "I think you better come with us. We'll help you." Lalo shook his head.

The rest of the boys went on ahead with the truck driver. When they reached the door of the church, they heard Lalo calling to them, "Hey, wait for me!"

Felipe went to help him while the boys waited at the entrance of the church. The half-opened door revealed communion time. Miguel could see the people returning to their pews and Father Santiago giving communion to the last group. When Felipe and Lalo reached the other boys, Miguel opened the church door wide; then, leading the line, he walked slowly down the aisle. He could hear the people whispering in surprise. Then, suddenly he saw Diego's mother stand and put out her arms, "¡Hijo mío!"

Diego ran to his mother. She put her arms around him and began to cry. The mothers of the other boys did the same. The men looked stern and unforgiving, eyeing the boys for some explanation. Father Santiago looked from one bedraggled boy to the other. Miguel left his mother and went to the front of the church. One by one, the other boys joined him. They were a strange sight. Dirty, unkempt, with Lalo holding on to Felipe they stood facing everybody. A deliverance from God and an intrusion upon God. The people's faces wore astonishment mixed with puzzlement. At first the boys felt ashamed and embarrassed, but that did not last long. When Miguel stepped forward to explain to everybody what had happened, all the boys seemed to stand firm on some strange truth. Miguel spoke, "We're sorry we worried all of you. Is this Mass for us?" His eyes questioned the whole congregation. Caramba; he hoped not. The congregation only waited for further explanation. "We went into the cave of El Indio Tolo to look for the map of the green valley so we could give it to you. If all of us leave Smeltertown, like Fito says, we have a place to go. We found it." Miguel took the slab from beneath his shirt and held it up for everybody to see.

The greater part of the murmuring was still a question. Miguel continued, "We found the way out of the cave about twenty miles away in New Mexico . . . but the important thing is we found the map of El Indio Tolo that tells of Gotallama's green valley. We don't understand what it says. There's something written on it."

Father Santiago listened dumbfounded. The Mass had been interrupted by five boys who talked of pagan gods. They had brought their pagan gods into the church. For a long time, "God" had forbidden it. Father Santiago smiled. The ways of the world had a funny way of reconciling gods and ways of thinking. He looked at the boys who were looking at a piece of stone with such green faith. That was enough for Father Santiago. He sat down to listen to the boys. Miguel continued: "The map does not say much, but I'm sure Papa At knows what it means. If it tells about the green valley of the gods, then there must be a green valley. It's sort of becoming what we were once . . . like Indians who could talk to the earth."

Father Santiago was full of wonder. Here were five boys talking about a holy communion with the earth, about lambs who were no longer and never again could be lambs. They were a life force, fierce and strong. Why then? "Lamb of god . . . lamb of god . . . how long would people believe in sacrifice? In worthlessness?" Perhaps the time would soon come to put those things aside. El Indio Tolo and Gotallama were apparently real to these five boys . . . such was the propulsion of faith. The mass had ended and people gathered around the boys to understand a little more. . . .

The red wind saw the rain boil away. The desert was his again. Eons . . . who thinks in eons? Mountains fall and rise again. Who thinks of eons? The red wind asked, "Is there a green valley;"

Gotallama laughed, "Is there a green valley?"

Drowned or dry, hope burns. There is a surgery . . . men building, men killing.

There is a healing . . . men loving.

Gotallama circled with the force of life, sloping ways.

One day Gotallama talked to El Indio Tolo who was the full circle.

The red wind fell into the arms of an orange sky while Gotallama carved the sea. . . . Never is the sea full.

The face of the earth is soft and giving.

Air is an ocean that gags the mind . . . to leave a lightless deep . . . deep. Ask light, the aurora.

CHAPTER X

Unbelievers . . . the people had been unbelievers. They had scolded the boys, but they were not punished. Everybody was happy the boys

were not under the fallen hill. They had not listened to Fito's plan with
enthusiasm; they did not believe in the nonsense of a green valley. They
were people of today. Nevertheless, deep, deep in ancient instincts
something was felt, a tremor of their own earth. Perhaps they would
not say they believed. It would be nonsense . . . to say they believed.

Main Street was full of people helping people to make life livable
again. They were scrubbing. Those with a few extra dollars were
painting the inside or outside of buildings. Not the presidios, however.
These belonged to a rich landlord that had forgotten them already.
Things were made usable again. Nothing was new and shiny, but the
hearts. The heart felt glad to be alive and planning one more time.

The five boys were in Pepe's Bar varnishing tables. Champurrado was
supervising the job. Champurrado wanted to hear all about the cave and
about the map of the green valley.

"There is only one word on the stone you found?"

"It's an Indian word. It is the word, Kear . . . I don't know how to
say it."

"In Roman letters?" Champurrado asked.

Miguel nodded his head. Papa At says it's because El Indio Tolo
learned the white man's language in a mission school when he was a
little boy." Champurrado agreed, "That could account for it."

Champurrado looked at the tables almost finished and felt satisfied.
It would be good for the place to have beautiful tables. Champurrado
noticed that Manolo, the salesman, was at the bar talking to another
stranger.

"It could be a tourist attraction," Manolo was dreaming again.

The stranger was shaking his head, "Who would come to see some
dead scorpions?"

"No . . . no . . . it would not only be mud and dead scorpions but
there would be a big sign that would tell the story of the rain of
scorpions."

"An amusement park . . . possibilities. . . ."

"It didn't really rain scorpions. That's a lie."

Manolo's eyes shone with excitement, "That's just it! People love to
buy lies!"

"A restaurant. . . . It would be no worse than the ghost towns around
here . . . but better . . . like a miracle. We sidetrack some of the tourist
trade going across the border to Méjico."

The two continued the dream as the five boys went to wash up
before going to Papa At's.

"Want to come along with us, Champurrado? Papa At is going to
explain the map over at his store."

Champurrado showed the beginning of a surge of enthusiasm, but
then, he hesitated.

"No . . . no . . . you boys go along. You can tell me later. I have things to do. Pepe needs help if the place is to be full again."

The five boys walked to the store almost in silence. They were thinking about a time that would end tomorrow. That would be the beginning of the usual things. The adventure of the last few days would be put away. Today the portals had been slowly closed. They were disappointed by the town's reaction to the finding of the map. Felipe, Sergio, Diego, and Lalo believed there was some mystery to the slab they found. To Miguel it was no mystery. It was the secret of the green valley. He did not doubt. He had seen Papa At's eyes when he had handed him the slab. They were full of a strange excitement. El amigo de los pobres was full of children again. There were a few ancianos who had come to listen. Later on, parents would listen to their children intently.

The truth of pagan gods was still a truth. Everybody sat around Papa At who was holding the slab very carefully. He traced it with his worn hands. He was deep in thought.

"Do you know what the words means, Papa At?" Miguel asked eagerly.

"It's a simple Indian word."

"K . . . E . . . A . . . R . . . ."

Everybody clamored, "Tell us, tell us!"

"The word means 'you.'"

They were disappointed. All, except Miguel. He knew there was more. He didn't say any thing, but he looked at Papa At anticipatingly. Papa At smiled reassuringly. "It's a piece of wisdom beyond years."

Miguel became excited, "It's a symbol, or a secret code?"

Papa At shook his head. Papa At had placed all the things they had brought back from the cave on a small table for people to see. The orange jars, the beautiful stones, and the slab. They were not worth money. But people would wonder when they came into the store. The water of the cave had made another world, another kind of light in the stones and rocks. People would feel an old mystery inside themselves. Papa At felt it and he wanted the people to feel it too. It was like centuries discovered inside the heart and in a silent mind. He held up one of the stones, "This used to be water, but the light made it stone."

He handed it to Felipe and he passed it around for everybody to see. Miguel's voice was impatient, "The Indian word, Papa At . . . what else does it mean?"

"It's a fire." Papa At almost said it in a whisper.

The children asked, "The stone?"

Miguel asked at the same time, "The word?"

Papa At smiled, "Both."

Light . . . water . . . stone . . . fire . . . people. There was more bewilderment than understanding, but there was a feel, a strange feel as if a door had opened unto something to be realized.

"It is all a composition. What made the crystals; what made you. All things are the same."

"That's the explanation?" asked Felipe with disappointment. It was obvious that all the boys were disappointed.

"Man is the most green, the most alive." It was an affirmation. Miguel groped for understanding. He asked hesitatingly, "We are the green valley?"

Papa At nodded. Miguel said assuredly, "I am a green valley." His voice was so solemn that everybody laughed.

Felipe commented, "My father was sort of proud I had gone into the cave. He said we had the boiling blood of adventurers."

Papa At agreed, "You have."

Miguel was pensive, "But I don't think that is being a green valley." He turned to Papa At questioning, "Is it?"

Papa At spoke softly, "That is part; it is the part for the young and energetic like all of you. Then, there's a more important adventure . . . with time. When El Indio Tolo found the cave, he was an adventurer. He had done many things in his life, bad and good, but most of all he remembered the part he played in the universe. This was the message of his blood, of his earth. In the cave, he sifted the blindness from his eyes and found a simple clarity called peace. He wrote this experience on the stone."

The boys remembered the crystal room, the miracles of light and the many feelings that mixed with their blood during their search and their finding. It was good. It was good.

A rain of scorpions was a clumsy thing . . . it was a humor, a play of change. The rain of scorpions was something else . . . to some an extravaganza; to others a horror . . . to some an omen . . . to some a lie . . . and there were many who knew nothing of a rain of scorpions. The earth moves towards embracing truths, the full circle of all things.

The boys had gone to a cave to find a part of themselves. There would be time to share the green valley.